Prologue

Desolation had a new meaning when looking across the basin. Stark and bare, the basin was chilling to look at. A white mineral powder covered the basin's reflective, blood-red ground like snow. A storm that had the mineral fall from it stood out in the distance above a city nestled into the cliffs. Lightning flashed above the city.

At the mountainside opposite to the city, a portal appeared. Three figures walked from it. Each wore dark brown clothing and dark travel cloaks. Their faces were concealed by hoods and scarves wrapped at their necks. The three figures stared at the city before them. The city was in ruins like so many others in this world. Parts of blackened spires had collapsed in on itself leaving large gaps in the city where rubble now stood. It would've been beautiful if it weren't abandoned and halfway destroyed.

"What makes this ruin different, General Pane?" asked a small man.

"It's where Death lived decades ago," answered Pane, "He hates this place as much as he yearns for it to answer your question Anders. He was banished here for nearly a decade."

"I knew that," said Anders, "I meant that this place is near worse condition than the rest of the cities that still remain standing. We could find another city that hasn't been nearly destroyed, just abandoned."

"The city is much larger than the rest," said the third figure, "Should Boreas and company come walking, they have a lot of ground to cover and we have cover from the world engine's bombardment."

"Agreed, Volk. Let's see what we can use," said Pane. He conjured another portal in front of them. They walked through. They were at the edge of the city. The golden spires that lay in front of the three figures could have been once beautiful like the rest of the city. Now they lay scorched and parts were blasted to rubble in battles.

"Damn," Anders said, "I don't think we can use the outer parts at all."

"As long as the center works, we can use it," Volk said.

They began to walk through the city. Flashes of lightning cast shadows across the spires and the only sound that came was the deep thunder. Everywhere they turned, they saw only the darkness of the alleyways and the abandonment of the city.

Soon they came upon the largest building. It was once the palace. It was embedded upon the quartz cliff behind it. Despite the state of the rest of the city, the palace looked mostly undamaged. There were hardly any holes from the attacks and there was no visible rubble at the front.

They walked toward the palace and walked through the entryway. Faded decorations that could have been once beautiful surrounded them at the walls. Blue orbs stood at the edges of the rooms. Lights at the ceiling of the palace flickered on. The lights cast the room in golden light.

"I told you we could use this," Pane said to Anders, "We might be able to work with the entire palace if this is any indication."

"Alright," Anders said, "I was wrong. I wonder why this place was abandoned if there was still power."

"Lets see if there is any evidence why," Volk said. He walked toward the first of two other passageways apart from where they entered. It was a dark hallway where the light from the ceiling did not enter.

Pane and Anders followed him to the hallway. Volk stopped in front of them as they made it to the hallway. He made a light in between his fingertips and flung it out into the darkness. The light floated across a bare hallway leading them to a door at the end.

It was a library or an archive. Rows of shelves covered the whole floor. Dust, papers, books, and broken glass from the lights covered the floor. Volk walked to the right. Pane conjured a light in his fingertips and walked to the left. Anders behind him walked away with Volk.

Pane walked alone, scanning the shelves. There was little among them but the books. He wondered what was in each of them. Most were the only copies left in the world, he assumed. He soon surmised it was empty. He followed the shelves looking at the light Volk had conjured.

"What do you think happened?" Pane heard Anders whisper.

He came upon them looking down at two bodies. The two skeletons lay on the floor in the corner of the library. One skeleton was wrapped in the arms of the other.

"They came here starving looking for food," Pane whispered, "And found none."

Volk crouched down to the floor and picked up an old, rusted knife. "And did themselves with this to save themselves the pain," Volk finished.

"We'll bury them when we leave," Anders said.

They exited the library and traveled back to the entrance. They walked toward the other passageway and entered. This time the light flickered on. They continued to the end of it.

They walked toward the door. Volk opened it and they stepped through. Lights flickered on around them. They were in a cavern carved directly into the cliffs. Walkways surrounded them, surrounding each level and they crossed to and from each surrounding walkway. They walked over to the railing on the walkway in front of them.

"Wow," Anders said.

Below the railing was a massive complex of machines that appeared to be vehicles capable of flight. They stood silent in rows across a massive platform that supported the whole structure. Each machine was a deep blue or teal and strikingly resembled a dragonfly complete with two thin narrow wings on each side.

"Let's go back to the Last City and give them what we have found," Pane said, "I think we have our base."

Chapter One:
The Titan-World

Lily looked out across the woods in front of her. It wasn't anything comparable to Earth. Covered in snow, the trees were made from a blue crystal that twisted and turned into incredible shapes while others looked exactly like that of a pine tree. Behind the woods, a dark snow-covered mountain range surrounded the basin covered by dark clouds that loomed overhead.

She was sitting on a wall that surrounded the Capital. It consisted of dark silver pillars that rose up to where she stood. Her feet dangled at the ledge above the snow twenty feet below. Her brain was in a haze. She tried not to think of everything that just days ago happened. Boreas not only had the Crimson Blade, he also resurrected her father Death.

Since the attack at the Last City, Lily had often blamed herself for everything that had happened despite Sage constantly telling her otherwise. Her visions of the future hadn't helped her stop Boreas from getting the Crimson Blade nor had they stopped Boreas from resurrecting Death. Sage had always told her in the past few days that they were being too cryptic but now being after the end of the visions it was too painfully obvious.

Since the attack, the group had been in a search for a new base. Lee had gone back to the Gates of the Storm and had gone north searching for an outpost. There were dozens beyond the gates and they were hoping to find one suitable enough to defend from the Storm Riders and to be able to fight off an attack from the North Wind's world engine. Pane, Anders, and Volk had gone to a world they had not told her to try and find a suitable base. All four of them had not returned yet.

Her dark hair billowed as a cold gust of wand came to her. She pulled it back and pulled her hood over it.

Lily looked toward the city. Elegant and tall dark silver spires stood throughout the city. Behind them, a palace made from the same dark silver substance like the spires stood in the jagged snow-covered cliffs behind them. The outside looked like an incredible stairway with large pillars covering the outside gradually rising to the top. At the highest point, there was a narrow walkway. She knew that walkway well. The Assassin had fallen from it after he had trapped Lily and her friends.

Across the wall, a lone figure was walking toward her. A pale girl with auburn hair was walking toward her. She was wearing a purple cloak that was billowing in the cold wind.

Lily stood up and looked at her. "Pane says he may have found something," Sage said.

"When are we meeting him?" Lily asked.

Sage looked at her. "He wants to see us now," she answered, "I just had a messenger give me a slip at the house. I think he was expecting to see you but he passed the message on once I gave him one of the codes."

"Alright," Lily said, "Let's go then."

They began to walk along the wall surrounding the city. After about a minute, they came to a stairway that descended through the two levels below. They descended to the bottom level and continued walking. The two levels below the top were lantern-lit corridors that turned with the wall.

Lily had always been confused by the architecture of the wall. Despite an armory below the ground, it had not been made for defenses whatsoever. There were no battlements even before Death had attacked years ago and she did not know what the second level was made for at all. It seemed to her that the wall was only made to keep out animals.

As she walked to the end of the wall, she found the doorway where she had entered earlier. The two of them walked through and they found themselves in the city far from where she had sat before.

They began to walk through the city. Throughout the walk through the city, Lily could only stare at the ground of the street. No snow ever collected on it, maybe due to the type of rock or maybe because of an enchantment. The bulk of it was a murky gray but there were splashes and swirls of other colors like blue, green, and red. With each step, the color around her foot changed: sometimes going darker, lighter, or creating a new streak of color.

Lily saw no Sorcerers in the streets as they walked by each spire. Even though many, at least a third, had left the Last City after the attack the streets were not crowded at all. Lily wondered whether it was because of fear of another attack or something else.

Soon, they found themselves in the main walkway, a path at least twenty feet in width and they began to walk to the end of the city. Once they passed under the wall, Lily felt snow beneath her shoes and she knew she could conjure a portal.

She did. The view of the Last City came in front of her as the portal appeared. They walked through the portal. They were on the end of the mountain range that stood above the city. Pine trees and snow surrounded them.

The city in front of her was disheveled from the last attack. Many parts of the wall were blasted to rubble. Much of the spires lacked the lights at their windows. They were abandoned, where the people went, she could only guess.

"It looks worse than yesterday," Sage said.

"People finally cleared out," Lily said, "I was expecting less to have left."

They began to walk down toward the city.

Below them, guards clad in golden armor stood in front of them. Lily waited for them to ask her for identification as they came down. They however didn't as she walked by.

Lily was confused but almost immediately realized why. The Last City was coming into a situation as if it was the new Capital. People were abandoning the city for other planets or the Capital itself. The guards, unless notified by Pane, must have known that anyone coming to the city was under orders by Pane or someone else.

As she walked toward the palace, she saw two people standing at the doorway. Peter and John were standing by.

Lily and Sage walked up and greeted them. "Do either of you know why Pane called us?" Peter asked.

Lily shook her head. "Where is Fonsesca?" Lily asked, but she knew why by John and Peter's faces almost immediately. He was too ridden by guilt. Two years ago Death had let him survive but had killed the rest of his friends in the police force. Before, Lily knew Fonsesca had felt guilty but now the only person whose guilt rivaled his was her own. "Should we go in?" she asked.

"Probably best," Peter whispered.

They walked through the doors of the palace. They were in a large, ornate room with floating blue, pink, and white lights giving light to the expanse. Two guards stood by the portal at the center of the room. Powered by the Luminous Creek, the portal could take you anywhere in the universe without going through the Spectral Boundary. While the portal was a major help two years ago, it was now obsolete except to children who were unable to fully conjure portals considering there was no turmoil in the Spectral Boundary.

Lily walked toward the stairs at the side of the room and walked with the group. After walking through the palace's golden walls, they came upon a room with a collapsed floor that was at least twenty feet wide. Avertree, the traitor had blown a hole through the floor when he was escaping. In front of the crevasse was Lee in the golden armor of the Last City rather than the furs and blacks of the Black Strider uniform.

"Come on," Lee said, "Pane found a base we could use."

"Where is it?" John said.

"That is what we are here to talk about," Lee said.

He led them along a narrow walk around the crevasse into the war room. General Pane and General Anders were both at the two ends of the long table that spread across most of the room. Commander Volk, the man who led the Gates of the Storm, sat at a chair next to Pane and Graves sat opposite to him. Graves had never forgiven Lily for giving up the Crimson Blade for their lives at the dead world Torfaa a few weeks ago. He tried to take no notice of them, her specifically as they walked in.

"Lee says you found a base," Lily said, "What did you find?"

"Well, there are a lot of things that we need to talk about, mainly our plan forward," Pane said, "First we should start off with the base. It's abandoned, there is technology that we know we have an edge on with Boreas. But there is a catch."

"What is it?" Sage asked.

"It's on the Titan-World," Volk said.

Lily looked at Pane and Volk confused. Every major city was destroyed to ashes in the war or was destroyed by Death after in his rage. How they found a base large enough to fight Boreas and support their soldiers was a mystery.

"How is that possible?" Lily asked.

"When Death made his 'vow' as he put it, he burned down much of the outer parts of the main city," Anders said, "Pane filled me in on those details. However, much of the inner parts of the city were not only intact, but in pristine condition with supplies and vehicles."

"What is so bad about this?" John asked, "If we have a base on the Titan-World then that means we have support from multiple bases across the universe?"

Peter was the first to answer. "While this idea would have been perfect a week ago, it is a serious gamble now. With Death alive, he'd do whatever he can to get us off of the world. He hates the world as much as he wants to save and return it to what it was before. Lethality controlled is deadly, lethality in rage is much worse."

"Are there any other worlds we can use to avoid this problem?" Lily asked.

"Not really," Pane said, "Of the five worlds not our own or the Titan-World, we can't use Earth, too many lives that could be lost. I would not want to send anyone to Torfaa. The other three we can't use or they are inhabited without knowledge of us."

"What do you mean, 'without knowledge of us'?" John asked, "Are there more worlds with humans?"

"Just one," Anders said, "But we can't go there. We can't go to a world, tell them of our existence and then expect them to take it well. Just look at Earth. A decent amount of people would rather have never known we existed and have us leave rather than help each other."

"So there are no other options," Peter said, "What is so good about this base?"

"The buildings surrounding the palace provide protection against the world engine," Volk began, "Not only that but we may be able to take out the world engine as well. Inside the palace are small crafts for mining in the cliffs. We should be able to make some sort of adjustments on them and we may be able to stand a chance against the world engine which would leave only Boreas's forces."

"Yes but the real threat isn't the world engine," Lily said, "Death and Boreas are the most dangerous. We've all seen what each could do by themselves but together and with the Crimson Blade, they are just below unstoppable."

"And that brings us to the other reason why this base works well," Anders said, "In the palace there is an escape route through the mines. In the hangar before the entrance is a blast shield, at least four feet of metal. If we can get the Reality Stone, we can close the shield while they are attacking and get the stone somewhere else through the mines."

"And this leads us to the problem of getting the Reality Stone before Boreas," Lee said.

"Do we have any idea of where the stone can be found?" Peter asked.

"Actually we do," Lily said, "Boreas said the reason he revived Death was that he could only obtain the stone with a titan on hand."

"That is actually helpful," Pane said, "On one of the worlds called Harenae, there is a place; a massive jungle full of life that shouldn't exist considering it is surrounded by a desert full of sand and droughts. The locals hate it there."

"So the Reality Stone has an opposite effect on the world around it," Peter said, "Unlike the blade which withers away all life, the stone must fuel life beyond anything seen before."

"That is the prevailing theory combined with the fact that the jungle always appears as if it moves away from someone coming to it," Volk said.

"What do you mean appears to be moving away from someone?" John asked.

"Well the illusion is that the jungle appears to always be at a certain distance from someone who does not have prominent titan blood," Pane said, "So we know who will be going to the world to help some of us in."

"Me," Lily whispered. She didn't want to be reminded she was Death's daughter now that he was back but for this, it was critical.

"Wait, what do you mean help some of us in?" Graves broke in, "Is she not going?"

"Hang on," Lily said after Graves realized what he meant, "Why am I not going?"

"You're the only one that has been at Boreas fortress," Volk said, "You'll be with Lee and I when we go to the North Pole. If we take out his base he won't have anywhere to go but on the run."

Lily did not find the idea that fun but, nonetheless, she didn't want to be racing to find the Reality Stone before Boreas. "All right," Lily said.

"We can go with you," Sage said.

"I'm going to be honest with you," Lee said, "The journey to the stone would be much more appealing than going through the north. The cold is hellacious and that was in October and November. Now, near December, there is no day, instead there is only night. The cold either isn't our only problem. For the week of journey that we have, we will be followed and ambushed by dozens, perhaps hundreds of the Storm Riders trying to catch us."

Sage, John, and Peter all began to argue with Lee, Volk, Pane, and even Graves.

Lily thought it over. Having Sage, John, and Peter near her would be a comfort without a doubt, but she knew that Lee was telling what he thought was best. The odds of coming in contact with Boreas were slim, at least until the end of the journey, but up north, they would be in a constant battle with the Storm Riders.

"Sage," Lily said above them, "You'll go to Harenae. Like Lee said, it is too dangerous to go north."

Sage clenched her jaw and sat down in her chair. She said nothing. Lily was surprised by her confidence in going with her. Love was a part of it, but the Sage that she knew years ago who would cry after seeing the news every few weeks would never go in by confidence.

Pane seeing that at least verbal tension was gone, started going over the plan. Lily would go to Harenae with the bulk of the group. Lily would go back with Pane. Lee, Volk, and Lily would then go up north with the volunteer Capital and Last City guards and the Black Striders that remained as well as a large group of soldiers from certain countries on Earth. Pane had been able to cut a deal that allowed some nations that were against Boreas's attacks to send a large number of soldiers to the north, nearly adding five fold to the Black Striders. They would take horses across the wasteland passing and staying at the abandoned outposts of old as they went. No one had seen the fortress's outer exterior long enough to have a picture in their mind to make a portal to it. When either party finished their intended goal, they would leave for the Titan-World.

Nobody else spoke about the plan nor did anyone try to argue. After Pane finished going over the plans, Lily and Sage left.

They remained quiet for the remainder of the walk. Lily didn't want to speak because she knew it would lead back to the argument. Outside the cold air hit her along with the cloudy night.

"Why won't you let me come with you?" Sage asked.

Lily didn't want to repeat the same point but she knew she had to. "It's not safe," Lily said as they came upon the rubble of the wall. "If the Reality Stone has an opposite effect on the land around it then maybe you could as well take a portal at the heart of the jungle. You could escape at any given time. But up north at the fortress, there is no escape. If you get captured then that is final. No one can help you. *I can't help you.*"

Sage remained quiet as the two of them stepped into the snow. Lily conjured a portal in front of them. The intricately bizarre crystal woods came in front of them. Lily walked through the portal. Sage followed her.

"But what if you get captured?" Sage asked quietly. "Who will help you?"

Lily thought it over. "I won't get captured. I'll come back. I promise I will come back."

Sage nodded. "All right," she whispered, "I'll go to the jungle."

They walked back to the city.

Chapter Two:
To Diverge from Destiny

In the blackness of the night, a storm descended upon the encampment. The blizzard blasted the dozens of soldiers in chilling gails and flurries of snow. Around Lily, dozens of soldiers were covered from the snow only by the tents they stood in. Others huddled around campfires that blew to the side in the harsh wind. The thin branches of the forest provided little protection in the night.

A strange noise went through the storm around her. The wind stopped followed by the snow. Lily looked around her. A faint light began to grow above her in the clouds. It was a deep purple that grew in the seconds that followed. The soldiers around her stood up and looked above toward it.

A new strange noise went across the snowscape. A brilliant explosion came from the light above. The light grew brighter followed by a massive purple shockwave. As the shockwave expanded, Lily covered her eyes.

The shockwave hit the encampment but Lily never felt a thing. Lily opened her eyes. The storm was gone as well as everyone else in the encampment.

Lily was in a dark room lit by the flicker of lanterns. She recognized the stone that stood upon the walls of the room. At a table in front of her were Boreas and Avertree both sitting on chairs. Her father stood in his human form, Aethor underneath a lantern. Two other figures brought a third figure in the room.

The first two were both in large amounts of furs and covered in snow. She didn't recognize either of them but she could guess they were both Storm Riders. She knew however the third. Lee collapsed onto the floor bloodied, bruised and weaponless.

Aethor walked up to Lee as the Storm Riders left the room. Lee looked up toward him. A long blade appeared in Aethor's hand. Lily ran up to Aethor to stop him but it was too late. Lee was killed in an instant.

The dream ended with his death.

...

Lily bolted awake from her covers. The only thought that she had in the darkness of her room was that Lee was going to die.

The rest of the night was a dreamless blackness. In the moonlight, her mind whirled with possibilities. She couldn't get her mind through the fact that Lee would die up north. Her mind began to go over possibilities of how it might happen. Maybe he was captured and handed to Boreas. Maybe he was killed trying to get to the north pole.

Then a thought went through Lily's mind. *What if she tried to stop him from going to the north.* At least for Lee, she could try and persuade him to go after the Reality Stone rather than try and break through Boreas's defenses.

Her mind went through ways of trying to persuade him. She didn't want to terrify him with the fact he would die. But she couldn't find a way to twist so that he could believe her without having to tell him he died.

There was only one way in which he'd survive and she began to see it as the only outcome. She would have to tell him he would die.

As the night began to dwindle she stood up and looked out through her window. Golden rays of light came into the basin of the Capital. In an orange sky, she saw the single moon of Alveran near the end of its day.

She changed into her clothes and went downstairs to find Sage already waiting for her. She handed her Lily's cloak.

"What happened last night?" Sage asked. "I see it in your eyes. Something you saw last night terrifies   you."

Lily stared at her. The truth was inevitable. "I saw Lee die."

"What!?" Sage asked. "How?"

"We were up north. I was in Boreas's fortress and I saw them drag Lee in front of Boreas. And they killed him there."

"We need to tell Pane and Lee now," Sage whispered.

"I just don't know how," Lily said, "You shouldn't tell someone you foresaw their own death. But we can't let him go north either."

"We have to tell Pane," Sage said, "At least tell him. We don't know what to do. He might know what to do."

Lily thought it over but eventually nodded. They left their spire in a hurry. In the shadows of the elegant silver spires, they ran toward the wall where they could leave and hurry to Pane. As they made it to the snow line outside the wall, Lily conjured a portal.

They walked through and rushed down the snow-covered hill above the Last City. Avoiding the last of the pine trees, Lily stopped in front of the guards.

Recognizing her and Sage, the guards let them through and they passed. The two ran beside the Luminous Creek over toward the palace. In the sun, the palace gleamed in golden light. The two of them stopped in front of the two guards at the entrance of the palace.

"Where is General Pane?" Lily asked.

"Is this urgent?" The first of the guards asked. "Just yesterday, someone demanded for an escort of guards to defend her at her holiday home."

"Yes, this is urgent," Lily answered, "It's about the integrity of the mission up north." Technically, it was partly true. Should Lee be captured and Volk killed, Lily didn't even know who would fall under the chain of command.

"How do you know about the mission in the north?" The second guard asked.

"She's one of the people leading it," Sage answered.

The two guards looked perplexed from Sage to Lily.

"If it is so important," the first guard said, "He is in the war room. If you are who you say you are, then you'll know where that is."

Sage looked at Lily before they burst out running. They passed by the portal powered by the Luminous Creek before running up the stairwell. They began to walk through the maze of hallways until they came upon a large hole in front of the war room.

Beside it, Pane was parting ways with some other high ranking soldiers she did recognize. He saw them and his face was surprised.

"What are you doing here?" Pane asked as they came over.

"We need to see Lee now," Lily answered, "I saw him last night."

"What did you see last night in your dreams?" Pane asked.

"I saw him die," Lily answered.

Pane's face was shocked. He looked around them apparently to see if anyone else was around and cornered them into the war room. "Go over everything right now," he said. Lily retold him how she was in the north before the scene then changed later to Boreas's fortress before he was killed there. Pane walked briefly out of the war room. "Send Commander Lee here, alone," he said to a guard.

The guard ran off and they waited in silence. After a few minutes Lee came rushed into the war room alone. He looked from Pane to Lily and Sage. "What happened?" he asked. "Where is everyone else?"

"Lee, you might want to sit down," Pane said quietly.

"What happened?" Lee asked again.

Lily retold her dream to Lee. She imagined it would be hard to tell someone they were going to die but it was so much worse. As Lily ended, she could see the shock on his face when she said he was going to die. The moment, however, passed and he looked more perplexed than worried.

"Did you ever consider that perhaps, whoever has shown these visions has intentions against our own?" Lee asked. "That, perhaps, someone like Boreas wanted you to see these visions in order to change our own choices at the last second? Thereby changing the outcome of this."

Lily thought it over. It was an interesting theory. But somehow she knew it wouldn't add up. Boreas would never have shown as much as the visions had. Subtlety was his specialty only until he required something he could only get by being open; such as reviving Death and using the rest of the North Wind as a cover.

"No, it couldn't be Boreas," she whispered, "He has had too many things go wrong with his plans. While the outcome of them always ended in his intention, Boreas would never risk losing his plans in such a way."

"Okay, so then what?" Lee asked. "What do I do? Do I just believe everything you just saw was nothing more than an outcome too late to come now? I should perhaps go to Haranae instead?"

"That is exactly what you should do," Sage broke in, "If we can stop you from going north, then you won't die."

Lee slumped into the bottom of his chair and for the first time to Lily, Lee looked tired. His old features were exhausted as he thought through everything that he had just heard. She knew it would be hard on him but she had always expected Lee to have been able to handle it.

"The paths we walk, demons past, present, and to come lay beneath," Lee whispered. "Each path may diverge from each other in some way but what we run from always will come to greet us at some point along. Maybe, every outcome will end with the same fate. Some people believe that time and destiny are always set in place no matter what you do to stop it. That time is like a river and no matter how many stones you throw in, the flow will never change. Let me ask you, Lily, right now, do you believe in such things?"

"I don't believe in destiny, or fate, or the flow of time," Lily answered softly, "Our own choices brought us here, whether believing in such things or not. Nothing is set in place and that is why I am here now to try and save you."

"And yet, as a child," Lee said, "You ran from Death after you heard you would cause The End. And we were only minutes from that even after you tried to change it."

Lily's argument was killed then and there. One of her biggest choices she ever made, to run away from her father, was as Lee said, a diversion of destiny.

"Lee," Pane whispered, "We are trying to save your life. And whether it affects our end mission, we still have to try and bring everyone home."

"And I am eternally grateful for that," Lee whispered. They remained quiet for some time. Lily didn't want to add anything to the flames of the argument. She could tell Lee was thinking it everything even further over.

"Can you promise me this will end well?" Lee asked.

Lily looked at him confused. What had caused the sudden change, she did not know. "What do you mean?" she asked.

"Can you promise me that when this is over, we will end on a victorious path?" he asked her again.

The question hit Lily hard. *Was he accepting his own death?* She asked herself. If this was the only way to have to go for the Reality Stone, she knew she'd have to promise.

"We will," she whispered.

Lily stayed quiet for a second but nodded. "I'll go to Haranae," Lee whispered. Quietly, he walked out of the room without saying another word.

But the only two things going through Lily's mind now was whether she had made the right choice to tell him and whether he had just chosen to accept death.

Chapter Three:
In the North Pole

Boreas opened his eyes. He sat up in the dim, lantern-lit room. He had just seen the same vision he knew the daughter of Aethor had seen. His mind went through the fact Commander Lee had died in front of him in his fortress. Floating at his bedside, was the Crimson Blade.

The vision, however, had revealed to him information the enemy would rather not have wanted to see. He now knew that a large encampment of soldiers would attempt to attack his own fortress at the north pole. *Let them try*, he thought to himself. With that said, he doubted that. Their connected dreams often changed or over exaggerated themselves.

The peculiar connection between him and Lily had been of benefit for not just her but rather him, as well. His secrets would often show them what he would do and then he would adjust after he would see what they attempted to do at the same period.

Boreas held out his hand and the Crimson Blade floated into it. He put on his cloak of midnight blue and silver, the colors of the North Wind, and left his room. He was at nearly the top of the fortress. Outside, he could see the black of night in the snowstorm that descended upon the fortress. As he walked down the steps, he ran into a non-magic. He could tell immediately this with his robes tucked in correctly.

"Lord Boreas," He said, bowing his head. Boreas nodded in return but caught his arm as he passed.

"May you send word to a man named Aethor and bring him to the engineering level?" Boreas whispered to him. "He is two floors up in the room two doors to the right. Tell no one of this task."

The man waited a few seconds taking the information in and nodded. "I'll bring him right away," he replied.

Boreas walked away from the man and further descended across the fortress. He passed more groups of his followers, both non-magics and Sorcerers as he passed. The fortress, which nearly was abandoned except for his three main followers, Corvus, Ariadne, and their son Percival, now felt much more welcoming. The lanterns along the walls were always lit and it was nice to see a passing face.

Soon, he finally descended upon the engineering level. Below the fortress was a massive cavern where the world engine stood connected to supports at the ground. Workers were helping fix the menial damage it had sustained during the battle at the Last City a week ago.

As he stood looking at the view, Aethor came in behind him. "You had a non-magic sent to me?" he asked.

"This fortress is full of non-magics and Sorcerers alike," Boreas said, "Get over it."

"Why was I sent?" Aethor asked unphased as if he hadn't heard.

"The Reality Stone," Boreas whispered, as a Sorcerer passed by them. "I have someone else helping us. One who will help us find it."

Aethor looked at him confused. "Who?" he asked.

The two of them descended to the ground level of the cavern. They began to walk across the cavern floor. They weaved through the desks strewn of workers attempting to combine Earth's technology and his own. Boreas thought of the marvels that could be created that could tip the tides of the war in his favor, but he could tell Aethor thought otherwise.

Soon he came upon the last of the work stations in the cavern. It was at a corner of the cavern, and one of the parts of the table touched the rock face. Boreas had wanted absolute secrecy in this man's work.

"Dr. Quentin Johannson, meet Aethor," Boreas said. A long haired, bearded man appeared from below the work table. He was in a white lab coat, some of which was smudged or singed black. Boreas knew that him being from Earth may be a problem with Aethor.

"Lord Boreas," he said bowing to Boreas, "and Aethor, was it?" He held out his hand to Aethor. Boreas looked at Aethor, half expecting him to not take it. Soon, however, he gave in and shook it. "Have you come for the…" Dr. Johannson whispered, "detectors?"

"You don't need to whisper around him," Boreas said, "He is on the same path we take. Now, let us see the detectors."

"My husband Ray will bring them over in a second," Dr. Johannson said. He shouted across the cavern and another man came running down toward them. Ray Johannson was a slightly overweight, kind faced man with the same, slightly singed lab coat as his husband.

"Where did you put the lock box?" Quentin Johannson asked.

Ray Johannson shuffled along below the work table looking for what he called the 'lock box' and soon he came upon it. He pulled up a small metal box with a small keypad at the end of it. He inputted a few digits into the keypad and the lock box clicked open. He set it in front of Boreas, rather than opening it.

Boreas walked forward and opened the box. Inside were four sleek black pads. Attached to them were straps like a watch.

"How do they work?" Boreas asked. He put the pad at the top of his wrist and fastened the clasp around it.

"The Annihilation Detectors," Quentin Johannson began, "As I named them after the creation of the stone and the blade are a type of tracker to locate the Reality Stone and the Crimson Blade. As we know, the two were created by opposite forces. The Crimson Blade created by a harnessed singularity of antimatter and the Reality Stone made by a singularity of constant matter. I came up with the theory to track the two opposites."

Ray Johannson broke in. "He gave me the theory, I designed the detectors. I came up with the idea from the police detectors that are used to find one another. I modified it to track the singularities."

"I've seen one of those... " Aethor whispered before trailing off.

"You have?" Ray Johannson asked. "Have you stayed on Earth before?"

Boreas looked toward Aethor and knew where he had. He had killed a few dozen police officers from Earth before acquiring blood matter and nearly succeeded in wiping out humanity.

"I have," Aethor lied quickly, "Two years ago I believe."

"Oh, where did you stay?" Ray Johannson asked again.

"Sunlight Grove, in a disguise, however... all to briefly I must add," Aethor answered, "I was hoping to stay longer but I found the silence of some places better."

Boreas winced at his answer. It was treading dangerous water but at least he didn't lie because he could have made a false statement. Both, however, were unable to tell by the clues as Ray Johannson started again.

"I took the tracker and took out the signal beacon that connected the pads to each other," he began once more, "Before modifying it to match the two singularities' energy signatures. May I show you?"

Boreas looked around and found the engineering level nearly vacant. He pulled aside his cloak and he let the Crimson Blade float freely in the open in front of the four of them. He then held out his wrist in front of Ray.

Ray Johannson walked in front of them and turned the detector on. The screen lit up. The screen showed an arrow where Boreas stood. A red dot stood where the Crimson Blade was floating. Boreas moved it slightly to the right and the dot followed.

"Nicely done," Boreas said.

"There is a slight problem, however," Quentin Johannson came in.

"What is it?" Boreas asked, looking at him perplexed. Everything as far as he could tell worked all right.

"The energy signatures are quite faint," he answered, "Had I had more time, perhaps a few weeks rather than just one, I could have been able to increase the range of the tracker."

"What is the range?" Boreas asked.

"A few miles," Quentin Johannson answered, "Maybe ten."

Aethor looked at him. "Do you know how far we are looking?" he nearly shouted. "Perhaps you do not understand where they were put. There are hundreds of miles between the center and the entrance. And, unlike the Crimson Blade, we do not have a map to search for it. You are asking us to search for a single blade of grass in a field!"

Both Ray and Quentin were startled by his shouting.

Boreas intervened before he could say anything else. "Ray, you were working on the world engine before coming over here. How far are you into fixing it?"

"The hull contained little to no damage in the battle but the engine overheated from the consistent rate of fire," Ray Johannson answered, "In a week, perhaps, I can fix it. This technology is new to me."

"Then do it quickly," Boreas said, "Aethor, might I have a word with you on the balcony."

They walked out of the engineering level. Neither of them spoke a word to each other until no one was near them.

"What the hell do you think you are doing?" Boreas asked.

"How can you trust the people from there?" Aethor asked.

"How can I trust non-magics?" Boreas asked rhetorically. "They are no different than the Sorcerers around you and I here.

"You don't know them like I do," Aethor hissed.

"I do in fact," Boreas said back, "They've taken what I have loved most. The only difference between us is who we blame for what we've lost. You lost your whole species due to one group's hands and yet you blame everyone else for it. Did you ever consider perhaps that your own choices led you to this fate?"

"My daughter once told me that," Aethor whispered.

"Forgiveness is the only way you can bring back what you lost," Boreas whispered, "And then you may build back what you lost."

Aethor laughed. "How many have you murdered for your 'justice' as you-so-called it? Vengeance is a hard thing to control in yourself. It's a shame you never had the same experience I did. Then perhaps we'd see eye to eye. My people are dead. The last of us are in the Sorcerers now. And what is done is done. There are no do-overs."

Boreas flinched at his last words. He couldn't handle him anymore. "Be ready to leave in a week."

Aethor didn't add anything else to the argument, and at least Boreas was thankful for that.

Chapter Four:
Isolated

"I wished you'd have come around sooner," Mary Ravenhill said to Lily and Sage. She was their foster parent they lived with before they went to college. Carlo Ravenhill, their other foster parent sat beside her. Lily had told them she was a Sorcerer years earlier but had never shown them out of fear that someone else would find out. She had lived with them just after she had run away from her own father.

Lily and Sage came to visit their foster parents when they could, but they hadn't in a while. They were in the sitting room at their foster parents' house on Earth. Sunlight was flooding into the room from a large window leading out into the green of the garden.

"We're sorry, just with everything happening with the North Wind, it has been hard to come here anytime soon," Sage said. Lily and Sage had given them some of the information about the North Wind and the past month and a half that had gone by. They told Lily and Sage about what politics had labeled the North Wind in their absence, the government naming them radicals and urging people to not join, but admitting the North Wind mustn't be what they said, and confirmed it was not illegal. Boreas even had another two rallies on Earth gaining hundreds more supporters.

"We are most worried about your safety," Carlo said, "We were never able to have children of our own until both of you ended with us."

"And with you going on an expedition to the north, we are so worried about you," Mary put in. Lily had left out key details to them about their raid north and only told the length and destination. She hadn't even told them Sage and she wouldn't be together for the next week or few.

"It is totally safe," Lily lied, "You shouldn't worry about it."

A loud beeping went through the sitting room. "That would be lunch," Carlo said and he pushed himself out of his seat to go to the kitchen.

"I'll help," Sage said and she left the sitting room.

Mary leaned closely to Lily as she left the room. "Are you two still hanging out with John?" Mary asked.

"Yes," Lily answered, rolling her eyes. "What are you implying with that?"

"I am just implying that they both have some soft spots for each other," Mary answered, "and I don't want her to end up with some sleight of hand Sorcerer to end up flirting with her."

"Don't worry, I'll keep an eye on her," Lily whispered. Lily felt the same concern Mary did but she knew that their concerns were unlikely, at worst.

They soon had lunch in the garden. Lily and Sage both tried to bury their concerns, but Lily had to admit she was spreading the lies pretty far.

Soon after, Lily and Sage were beginning to leave the home. "Stay safe," Carlo said, embracing them each.

"Bye, Mom," Lily said, hugging Mary. Sage did the same and they left. Their foster parents' house stood by the community a few miles outside of Sunlight Grove in the mountains. Their house had a view of the silver skyscrapers and the fields of the meadow next to the city where she had once read in quiet, before everything had changed. She even saw the specific tree where she used to read, although it looked very small in the distance.

"We should take a portal from here," Sage said.

Lily remembered what she had to do now, and it hit her hard. They had to try and persuade James Fonsesca out from hiding. Lily knew he was going through a depression after her father was revived.

"I hope what we see isn't too bad," Sage whispered.

"I have a feeling that neither of us are going to like what we see," Lily whispered back. She conjured a portal to the Spectral Boundary. The familiar purple haze was in front of them. She peered through. No demons. Since her father had come back she always wanted to check to make sure there were no demons.

They jumped through. The two of them fell through the boundary. There were no flashes of light that looked like lightning, which was what the demons and spirits fighting looked like. They soon fell through the ground at the bottom of the boundary.

Long, thin brown shapes came to Lily's vision before it adjusted. She had fallen upon the snow in a cluster of trees that were in the forest on the hills beside the Capital. Sage was beside her. She brushed off the snow and held out her hand to Sage and pulled her up.

The two of them walked down the rest of the hill until they came toward the ruined wall. The guards didn't ask for their identification again, so they began walking through the spires. A gentle snowfall began. The sun barely was able to pierce through. The snowflakes fell slowly before the ground but never made contact. They would vanish. While in the summer, blizzards occasionally came, but winter snowfalls or blizzards were frequent. Because it was nearly winter, there were many snowfalls to come.

As the two of them continued to walk they saw Peter and John across a street. Lily and Sage walked up toward them. "Have either of you seen Fonsesca?" Lily asked.

Peter shook his head. "It has been completely quiet," Peter answered, "We knocked on his door a few times, around ten minutes ago, but he didn't come out."

"That's not good," Sage said, "He would've come out if he wanted to see us. I don't think there is anything good behind that door."

Lily walked up to the door. She hesitated, but knocked. They waited in silence. After around thirty seconds, she knocked again. The same silence.

35

Lily conjured a disc and broke the doorknob. The door knob cracked in front of them as she hit it and the door creaked open.

"We should've done that earlier," Sage whispered, "We should've known he wouldn't answer."

Lily pushed it a little farther revealing the darkness of the spire within. They walked forward into the spire, as silently as possible. In front of them was a darkened stairwell that encircled the walls of the spire. The living room appeared to not have been touched in days and the ashes in the fireplace were piled up, also untouched.

They heard a creak upstairs. They looked up and heard another creak. "James!" Sage shouted through the spire. "James, we are here to see you! Can we come up?"

No reply came to them. "Let's go up quietly," John said.

Lily crept up the stairs before them. She tried not to make a sound, as much as she could, but she couldn't help the occasional creak on the stairs. She came upon the next room and she gently opened the door. Darkness without movement. She scanned the rest of the room and found no one else there. She heard another creak from above and motioned to the others above her.

She began up the end of the stairs once more. She knew that most spires in the city had no more than three floors. She came upon the final door where the stairs ended. She opened the door and to her surprise saw no one.

Lily had just enough time to scan the room before she saw the knife coming at her head. She heard someone scream behind her. She caught the wrist of the attacker and struck the knife out of his hand. With the same hand, she struck the assailant in the nose.

Lily looked at her assailant. She was shocked at who she saw. In the shadows, Fonsesca stared back at her.

"Lily," he gasped, "What the hell are you doing here?" Lily let go of his arm. With a trembling hand, she lit the room with a green orb between her fingers.

If she hadn't been so shocked at seeing that he was the one attacking her, she would have gasped after seeing him in the green light. His face was gaunt and his eyes were set in heavy shadows. His hair was mottled and messy against his forehead. When Lily scanned the room, she knew it was worse. Bottles were strewn across his bedroom.

"How much have you been drinking?" she asked.

Fonsesca looked around the room. "Too much," he answered, "I blacked out a few hours ago and I woke up to someone moving up the stairs. I thought you were the damn North Wind."

Lily put her hand against his cheek."What have you done to yourself?" She asked. Fonsesca stepped away from her. He didn't answer.

"Let's get him downstairs," Peter said.

They helped Fonsesca downstairs. Lily watched as he held the railing with each frail step.

Twice, he would have fallen over if it hadn't been for John or Peter catching him. Lily was amazed he had been able to attack her in his current state.

Peter and John helped him onto the couch on the bottom floor. Lily lit a small fire due to the fireplace being neglected of the ashes being cleaned out.

After a single log was crackling with small orange flames in the fireplace, Lily turned back to Fonsesca. "Why did you let yourself get to this?" she asked.

"I think you know why I am like this," Fonsesca answered.

"Then that is no excuse," Sage put in, "If we knew then we could've helped you."

"I lost everything two years ago," Fonsesca hissed. "I lost my friends, I lost Ritter, and I nearly gave my life. And I should have given it. And instead, the bastard that left me alive is back. He haunted my dreams for two years, and now he haunts my life."

Lily remembered what Lee had told them earlier in the day about changing the future. One line he said, she stood out. *The paths we walk, demons past, present, and to come, lay beneath*. His demons had come back and now they were here to haunt him.

"The only way we can make amends is by fighting our demons, not by fleeing from them," Lily said.

"I encaged mine in my nightmares," Fonsesca whispered, "But now they exist outside of my nightmares. The only thing that kept them back is behind the bottles. And even that doesn't work now."

"Come with us," Sage said, "Together, we can kill your demons for good."

"You expect too much from me," Fonsesca said. He stood up and walked to the beginning of the stairs. Peter and John grudgingly moved aside for him. "Just leave me alone. Please."

"We leave tomorrow," Peter said but Lily could tell it was useless.

Lily watched as he walked up the stairs away from them. Seeing him leave filled her with sadness. She could tell the others felt the same, even in the faint firelight.

"What do we do?" John asked.

"We have to let him go," Peter said, "I want to do this right. And that means we have to give him time. And not force him in any way."

"I think that is all we'll get out of him anyway at the current moment," Lily said, "If he sees the harm done by these people then perhaps he'll join us."

"He already has," Sage said, "He's just scared."

She stood up and walked to the entrance. Peter, John, and Sage followed. "I shouldn't have broken the door knob," she whispered as she looked at the broken piece of metal.

Peter shut the door. "It still closes."

Chapter Five:
The Sea of Sand

Lily looked out into the storm. The snow whipped against her in the harsh, chilling winds. In the ink of the night, the encampment stood still. Soldiers were huddled around campfires that gave just enough light to the whole camp. It was just like her dream before.

Lily heard the same strange noise she had heard before. She looked up into the sky. It was the same purple light. The purple shockwave followed the expansion of the lone light in the sky. She covered her eyes in the light.

The encampment was gone. She was in the fortress of the North Wind once more. She wasn't, however, overlooking from the side of the room. She was lying at the center of the room. There was no Lee in the room, or her father and Boreas. She pushed herself off of the cold stone. She realized the harsh reality of the dream. *She had taken Lee's place.*

In front of her, Avertree sat at the same table as before. He beckoned for someone to come forward. She didn't see who it was. All she saw was the sword that came to her head.

...

Lily gasped as she bolted up. Unlike normal, silence in the darkness didn't come. After about ten

40

seconds, she heard someone coming up the stairs. Sage entered her bedroom.

"I heard you scream," she said, "And I thought I heard someone going down the stairs. I thought maybe someone else was here."

"No one else is here," Lily whispered, "I just heard you going up the stairs."

Sage shrugged before walking closer to her. "Another dream?"

"Yeah," Lily whispered, "Another dream."

"That one was different, wasn't it?" Sage asked. She walked over next to the bed. She sat down beside her. She held Lily's hand in her own. "What happened?"

"I traded places with Lee," Lily answered in a faint whisper.

Sage gasped. "Does that mean…"

Lily put her head into her own arms. "Oh please, I hope not." She could feel tears coming down onto her palms. What if she had done the wrong thing by telling Lee he was going to die? Had that set up herself on the cold floor in front of Avertree. She felt Sage crawl into the covers beside her and put her arm around her shoulders.

"Was there anything else different in the dream?" Sage asked.

Lily thought it over. "My father and Boreas weren't there," she answered. "That was all."

"That tells us one thing at least," Sage said.

"What is that?" Lily asked.

"Well it means we may be able to affect what will come next," Sage whispered, "Perhaps if we were able to affect Lee and your father not being in the dream, then we could take you out."

"How would we do that?" Lily asked. "We are leaving for Haranae today, and then I'll be going to the north tomorrow."

"I don't know," Sage answered. "Perhaps we could find an answer for that. But I don't want you to go. Go with us to Haranae. We can tell Pane and he'll say the same."

Lily waited for a moment before deciding. She was the only person who knew the fortress despite being in it briefly. "Maybe we should just leave it," Lily whispered, "And don't tell anyone. We may have saved Lee. I don't want him going back north and him being killed once more."

Sage gripped her hand. "Promise me you will stay safe," she whispered, "Please promise me."

"I will," Lily promised. They waited without saying a word to each other. Lily looked outside. The dark night was finally lighting up into dawn. Glints of orange were above the mountain range. "We should get ready," Lily whispered. "Pane will want us soon."

Sage lifted the covers off herself. "All right," she said, "I'll get ready below."

Lily began to get ready, once Sage left. She changed and washed herself before grabbing a light brown cloak for the desert travel. She wouldn't have to wear it for long. As soon as she was able to get the group into the jungle, she could leave at a moment's notice. Then she would gather her things for the north and would leave with Pane.

She left her room and went downstairs. Sage was attaching a sleeping bag onto her traveling backpack. "Are you ready?" Lily asked.

Sage finished attaching the sleeping bag. She put on a similar light brown cloak and slung her backpack onto her shoulders. "Yeah." She answered.

They walked outside. The cold attacked her. Her cloak was designed to repel heat, not keep it. The sky was a brilliant orange as the sun was lifting into the sky. They walked through the silver city. Soon they came upon the city's edge.

Lily conjured a portal. The Last City's golden spires came into view at the bottom of the hill they stood upon. Lily and Sage walked through the pine trees to the bottom of the hill. The soft new snow collapsed with each step leading to the hard icy snow below. She had to keep her footing or she would've slid through the snow.

"We should have brought sleds," Sage said as she tried to keep her footing. She held onto a tree to keep herself from sliding down.

Lily laughed. "Yeah, that would make this so much easier."

Below them was Graves and Lee. They were waiting at the rubble of the ruined wall. They were also in similar lighter clothing. Fonsesca was not there. "Who are we waiting for?" Lily asked.

"Pane," Lee answered. "He's giving some final orders to General Anders. You'll be leaving almost immediately after you return to go north. No idea what Peter and John are waiting for."

Soon, Pane came from the Capital. He was with General Anders but he left as Pane came upon the group.

The minutes began to tick by. Lily and Sage began teaching Lee a card game from Earth, and Graves began kicking around a small rock in the rubble. Soon, Peter and John came running from the streets of the Capital toward them. "We're not late!" Lily heard John shout through the streets before they stopped in front of the group. "We're not late." He took another breath. "We were always here. Just keep going over the plan."

"We didn't go over the plan," Pane said, "but we have made some changes. For those who haven't been in the loop, Lee is going with you to Haranae, rather than the north. I thought it better to have a second Sorcerer in the group, if you have any questions." He had added the lie convincingly. Lily didn't know who he told but she doubted he had told Graves or Peter and John, based on their surprised looks.

"If I might add," Graves said, "but I think we'd like to know where you were." He motioned toward Peter and John.

Peter held out his wrist. A small wrist pad was attached to it. "Hey, I recognize that," Sage said, "Fonsesca had one when we first came to this planet two years ago."

"So did I," Peter said, "I went over to his place to ask for his." He paused. "He's not coming but he wasn't reluctant to give help when he could. Look at this, however." He turned on the pad and the screen lit up. He pressed the screen a few times, until he showed them the pad.

Peter held out the screen for the rest of them to see. Two beacons were on the screen. He pulled a second from his jacket and moved it around. The second beacon slowly moved as his arm passed. He handed the second to Pane. "In case we get lost," Peter said. Pane put it in his own cloak. "We can also communicate, and the pad also has a drone, because you can't make portals to places you have never seen."

Graves looked at Pane surprised. "That actually makes a lot of sense," he said, "Not bad, kid."

"Of course it makes sense," Sage said, "Peter lives to make good ideas and to find the best solutions."

"I also live for other things," Peter said.

John, Lily and Sage laughed. "Such as?" John asked.

Peter stared up into the sky. "Let's get to the damn desert," he said quickly without answering.

Pane held up a photo in his hand. It looked as if it was torn out of a book with the edges rough and misshapen. "Is that the world?" Graves said. "Looks like a couple of dunes."

Peter looked over at the photo. "That could be half of a continent on Earth. Are we sure it is from Haranae?" Lily went over and saw a sea of dunes. Peter was right. It could be a desert anywhere on Earth.

"Planets aren't as diverse as we all think," Lee said. "Look at my own. We are the same distance from our star albeit, a much colder star so that half of our oceans freeze over in hundreds of feet of ice and nearly all of the land is covered in snow apart from the equator." Only once had Lily ever been away from the snow on this world. It was when she was a child and was horribly sick, so her mother gave her own life for Lily. She had been taken to a nursery on a mountain range.

Lee continued on. "Earth is an exception. They have deserts of harsh heat, but they also have miles of ice at the poles. Haranae has only the former. Overuse of the world has turned it into a dust bowl of sand across all parts."

That last part hit Lily. It was exactly what her father had foretold on his own world. *And look what happened in the desert,* Lily told herself, *he was right.*

"Sounds nice," John said. "As Peter said, let's get to the damn desert."

Pane lowered the photo and conjured a portal. The Spectral Boundary was in their view. The familiar purple haze was on the other side.

"Follow me," Pane said. He jumped through followed by Lee and Graves.

Lily gave a last look at the rising sun above the peaks and jumped through. She was met soon by sand. As she landed, she tumbled down a sand dune and fell at the bottom. She landed beside Lee and Pane.

She heard the shouts of Sage and John, as they tumbled down behind her, followed by Peter.

"Well I think we are here," Lee said. He stood up and helped Lily up.

Lily brushed the sand off of her clothes. She surveyed the area around her. Under a blue sky was miles of sand dunes. The hot sun beating down upon them was at a midpoint in the sky.

"Let's get to high ground," Peter said.

Lily began taking steps up the dune. With each step, she sprayed a light sand in front of her. Soon she made it up the dune followed by Peter and everyone else. The first thing she noticed was a long moving spray of dust a few miles out in a flat land.

"What are those sprays?" she asked and pointed out to the flat lands. Peter already had binoculars out and was looking. Pane and Lee also were looking through their own.

"Humans," Pane whispered. He handed his pair to Lily. She immediately looked through. The sprays of sand were from multiple long thin metal vehicles with metal railings touching the sand. Humans in a dark sand colored coating rode them much like a motorbike.

They were chasing a herd of grazers that looked much like gazelle. Lily looked as one of the lead riders threw out something toward one of the grazers followed by the collapse of it. Soon a rider left the spray to meet the poor creature.

"Well we aren't on Earth," Lily said. She handed her binoculars off to someone else, but she didn't know who. She was still entranced by the chase.

"How far are we from the jungle?" Graves asked.

Lily looked around. All across them was the sea of dunes, except for the flat lands where the chase occurred.

"I sure hope it isn't near the flat lands," Lee said, "I haven't met anyone in this world, but I wouldn't bet they would be much kinder to outsiders."

Peter already had his drone zipping around. He flew it out in the direction opposite of the flat lands. They stood there for several minutes as the drone flew out of sight. Soon it was nothing more than a speck in the sky.

Lily took several glances at the screen and noticed Peter always avoided the cliffs and mountains when he controlled the drone. Lily guessed he must have thought the jungle was in the middle of nowhere, not beside a cliff.

"Can someone get me a portal?" Peter asked. "It'll be easier in the shade. And I don't want to find out how bad the ultra violet radiation is here."

Lee looked over at the pad and conjured a portal. Through the portal was a cliff face off a dark color. Rocks were strewn across the floor under the shade.

They walked through, under the shade. As the portal closed behind her, Lily saw the drone zip away.

The wait began once more. Even under the shade, it was still deathly hot. Lily once more began to teach Lee the card game she had done earlier with

Sage and John. Even Pane and Graves began to watch, in the boredom under the cliff.

After some time, a herd of grazers they had seen before came upon the group. Lily finally saw them for what they looked like for the first time. They were similar to gazelles with a thin light brown fur and small black eyes. At the end of their head were two razor sharp black prongs. The few in the herd began to feed with long tongues on the thin brush and leaves that grew along the cliffside.

Lily watched, as Sage stood up from the game and walked to an unattended brush, and snapped off a sprig of the brush. Sage walked over to one of the grazers. It lifted its head at the girl. Sage held out the sprig and watched as the grazer's tongue fed off of the small leaves. Sage giggled as the tongue brushed against her hand and Lily couldn't help but smile.

"Wow," Peter whispered. Lily turned toward him and knew what he must've meant. Lily walked over to him and looked at the pad. A vast jungle of green spanned nearly the entire pad except for the bottom where sand still stood.

Lily looked off into the distance and realized just how important leaving was. Sprays of sand were heading directly toward them from less than a mile away. In front of them were three of the metal vehicles.

"Let's go," Lily said to the group, "I think they see us." She conjured a portal from the image. The jungle awaited her on the other side. As the others jumped through, Lily noticed the grazers didn't have their attention on their chasers but rather the portal.

Without a second guess, one by one they jumped through the portal to their shock. Lily gasped and marveled at their intelligence. When the last one had jumped through and scampered off into the sand, Lily was still shocked. She could tell the others felt the same.

Lily looked toward the jungle and felt another wave of shock. The jungle was massive. Much like the mist that occupied the edge of the space that held the Crimson Blade, the jungle spanned in a circle across the horizon. At the edge of the jungle, the ground turned almost immediately to sand to grass and flowers on wet soil. The trees that towered in the jungle were at least a hundred feet tall and their canopies covered nearly all of it.

The group began to walk over to the jungle. As the group came closer, the jungle loomed overhead exponentially. And that was when Lily noticed the flowers. There was a ring of flowers that was at the edge of the jungle. Except she knew they shouldn't exist. Different types of flowers grew upon the vines of the same plant.

Peter stopped in front of the row of flowers. There were three types that grew on the same plant and the ring was itself a foot wide. The first was a small blue-purple flower called an iris. The other two were a white orchid and purple hyacinth that both grew above the iris. "Strange," he whispered, "Something changed their DNA and structures to grow together on the same plant."

"The Reality Stone," Pane whispered. "At least, there is no mist this time."

Lee looked toward Lily. "We can't move forward until you do," he said. It was part of the enchantment and she knew it.

She walked forward over the flowers and laid a step into the jungle. One by one they followed her in, almost as if the enchantment hadn't been laid there.

"Say your partings and let's move," Graves said. Lily looked at him in anger. She could see some of the others giving him the same look.

"Graves, give the kids their time," Lee said.

"We have a chance to stop Boreas from getting the Reality Stone," Graves said, "I only want to ensure that. I don't want to be in a universe in which Boreas has the ability to do and get whatever he wants."

Graves walked off into the jungle. While Pane talked to Lee, Lily talked to Peter, John, and Sage.

"I am going to miss you," Sage said and she hugged Lily.

"Me too," Lily whispered. Lily felt John wrap his arms around them. Soon, they let go of each other. "Stay safe," Lily said.

"We have it easy," John whispered, "You're going to war in the middle of a tundra. We get a vacation in the jungle with a few psychopaths chasing us."

"Thanks for reminding me," Lily said. "Stay safe," she said to Peter. She hugged him as well despite his brief protest.

Lily let go of him. Sage gave her another hug. "Keep your promise," Sage whispered into her ear, only just to her.

"I will," Lily whispered back. She let go of Sage and looked back toward Pane, who was waiting for her. She looked toward Lee, who was just feet from him.

Lee nodded to her and gave her a weak smile. "We made the right choices," he said. Lily nodded.

Pane and Lily walked out of the shade of the jungle and the ring of flowers into the desert sun. Pane conjured a portal to the Spectral Boundary.

Lily gave one last look at her friends in the jungle. They were smiling at her. She looked away and leapt through.

Chapter Six:
The Raiding Party

Lily fell through the boundary. Soon she was greeted by the stretched out image of the crystal woods beside the Capital and followed by the cold of the snow.

Pane was brushing off snow behind her. "I'll be back soon," he said. He conjured a portal and was gone. Lily looked up into the clouds. The sun showed it was already past midday.

She looked toward the city. The wall of pillars that encircled the city loomed in front of her. Behind it was the still silver spires of a quiet city and the looming palace in the mountains. She saw a few faint lights in the palace and Lily wondered who was in charge of the Capital now that Pane was leaving north and General Anders was leading the Last City.

Lily began to walk toward the city. She walked through the entrance of the city. She watched as the pathway's color changed with each step. She saw a mother watching her two children, no more than toddlers, laughing as they danced along the grey path, changing the colors of the swirls and streaks around it.

She remembered the first time she had come upon the beauty of the pathway. After her father had entrusted her life to Pane and his wife Adrianna, she had lived where they had for some time. When Pane had been promoted to Commander, they had moved to the city. She remembered as she entered the city, her hand in Adrianna's and she couldn't have helped being transfixed by the path. She smiled remembering the memory; remembering a time when Adrianna was alive and she had no sorrows of her own except what little memory of her parents she had at the time.

Lily soon left the main pathway to her own spire. When she got home, she stripped off her light clothing and entered a hot shower before changing into her heaviest clothing. She packed extra pairs of clothing in a small bag. She also packed a small sabre of her own that she had carried when chasing The Assassin years ago.

As she left, she felt warm for once but she knew that it wouldn't last long the moment she felt the cold of the north. As she walked through the silver spires, she felt a cold gust of wind pass through the city. She heard the small ringing off chimes overhead, perhaps on some balcony. The sound of the chimes calmed her in the quiet city. The gust and ring of chimes were gone as she came to the main walkway.

Lily looked around for the children and their mother laughing in the streets but saw they were gone. She walked toward the edge of the city. Pane wasn't at the city's edge nor in the crystal woods. Perhaps he had another issue to resolve in command.

She walked to one of the trees at the border of the woods. At the trunk of the tree, the base split into two which lead to the branches overhead. She wrapped her hand around one of the branches and pulled herself up onto the split.

Lily began to watch the quiet city. She began to wonder why the Capital was near empty. She knew many would never come back after whatever trauma they received years ago when her father had attacked the city. But after that, she had no clue. She knew people had left the Last City after Boreas had attacked, but she had assumed they had moved here and yet the city still stood quiet. Maybe they feared an attack here and decided on leaving all major cities or to another world. She knew that fear was stronger than the heaviest of hammers or wounds from the sharpest of swords, but it was still a mystery.

Another gust of wind befell her. Even in her heaviest of clothes, she still felt the chill. She knew she should relish the moments before she traveled north. Only once she had felt so cold that fear had cut into her. When she ran away from her father, she had traveled across the world to the Last City. The Assassin had shown her the memory two years ago. She remembered how hard it had been to even do the simplest of tasks in the cold.

Footsteps came behind her. Her head whipped around and she saw Pane limping from behind a tree. He was wrapped in a black fur cloak rather than the Last City's own gold.

"I am terribly sorry if I startled you," Pane whispered, "I had been taking a walk through the woods."

Lily nodded. "Will we go to the Gates of the Storm?" she asked.

Pane opened a portal. Lily slid down from the tree. She brushed off the snow that had stuck to her cloak.

"I am sorry if this is hard for you," Pane said, "Leaving your friends. Your family. We were so worried about you when Boreas took you."

"I didn't want them to come with me here," Lily said, "I know the risks. It would be better if they search for the Reality Stone."

Pane conjured a portal. "That is why we are here instead of them. They are safe with Commander Lee and Graves," Pane said.

"What do you think they will find?" Lily asked.

"I don't know," Pane said. Lily saw him look to the sky briefly. She saw a small crystal sparrow, glitter in the faint sunlight that pierced the clouds.

"Life perhaps. Strange wonders that few have seen and fewer can comprehend."

He beckoned for Lily to go through. She walked through and he followed her. Lily was met by a bitter wind and a cold she had felt only so terrible a few times before. The sky around her was a dark night in the clouds unlike hundreds of miles below at the Capital. She was met by what may have once been a massive wall, now rubble. A narrow path, no more than ten feet wide had been carved into the rubble. Wooden spikes larger than a man were shoved into the ground in half-rings around the outside of the rubble. Crude towers of stone had been erected at the rings where she saw small groups of Black Striders huddled around the warmth of glowing orange braziers. She saw large weapons of war positioned on top of the towers surrounded by dim torches as well as panels of hinged wood for archer posts.

"Is it too late too maroon, for those strange wonders we were talking about?" she asked.

"Not unless you want to be an outlaw and deserter," Pane answered, "Follow and attempt not stare at the destruction." He added that second part in a whisper.

Lily followed him through the rings of the shafts of the wood. As she passed each watchtower, many of the groups or pairs of guards bolted up expecting orders as Pane came near. Lily even saw a lanky girl and two bearded men make a poor attempt at hiding a game of cards before standing to meet him.

Soon they came to the end of the rings and began to cut through the rubble. Despite new layers of snow, Lily could still tell the unevenness from the attack from the world engine a few weeks ago. A few blackened ghosts of pale trees stood out among the valley. In the mountains were two rows of the encampment that dug directly into the stone. Dim orange flickers of light from braziers lined the rows of encampments across the railings.

While she knew it was there, Lily could barely see the much larger northern gate at the other side of the valley, near a mile away. Much of her vision in the darkness was of the soldiers training on the ground. She saw Black Striders training soldiers who didn't wear the black uniform of them but rather a reflective silver beneath their black fur cloaks. She saw some shooting at targets lit by braziers with arrows with mostly poor results. Lily as well saw groups being taught combat with heavy wooden staffs and blunted steel swords.

Pane led her along the edge of the encampment toward a set of stairs. She walked along the stairs until they reached the lower railway. She then walked along the railway toward a room dug into the stone. Pane held the door open for her and she walked through.

Firelight from a fireplace lit Commander Volk who stood at a table with a map of the north surrounded by three people she hadn't met before. Behind Volk was a tall, lean man with long hair sitting quietly behind Volk with the colors of a Black Strider. At the other side of the table stood two people in the same reflective silver who must have been the commanders of the soldiers from Earth. One was a tall blond man with receding long hair and the other a young woman with short black hair. The blond man had been in a tense shouting conflict with Volk.

All but Commander Volk looked at her tense but relaxed when they saw Pane. The four of them sat back in their chairs. "Sorry Lily," Commander Volk said. "We had told the soldiers we had come up with a plan. We had hoped no one would walk in while we were debating." He motioned toward two seats next to him and the woman commander.

"I thought we had a plan," Lily whispered as she sat beside the woman commander.

"Well we did," Volk said, "But in the compromise of diplomacy with Earth we decided to share command of the raid. My lieutenant commander, Commander Reeves is beside me." Volk said motioning to the quiet man in black.

The woman beside her stood up. "Commander Lin," she smiled in an accent holding out her hand. Lily shook it, noticing the Chinese flag at the breast of her jacket.

"And the bastard I love so dearly is Commander Nolan of the Unified Domains," Volk said.

Commander Nolan stood up and held out his hand. "United States, not even close." Lily shook his hand as well. "Commander Lin and I can scarcely agree on a few things politically but we both support this cause."

"What haven't we decided on?" Pane asked.

"Here is what we have decided on," Nolan said. He pointed at the bottom of the map labeled *The Gates of the Storm* in neat writing. "On a day clear without blizzards or snowfalls, hopefully tomorrow, we take experienced riders northwest toward a walled outpost called Crows' Hill and teleport other soldiers under my own and Commander Lin's command to the hill." His fingers traced a path through valleys, plains, and even frozen lakes avoiding mountain ranges toward a small marking on the map labeled *Crows' Hill* in the same neat writing.

"Then we take the soldiers northeast through the Forest of the Ghosts before coming upon another outpost called the Fangs of Stone," Commander Lin continued, "Then we'll take inventory before coming upon the Ice Spikes, where Boreas is hiding somewhere at the North Pole."

"So what are we debating about?" Lily asked.

"About who we are sending on the first part of our journey," Volk said. "I want to send a large group of Striders and soldiers, alike, for the dawn to dusk travel to Crow's Hill."

Commander Nolan intervened, "But I and Commander Lin again agree to our surprise, that we should send groups of light parties of only the experienced of these lands to the Hill."

And the debate Lily and Pane had walked in upon began once more. She heard the pros and cons of both. Pane listened to both sides with only weighing slight unmentioned cons that would have been sorted through later. Volk always voiced the issue of how hard it was to battle any of the Storm Riders in groups and that a large party would be able to take on scouting groups with ease.

Commander Lin pointed out the lack of stealth and weighed in on how word might reach Boreas before they could reach the North Pole. Commander Nolan surmised, as well, that it wouldn't be a good idea to send his own soldiers who were ill-equipped for the north so quickly into the open. He added their own plan which was to send small groups like a normal scouting mission to Crow's Hill which wouldn't raise suspicion until after the large group by portal would arrive.

Volk then countered by saying that it would be likely to lose some of the scouting groups who would often only travel west or east to make sure no one was attempting to cross the mountains or to draw out groups in blizzards.

Like Lily, Reeves held his tongue, rather than argue with the others, only until Volk asked for his support. It wasn't until later when she realized Reeves was a mute who had his tongue cut out by the Storm Riders through a whisper from Pane at her left.

Lily spent the debate constantly avoiding confrontation from either side and studying the map. She looked through the hundreds of miles of terrain that lay in front of them. She was chilled by the grim names of some of the outposts and forests like *Death's Landing* on the east, opposite to the *Forest of the Ghosts* and *Demons Gorge*, a long ravine just below where the region of the Ice Spikes began. And then she realized what one of the names was.

She had glanced at Death's Landing all too briefly and then she realized something that shocked her. The name told her all. It was where she had been raised by her father. She looked across the map and saw the mountains she had crossed in The Assassin's dreams where in fact the range that the gates had been built upon. She looked at Pane trying to tell him something not in front of the other commanders, but even he had been wrapped up into the debate.

Soon, they came to a compromise. With the few of the flying vehicles left to them, pilots would scout from above searching for groups of Storm Riders and their scouts while a large group, albeit half the size Volk had suggested, would travel on their proposed route.

"Well, we know democracy is working," Nolan had quipped, "Neither side is happy but we'll both not throw a stone at the other the next time we see each other outside."

The meeting adjourned with Commander Lin and Commander Nolan to tell their soldiers the plan and arrange who would go in the first party, and Commander Volk would do the same.

Pane led Lily up to her quarters. "You did not seem too happy during the last half of our debate," he whispered so no one could hear. "What did you see?"

"I…" she paused, "I saw where I grew up. Death's Landing. It was in the name even. I glanced at it, at first, but then I remembered… everything. What I was to become, what my father wanted to become. It was too much." She grimaced at the thought of being anywhere near where her father had raised her.

"The Forest of the Ghosts is nearly a hundred miles long east to west and half that north to south," Pane whispered, "You'll never see it through the undergrowth." He paused and she saw the sympathetic look in his eyes. "I am sorry for what you went through. But you will never be what Death wanted you to become. I see it in you now and I saw it in you when I took you in all those years ago." He looked out into the darkness only lit by the fires. "I feel old when I talk about it. And yet I still feel the pain from my wounds and the sorrow of losing Adrianna." He gave a squeeze to Lily's shoulder. "But beneath all that, I also feel the flickers of happiness raising you like my own daughter."

Pane led her through the rest to her quarters, not adding a word to what he had just said. When she finally entered the stone room where she would stay, she parted with the man who had once raised her as his own.

Lily lit a small fire next to her bed before taking off her cloak and slipping into the furs of the bed. She thought about the words Pane gave her and yet the memories of Death's Landing came creeping back to her all the same. But she found sleep on Pane's own words.

…

And yet, Death's Landing came to Lily in her dreams. Upon a harsh wind, she stood looking down below the fortress, black as night that reflected the moonlight and orange lights of the braziers. Below, hundreds of demons swarmed inside the fortress lands crushing snow to powder and on the walls surrounding it, specters floated around like shadows without the hosts. Across the snow stood a pale white forest that surrounded the west.

Beside her was Boreas. The wind whipped his pale white hair across his face and he was staring at her. She saw the glow of the Crimson Blade in his own clothes. "Are you real?" he asked.

Lily looked at him and realized he was in the dream as well. "Why are we here?" Lily asked him.

She looked behind him and the shock told him all. Lily stared not at Aethor, but at Death who walked through a portal. Boreas spun around with discs already conjured, but lowered them when he saw that it was Death who walked through the open portal.

Beside Death was Lily, as she was when she first met Death as a child. She walked with him on the top of the fortress, his hand in hers.

"What the hell is this?" Boreas asked her, "How is the past in our future?"

Lily looked at the pair of them walking toward her and Boreas. And then the noise she heard twice already rang through the fortress. But with each step, Death came forward and the sound grew louder.

Boreas raised his hands again and Lily conjured her own discs.

The purple shockwave came directly from Death blinding them both just before throwing them from the fortress. The last thing she saw was the tower and the world around her began to collapse.

Chapter Seven:
Memories of the Sea

Boreas bolted from his sleep. He rubbed his eyes. "What was that?" he asked himself in a faint voice. He rolled out of bed and noticed the dying embers in the fire. The lanterns had given him little warmth in his sleep, and they served no purpose but to keep him up. The room, however, was given a faint red light. He lifted the Crimson Blade from his bedside table and let it go. He watched, as it floated slowly across the room bathing him and the room in red light.

He thought of everything that occurred in the dream. The fortress top with him and Lily side by side facing Death and Lily's younger self. And that noise. He was shocked and baffled to hear it, and, yet, he had no idea what it was. He, as well, had seen the shock on Lily's face when she heard it. Perhaps, she knew.

Boreas thought over the dream once more and realized what he'd do. He let the Crimson Blade float into his hand dimming whatever light it gave.

Boreas grabbed his cloak and wrapped it across his shoulders.

He walked out of his room and traveled across the lantern-lit hallways through the fortress. He took flights of stairs up and down until he came upon a hallway overlooking the courtyard at the left. He knocked upon the second door to the right of the hallway.

Almost immediately did Aethor respond by opening the door. Aethor looked around the hallway before looking at Boreas. "And to what do I owe this pleasure?" he asked Boreas.

"I need your help checking something," Boreas said.

"You already need my help finding something," Aethor said. "What do you need to check?"

"I had a dream again with your daughter," Boreas said. "I need to see Death's Landing."

"Was I in it?" Aethor asked.

"No," Boreas said. It was only a partial lie. Death was in the dream, not Aethor. But he still didn't want Aethor knowing that he was in it, nor did he want to find out why the shockwave had come from him, as well. "Were you not sleeping?" Boreas asked attempting to take off suspicion.

"No," Aethor said. He looked back at his bed which was at the corner of the room. "I slept when I was dead. And now, I am alive."

Boreas and Aethor walked in silence. They strolled through the hallways before coming upon the main hall. No one was at any of the circular tables bathed in lantern light. They walked out into the courtyard outside.

Boreas was met by such a cold that even he was touched by the near permanent storm of the north pole. He pulled his cloak close to his body. Wind whipped his long, pale hair and snow battered his vision. Blue flames arose from the braziers that lined the path with each step. The wind whipped the flames into brilliant shapes before Boreas passed away and the flames went out.

Boreas looked up at the wall that surrounded the fortress and saw sentries in heavy furs and mail staring down at them. They turned back toward the exterior of the wall when they realized it was him.

"I put the same enchantment the city watches do, that doesn't allow portals to be conjured inside the city," Boreas shouted over the wind to Aethor. "Just in case. Your daughter had been here, and I didn't want her to bring an army behind her."

"As you told me," Aethor said. Aethor and Boreas had crossed under the other side of the wall. In front of them lay jagged pieces of ice that jutted out of the snow, some as large as fifty feet.

"Can you conjure a portal to Death's Landing now?" Boreas asked over the wind again.

Aethor looked out into the cold and conjured a portal. Boreas looked through the portal and saw a tranquil night, opposite to the blizzard he was in now. Aethor walked through and Boreas followed him.

The night was decorated with the bands of the galaxy and thousands of stars. Moonlight lit the pale landscape, as well as the black fortress that loomed in front of him. The main castle loomed hundreds of feet high in the center of Death's landing, with a structure of smaller towers connected to such. Around the vacant fortress, stood a circular black wall twenty feet high.

No specters, Boreas thought, thankful for remembering his dream.

"Where will you need to go?" Aethor asked him.

Boreas looked toward him. "I need to check something from the dream," he answered. In truth, it was more than that. He wanted to see if the fortress was available for his own use. The nightmares that connected him and Lily often exaggerated the future, with grim tones. The specters may, in fact, be his bands of Storm Riders and the demons in fact their wolves. Boreas was not, however, sure if he had been at Death's Landing in the dream. While the image was shockingly similar, he needed to see from the top tower at the center of the fortress. Boreas looked behind him and, indeed, saw the vast, thin pale shapes of the Forest of the Ghosts.

Aethor and he began to walk toward the entrance of the fortress. They walked in silence under the stars, the only sound was the crunch of snow under their boots and the faint blow of wind. Soon, they crossed under the gate of the forest entering the courtyard. A blanket of snow covered the hard soil under the courtyard.

"I am going to walk around," Aethor whispered. "I haven't been here in a while. I'll be at the gate when you are ready to leave."

Boreas nodded and walked off into the fortress. It was similar to his own, with the main hall being the front entrance of the fortress. Orange firelight flickered into existence, opposite to his own blue, as he walked to it. The orange light danced across the smooth black of the fortress. The hall's doors were ajar and snow had fallen into the beginning of the hall from the wind. No light carried into the hall from the fires.

Boreas lit a small orb of light in his hands and walked through the desolate hall which was barren of all tables. Boreas soon found himself gone from the hall and walking through the hallways lit by moonlight slipping through windows shattered by wind. He stepped over broken glass through the hallway and soon found himself looking over the desolate landscape from above at an outside overview that connected to a tower.

Boreas tucked in his cloak close to his body, but realized the habit wasn't needed. At Death's Landing, the night was beautifully tranquil and silent. He entered the tower and climbed up a circular stairway, and soon the stairway ended upon a door. He opened it and found himself at the top of the tower.

A large panel that cut from the ground to the top of the domed roof was cut out of the tower. The panel led to a narrow balcony outside where metal railing stood. A large object pointed directly out into the sky under a tarp.

A weapon? Boreas asked himself. He walked slowly over to the tarp covered object, hesitant of any danger. He pulled the tarp from the object and let it fall to the ground.

"A telescope," Boreas whispered. Boreas looked at the glass head that peered to the sky. "I never took you for an astronomy guy, but what were you looking for?"

Boreas walked to the end of the telescope and peered through. It was a small cluster of stars in the middle of the bands of the galaxy they were in. *It was beautiful but… nowhere*, Boreas thought to himself. Boreas tried to clean the lense to see if he found anything else. But he found the same results.

Boreas looked around the mechanism of the telescope and immediately saw why the telescope was there. He held out his hand and took a piece of paper that was propped on the telescope. It was of a girl smiling while looking through a telescope.

Death hadn't been looking for something, Boreas thought, *he had been caring for his daughter.* He set the photo back where it had been propped up.

Boreas walked to the railing outside the observatory. He walked along the side until he saw the tower at the center of Death's Landing. He conjured a portal and walked through.

The top of the tower overlooked all of Death's Landing. And what Boreas saw, frightened him. It was the exact same view as in the dream. Boreas took out the Crimson Blade. It floated around him. Boreas closed his eyes. *Why had we seen Lily's younger self?* Boreas asked himself. *If only I could've held my own daughter's hand and watched her beside me. Instead, she's with the cold sea and I am here to mourn.*

Boreas opened his eyes. He wasn't alone. He wheeled around, where the Crimson Blade floated. He conjured two discs in front of him.

Where the Crimson Blade should have been, was a woman cradling their child. Despite the calm windless night, her auburn billowed in the wind.

"What kind of trick is this?" Boreas asked. His hands shook and the discs in front of him fizzled out.

'It's no trick,' his wife whispered, *'I am your memory.'*

"The Crimson Blade caused this," Boreas whispered, "Didn't it? Why are you here to haunt me?"

'I never meant to haunt you while you mourn,' the shade said. She smiled. *'You thought of your child and it was what you wanted. The Crimson Blade knew this and that is why I am here.'*

It can think? Boreas thought. *And it knew.* Boreas could feel tears against his eyes.

The ghost seemed to realize Boreas was angered. *'The Crimson Blade connects to our thoughts. It has no consciousness, no desires. That is how Lily broke free from the cave. It tapped into her thoughts and helped her with a projection of someone who could.'*

"She was hundreds of miles away," Boreas whispered, "There was no way she could tap into it."

'She was already in its grasp,' his wife answered, *'And she is terrifyingly strong. She is after all the daughter of Death.'*

"Is this what my dream meant?" Boreas asked. "Talking to you? Death is below and Lily is not here."

'You should never assume such things,' she answered, *'Lily did. And look what occured in the catacombs.'*

"What do you want me to do?" Boreas asked.

The shade smiled. *'Remember me,'* she answered and smiled. She held out her hand. Boreas took steps over to her and held out his hand. Their fingertips would've touched but they passed each other. Boreas's hand passed through her's. Boreas looked up to her and all she could do was give a sorrowful smile. *'Say 'hi' to her,'* she said.

"To who?" was all Boreas could choke out, to the last words she had spoken on the boat. The flames of the explosion that took her life years ago consumed her. Her image was gone.

The Crimson Blade floated where she had been. Boreas wiped away the tears that had begun to come across his face. He held out his hand and it floated back into his hand.

"What did you mean to say 'hi to her'?" Boreas asked, flipping the blade in his hand. He put it back in his cloak. He had no idea what the ghost had meant. The last words she had spoken years ago were to their infant daughter, telling her to say 'hi' to Boreas. Boreas remembered his wife's smile and looking at his daughter, just before the bomb went off.

He put the handle of the Crimson Blade into his cloak and his mind whirled with plans of what to do. From the last dream where he saw Commander Lee killed, he knew soldiers would come north to his own fortress.

He looked up into the sky filled with a thousand stars. The moon had passed through the horizon and dawn would soon greet him. He conjured a portal, knowing what to do.

He was at the entrance of the fortress where he had entered.

"Did you find what you were looking for?" A shadow asked in front of him. Aethor was looking toward the Forest of the Ghosts.

"Yes," Boreas answered. He walked up to Aethor.

"I always loved to stare into the stillness of the forest," Aethor whispered, "It was always calming to see it stand still, untouched by anything but wind and snow."

"It is quite beautiful," Boreas said, "I am going to call a meeting."

"What type?" Aethor asked. "One of strategy, or one of battle?"

"I would hope it is only strategy," Boreas said, "But, it may lead to battle. I need you to find Avertree and bring him to the conference room."

Aethor did not seem pleased, but nodded. Boreas conjured a portal and walked through. Aethor followed him into the howl of wind and snow.

They walked through the entrance of the fortress and soon entered the quiet hall. Few sorcerers were awake, except those who had manned the wall over the night. Boreas saw the same guards at the entrance, huddled by one of the fires. He walked through the hall and found Percival talking to some of the guards at a lantern-lit table.

Aethor stalked off, to wake Avertree. Boreas walked over to Percival's table. Boreas noticed the near-healed gash on Percival's forehead where he had hit his head upon the rocks at the cliffs on the dead world. The four at his table were all in the dark blue of the North Wind.

They all stood up, as Boreas came to their table. "Sit down," Boreas said, and he motioned for Percival to come walk with him.

"What do you require of me?" Percival asked after he had parted from his friends and no one was within earshot.

"Many things," Boreas answered, "Which is why I am telling you them now, rather than at our meeting." Boreas waited until they were in a vacant hallway. "First, I ask of you to remain here while your parents, Aethor, and I travel to find the Reality Stone."

Percival was shocked based on his reaction. "But why?" he began to stutter. "Surely, I must be of more use to you at Haranae than here?"

A group of guards came from the main hall toward them. "Not here," Boreas said, and they walked through more hallways until they were surely alone. Boreas and Percival were now overlooking the main hall and the growing amount of people entering. "I want you here because I don't trust Avertree," Boreas answered.

"Then why don't you take him with you?" Percival asked.

"Avertree is the face of a leader," Boreas answered, "While I, myself, am the face of leadership and authority here, few others can do the same. One of these people is Avertree. Should I leave, say Corvus or Ariadne, your parents, then people would not take their orders as seriously because they are not known for their authority."

"Why do I need to watch over him then?" Percival asked. "What gives you suspicions against him?"

"Avertree changed sides," Boreas said, "While that was nobly done by him, I surmise, however, it was out of cowardice, not loyalty. He is the very definition of the person we stand against, after all. A man with people around him, whether bribed or blackmailed, he seeks power only for himself, and none else. A man like that with people inside a group like us is very deadly. He could have paid off guards loyal to me, perhaps, to spy on myself, yourself or others.

"Our game with the good Sorcerers of Alveran is a game of intricacy. But beneath my own pieces, is a rogue with spiders of his own. That is Avertree. A man who can turn so quickly from the duty he was elected to, can do the same once more, but to us. Do not feel that I am punishing you, but rather I need you for this task."

Percival stared out into the larger group of Boreas's followers that were trickling in by the minute.

"Yeah, I'll do it," Percival sighed. "Do you have any other tasks for me to do?"

"Find your parents and bring them to the conference room," Boreas answered.

Percival walked off to find his parents. Boreas briefly watched his followers come into the hall before stalking off through the hallways of the fortress.

He soon came upon the conference room. He pushed open the door and found it vacant. Aethor and Avertree had yet to come. Lanterns at the side of the room flickered to life as he entered. Around a long marble table were shelves full of scrolls and books.

Boreas walked around the rectangular table at the center of the room and put his cloak around the head chair. He noticed the chill in the room after taking off his cloak. He walked over to the fireplace at the side of the room and started a fire with some firewood that remained at the side.

He began to look through the shelves for a map of the north beyond the Gates of the Storm. He soon found one and laid it across the table. He began to write down a list of stores and supplies for his plan.

The door opened and Avertree and Aethor entered the room. "My Lord Boreas, what a delight it is to see you," Avertree said courteously, "You look well." He held out his hand.

A false courtesy, Boreas thought. *He'll be courteous now but the moment he doesn't like a part of the plan he would lash out.* Boreas knew it would be no good to bring it up. He shook Avertree's hand. "You look well, also," Boreas said. Avertree moved to sit by Boreas's right hand at the table. Aethor moved to seat himself as far away from Avertree as possible.

Directly after they seated, the door opened once more. The gaunt face and cold eyes of Corvus walked into the room, followed by the dark hair of his wife Ariadne. Percival followed, behind his parents. They sat themselves down. Percival sat himself beside Avertree, which gave Boreas some hope Percival was playing his part well.

Boreas stood up as Corvus and Ariadne took their seats. "Thank you for joining me," Boreas started, "I believe that a group of Black Striders will attempt to come upon the fortress in the hopes of taking it. As I believe this, I have thought up a plan to stop them from reaching the fortress."

"Did you see these events in your dreams?" Corvus quietly asked him.

"Yes," Boreas answered, "I believe that our best hope is to hold Death's Landing and catch the north-bound group by surprise, nearby."

Aethor looked up to him but didn't speak a word. It was after all his own fortress which he had used for years. "Perhaps, I could hold the garrison there?" Aethor asked.

Boreas knew the question would come, and the answer Aethor would like even worse. "I believe that we should, in fact, ask the heads of the Storm Rider clans to hold the castle," Boreas answered. "They are accustomed to battle in the area."

Aethor gave him a look of pure anger. "Do you really think a group of savages can maintain the fortress?"

"They only need to hold the fortress," Boreas answered, "Storm Riders do not enjoy the inside of fortresses, either. They will only set up their tents outside of the fortress and the land inside."

Aethor did not looked pleased, at all.

"This is why I feel the other option was better," Avertree said. He looked at Boreas with a look of anger. Boreas knew why, and the other option was crossing the line too far, even for him.

"What other option?" Aethor asked.

None of them answered, immediately. Percival was the one to answer first. "It was a decision we made before we traveled to the dead world," he lied, "We decided that it would be best to leave the Storm Riders in their own territories, rather than move them closer to the fortress."

Avertree smiled at this, and Boreas was glad Percival was playing the part well.

"Corvus, Ariadne, will you join me as envoys to the Storm Riders, to convey our plan?" Boreas asked. Corvus nodded and Ariadne did the same.

"Perhaps, I may be able to accompany you, Lord Boreas?" Avertree asked.

"It would not be best to send the face of a former enemy to a meeting, while asking a favor," Boreas answered. "As well, I believe it right to inform you that Percival will stay here with you, when we leave to find the Reality Stone."

Corvus and Ariadne made no move to stop Boreas. Avertree looked toward Percival, to his left, and nodded. "An excellent idea, Lord Boreas," he said courteously.

This must have been how he came to power, Boreas thought. He took out the list of supplies he had written earlier and handed it to Ariadne, at his left. "Can you and Corvus take these to Quentin Johannson and his good husband, in engineering?" Boreas asked. It was a list of gifts he would give to the Storm Riders, before he presented his plan.

"Certainly," Ariadne answered. She and Corvus stood up from the table and walked out of the room.

"I do not believe my services are required," Aethor said before walking out of the room himself.

"I told you, we should have gone with the other option," Avertree said as Aethor closed the door leaving boreas with him and Percival.

"Get over it, I will never do that, even if my life depended on it," Boreas hissed.

"But what have your morals cost us?" Avertree asked him.

Boreas stood up and fastened his cloak over his shoulders. "What have my morals done, indeed?" he asked Avertree.

Chapter Eight:
Strange Wonders

Sage watched as the rain washed over their group. Just minutes after Lily had left, hours ago, a storm had descended upon the jungle. Peter had been able to use the drone to find a cave on a mountainside that overlooked the jungle canopy, and even the edge of the desert for shelter, but they were otherwise forced to walk. The rain did not allow the drone to work. Sage, John, and Lee were playing cards beside the fire.

Sage watched Peter come back into the cave with a metal water bottle in his hand. He closed the cap. "We are lucky we weren't in the desert when the rain started," Peter said, "I saw a mudslide occur on the dunes just beyond the jungle."

"How bad is the rain?" Graves asked as he sharpened his broadsword with a stone. "We need to leave as soon as possible."

"It doesn't matter," Lee answered, "The jungle is too wet for travel. We can stay here for the night. At least, this time we can see the sky."

Graves tossed the stone out of the cave. "I'm going to find some more firewood," he said. He walked out of the cave and passed Peter.

"At least, we have plenty of water," Peter said. He poured the water from the bottle into cups and gave one to each of them. "I saw a flock of birds fly by in the rain. I have never seen anything like them before. Dark green at the top, sky blue at the bottom. And they were big. At least a five foot wingspan."

"The coloring is for camouflage," Lee said, "It would be hard to see them from above and below. Birds of prey, not scavengers."

"Do you think that is all we will see here?" Sage asked.

"If Graves has his way, then I'll be doubtful," Peter answered. "But some things we'll find out here I doubt we will see ever again. I doubt three planets capable of life will have the exact same species."

That night, Sage slept peacefully until John woke her up. She found she was alone in the cave with all but him. "Come outside," he said. She followed him outside into the night. She was met by the sound of hundreds of cicadas in the night. Peter, Graves and Lee stood under a tarp they had propped up to cover them from the cool drizzle. They were looking out at the canopy below the mountainside.

The jungle was beautiful. In a cool gray sky, the night was lit up by blue and green lights that came from the jungle canopy. The trees around the cave glowed in some places the same. Sage joined them under the tarp.

"What causes them to glow?" Sage asked.

"Bioluminescence," Peter answered.

Lee took out a seed pod the size of Sage's hand from a satchel at his side. It glowed green in his hand. Sage held the seed pod in her hand. It was heavy for its size but smooth and hard.

Sage handed the seed pod back to Lee.

"When will the rain end?" John asked.

"Well it's diminishing now," Peter answered, "Perhaps, by morning. It is a shame. Part of me wants to stay and watch the view and find everything in this world."

But the rain didn't give away by morning. The rain increased as the sun would've crossed into the sky. The group spent their day in the cave. Their only task was to keep the fire going. The rain was cold to the touch, as well as the air.

During the morning a small herd of dusty-brown scaled creatures walked by the cave. They came to eat along the grass that grew outside the caves. Sage noticed a long spiked tail at the end of its body. She saw it used when one of the birds of prey flew along the herd trying to attack the group's youngest, which was no more than a foot long. The creatures smacked the bird across the body throwing it down the cliff. When the herd left, Lee said the bird's body was dragged off by an animal, below.

Just after lunch, a jungle cat Sage recognized as similar to a small ocelot came into the cave looking for food. It wasn't before long that they found out it was a baby and that a massive spotted cat that dwarfed the largest leopards on Earth came sniffing into space outside. Lee had shot off a gunshot into the cave ceiling and both darted at the sound.

The rest of the day was met by rain. The unceasing fall caused further anger in Graves and even the others, including Sage found that the increased time in the cave a problem. She had even grown accustomed to the rhythm of the rain as it fell.

Before falling asleep, Sage had looked once more upon the glow of the seed pods across the vast jungle. During her sleep, Sage was awoken not by a sound, but by the silence. She knew it once. It was late in the night and the rain had ended. She looked outside to find John sitting in the night.

Sage immediately saw what John was watching. It was a night of a thousand lights. The sky was filled with thousands of stars that glittered in the black night and she saw bands of a new galaxy to her, light up the sky. The glow of the seed pods didn't affect even the faintest star's light from reaching her. There was, however, no moon that flew across the night sky.

Sage stood by him and smiled. "I would have woken you, but Graves would have shouted at us to leave if he heard," John said quietly.

John looked at her as she sat down beside him. "I always thought that I would've gotten used to seeing a new night sky," Sage whispered, "But, I haven't. We've stood upon four worlds and seen four nights. And I couldn't even tell you which I enjoyed staring upon the most."

"What a world," John said.

"I bet Peter can name every one of those stars," Sage joked.

"We are on another side of the universe," John said, "Even if he could observe them from Alveran or Earth, I doubt he could name them."

"Then, I bet he has named them already," Sage said.

"All of them?" John said, trying not to laugh.

Sage looked over the night sky and pointed to a bright red star. "Yeah I bet he would start with that star by calling it 1-A and would go across from there," she answered.

The two of them spent an hour and a half naming stars and constellations and the stories behind them before the sun rose across the wet jungle. Peter even joined them thirty minutes before the light of the sun began to creep across. He had not, in fact, named any of them, but went along with their own names.

The three of them tried to fool Graves that they had just woken up but he doubted them from the beginning, until Lee lied for them and said he didn't see them an hour ago when he had gone to fill his water bottle.

The group packed up their bags after breakfast and stood under the tarp upon the damp stone and new yellow sky. Peter sent a message to Pane confirming they were on their way to locate the Reality Stone. Soon the drone was flying away, toward the center of the jungle.

"How fast does the drone travel?" Graves asked.

"I don't want to overuse the drone or then we would have to walk half way there," Peter answered. "The drone does have a limited battery, as well, that takes nearly a whole day to recharge. My guess is we can go a comfortable fifty to sixty miles an hour."

"At least, we don't have to abide by the paths laid out," John said, "We can just fly over mountains and cliffs. Walking by the sea to the cliffs was a decent part of our journey time."

So the group waited upon the cliff beside the cave. The group took interest in a flock of the birds of prey that swooped down on a small group of light blue macaws. Sage watched through binoculars, as each bird caught a macaw in their talons, as they attacked the flock. Only half of the flock of macaws had been able to escape. The birds of prey flew away with their kills.

That had been the only excitement in waiting. Soon, the sun was upon them and the air was only comfortable under the shade of the tarp.

Peter looked toward the group. "The jungle trees are thinning," Peter said, "Can someone make a portal just in case the drone runs out of battery and I don't notice."

Sage, John, and Lee began to take down the tarp, as Graves made a portal. As she was putting away the tarp, Sage peered through the portal and indeed saw that the trees were thinning. When that was done, they walked through and left the cave and cliffside.

The jungle sounded of bugs and the shrill cries of birds. The soil around them was damp and bugs crawled around the thick roots of the trees. Green brush of ferns and large flat leaves covered the area around them as well as small blue flowers that were near the trees that buzzed of bugs. Unlike the entrance of the jungle, the canopy didn't cover all of the sky as bright blue strips could be seen overhead.

Sage saw the drone briefly as it flew over the canopy and away. And the wait began once more. After ten minutes or so of waiting, the brush around them began to move. She looked toward where it began to move. She looked around and saw that both Lee and Graves had noticed it.

"Do you feel wind?" Graves asked Lee. Peter and John looked at them confused.

Lee took out one of his revolvers. "No," Lee answered, "No, I do not." Graves unsheathed his broadsword.

"Peter, how quickly can you get us out of here?" Graves asked.

"A few minutes," Peter answered, "The canopy thickened again."

Sage looked around. The brush moved in three areas. One to her back and two to her front. She could tell the others had noticed.

"Back to back," Lee said, "And cover your ears."

Sage ran beside John and Peter. Sage covered her ears as Lee fired a warning shot into the air. She pressed her hand onto John's wrist and he gave an encouraging nod of comfort.

Something peered through the brush at them. It was a spotted leopard, similar to the one she had seen yesterday at the caves, which had entered the clearing they stood in. It was nearly her own height and nearly nine feet long. It growled at the group of them.

Sage felt her fingers tighten around John's wrist. "Keep your eyes on the other two," Graves said. "They are the threats unseen, and, thereby, the deadliest. Peter, as soon as the canopy thins, show me and I'll get a portal under us."

"Duly noted," Peter said.

A high pitched yowl broke the air around them. Sage expected a second leopard to have broken through the clearing. Instead, the undergrowth remained unmoved. She heard the growl of a leopard and a deeper growl of another. Then silence.

Sage looked back toward the leopard and saw it sniffing the air, before growling. She looked back just as a body flew through the clearing. She expected the body to have landed on its paws in front of them but it fell onto the soil. She heard Peter gasp and Graves swear as the body landed. Sage saw the body of the dead leopard only briefly before turning away. It's neck and head had been covered in its blood and there were three, two foot-long claw marks that had cut across its stomach.

Sage looked back and saw the leopard behind them scamper away. She turned back toward the opposite direction trying to avoid the sight of the mauled leopard.

Her heart pounded, as two beasts raised their heads above the ferns. Their maws were bloody and the giant cats made the leopards look like kittens. Their fur was dark brown but their eyes were the color of the blood around their mouths. One carried the corpse of the third leopard by its neck and the body hung down limp.

The two beasts stared at them with their unsettling blood-red eyes. Lee raised his gun and fired bullets at one of the beasts. Sage saw blood that began to seep through the matted fur but it did nothing but anger the beast. It roared a ferocious cry, and Sage tensed.

The beasts crossed into the clearing. It was only seconds before they pounced. Sage lunged out of the way, with John by her side. John took her by the shoulder and pulled her up from the soil. They began to run from the beasts. Sage and John pushed away the plants that came in front of them as they ran. She turned back briefly and saw one of the beasts was bounding after them.

They had looked away for too long. Both of them tripped on the root of a tree and fell onto the soil. The contents of their packs spilled onto the soil around them. She felt John push her against a tree away from the immediate sight of the beast. She looked toward the beast as it entered the trees around them.

Sage truly saw the beast now. Its head stood nearly twice their height and the fur along its body had vertical black stripes much like a tiger. The tail at its end was nearly as long as her arm. It wasn't covered in blood and she knew it wasn't the beast Lee shot at.

Sage felt herself scamper as far into the tree as possible. The beast looked from John to her. John stood up. He put his fingers to his lips and gave a loud, sharp whistle. The blood-red eyes traveled back to him.

Her heart shook, as John held a flare from the fallen contents of the backpacks. John gave her one last smile as he looked toward the beast. "Run, and don't look back," he said.

Sage shook her head as she tried to tell him not to get its attention. The words never came out and the flare lit up in his hand. He waved the flare from side to side, as the beast's gaze followed it.

John was about to run when the back end of the beast's paw came at him. He was flung into the tree and the flare flew into the air landing on the beast's fur before falling onto the soil.

Sage screamed his name as the beast moved itself between her and John. She looked up at it and she knew then it was going to attack her.

She looked around her but she knew there was nothing she could do. The beast began to get into a position to pounce. She tried to meet John's eyes one last time but they were closed shut.

Sage's heart pounded, as she closed her eyes. She felt the beast growl as it began to pounce. She outstretched her hand just before it pounced.

Sage expected to die then and there. Instead, she heard the cry of the beast. She opened her eyes and saw the beast's fur aflame. It rushed away from the two of them, in pain and fear in it's cries. She saw the flare on the ground and knew why it had happened.

She rushed toward John, immediately. *He has to be okay*, was all she could think as she fell beside him. She cradled his head as she scanned his body. The beast had hit him with the back end of its paw, she was sure, but that had been from a creature of terrifying strength. His head had hit the tree and a gash bled from his head above his eyebrow.

"John," she whispered, "wake up." Her lip trembled as she spoke those words and she felt tears crawling down her cheeks. "Please wake up."

She cradled his body and stared at his face for what felt like an eternity. But her wish came true as John's eyes fluttered open.

She hugged him as his senses came to you. "I thought you were dead," she whispered into his ear. "I thought you were gone."

John put his hand to her cheek and looked at her. "The beast," he whispered, "Where is it?"

"It was your stupid flare," she answered, "It's fur caught fire after it landed on it."

She heard the rustle of ferns behind them. She tensed and was terrified only to find Lee run through the ferns sword in one hand, gun in the other.

Lee swore as he slid beside her. He dropped his sword onto the soil. "Are you hurt?" he asked Sage. She shook her head in response. He sighed. "How bad are you, John?"

John propped himself onto the tree and gently touched his forehead which was now covered in blood. "I think I broke a rib or two," he answered. Sage looked from him to Lee.

"Where are Peter and Graves?" she asked.

Lee relaxed. "We all made it," he answered and Sage felt the tension from her chest give way a little. "Can you walk?" he asked.

John couldn't. As he tried to stand up his legs gave away. Lee and Sage cleaned up the contents of their backpacks before they wrapped John's arms around them. Lee made a portal back toward where they had been before the attack.

Graves was propped against a tree root as Peter bandaged his arm. A long cut was being covered. Both of them looked relieved, as the others walked into the clearing. Peter was unharmed.

It wasn't until after she looked at them that Sage realized the carnage. The ground was covered in the second beast's blood and a paw twice the size of her head was cut from the body.

"It was a portal closing," Lee answered before Sage or John asked. "Graves opened a portal above me as it pounced. If it wasn't so big, it could have been cut clean in two. It pulled its leg out but it wasn't quick enough. It darted off through the brushes after."

Sage, with Peter's help, began to bandage John's head. Afterward, Peter began to pilot the drone once more, with Graves and Lee on alert watch. Even with a long gash on his arm, Graves was completely alert. Sage shakenely told them what happened, even though no one asked.

"Should we turn back?" Lee asked. "Peter and I can travel still to the Reality Stone and you can go to the Last City to get help for him."

Sage looked at John. He shook his head. "No, I'm fine. I can still travel. And, I doubt we can join you guys, as well, with Lily north."

"We'd probably just portal into a desert," Graves said grudgingly. "Are you sure? I can take you both back. Even I must admit that I am not looking to what lies ahead."

"We'll go," Sage said.

"The trees have ended," Peter said suddenly. "It's a savannah, but there are a few hills a few miles away and we can see anything that comes nearby."

Lee walked over to where Peter was, and made a portal. Sage helped John through and the others followed. Lee closed the portal. Even though they had just entered, Sage was already helping John rest. She sat beside them and soon fell asleep herself.

Chapter Nine:
The Snow Beyond the Gates

Lily awoke from her sleep. It wasn't until she pulled off the sheets and furs from her body stretched out of bed that she remembered the dream. When she had woken up in the middle of the night, she had fallen back asleep quickly afterward.

Lily rubbed her eyes. The dream had once again been shrouded in mystery. She hardly understood any of it, except for one part. *Death's Landing*, she thought to herself. The idea of being in the place where her father had raised her gave her chills.

Lily saw the folded black clothes and cloak of the Black Striders at the side of the bed. She had too much on her mind last night to notice them. She stepped barefoot on the cold stone floor and immediately felt the chill of the north below her. She quickly put on the black clothes over her. She wrapped her own cloak around her then the black one.

The cold greeted her outside. Lily knew she shouldn't have expected the sun but she hadn't expected this either. Even though it should have been dawn, the night was outside and so was the cold. She was glad she wore both of the cloaks around her but the cold was always there. Today, however, the wind was gone and it was still and clear.

Below the railing were Black Striders and the soldiers in the reflective silver, training in the snow. She wondered how many of them would be sent out today to ride north with her. She herself would join the group that would be traveling to Crows' Hill. Lily walked on until she found herself in the conference room.

Commander Volk, Commander Nolan, Commander Lin, and Pane were at the roundtable. Reeves was nowhere to be seen. They looked up as she entered. Lily saw a smaller version of the map of the north. Volk had begun to draw a route in red. "Are you ready for today?" Volk asked. "We are leaving in an hour."

"I thought it would be from dawn to dusk," Lily said.

"We are from Earth," Lin said, "And you are familiar with how seasons work. Both years and seasons are nearly the same so in winter the sky is nearly black all day."

"I miss the summer days," Volk sighed, "It would make work so much easier."

"We can't tell wars when they are to begin," Nolan said.

Volk finished drawing the route to Crows' Hill. Lily watched the red line travel through the snowy plains. They would go west by the cliffs that were parallel along the gates, then go north until they passed a frozen lake before coming upon Crows' Hill.

Commander Lin and Nolan both left to get the few troops they had coming with the first party. Volk grabbed his own sword which had been set upon Reeves's empty chair.

"Are you coming with us?" Lily asked.

"I can't sentence people to die without my own life among them," Volk answered. "I have already done that too much with this job."

Pane and Commander Volk both led her to the bottom of the encampment to the supply area. "I got a page from Peter," Pane said as they walked. "He sent the same message through a wormhole pager and the tracker. They are alright but stuck in the rain. They can't move forward until it ends. When they get the Reality Stone, we will meet at the Titan World to keep it safe."

Lily nodded as they entered the supply area. She saw a group of Black Striders getting a quiver of arrows and their bows.

Lily grabbed a shortsword, sheathed into black leather to match the rest of the black she wore from the rack. She unsheathed the sword just to check if it was sharp before attaching the sword to her sword belt. The blade had gleamed the fire light and she knew it had been sharp.

"Don't touch the steel to your skin in the cold," Pane said. "There are far better ways to lose some skin." Lily nodded.

She grabbed a quiver of arrows, as well as a bow, and slung it onto her back. She looked over at Pane who had no weapons with him. He would be taking command during Volk's exit.

Volk led them to the stables horses were saddled under the lantern light. A stable hand led a snow white horse to her. He gave her the reins. Volk was already mounted on his horse. Lily walked beside her horse rather than mount.

"Have you ever ridden a horse before?" Volk asked on horseback. He stopped his own, a coal black horse at the entrance of the stables.

"Yes," Lily answered, "I rode with my sister on Earth a few times."

"I hope you rode well then," Volk said.

They walked out into the cold. The Black Striders had formed into a group, waiting for their commander to greet them, as well as the few soldiers of Earth who rode in their silver, as well as a black cloak to mark themselves as one of them. Along the railing of the two levels of the encampments stood soldiers and the remaining group of Black Striders. Many of the Black Striders held torches dipped in oils that were set alight.

Lily mounted onto her horse. She followed Volk, as Pane joined Nolan and Lin away from the group. Beside the three of them were flying vehicles from earth. There were four of them. All were jet black with a three paneled window at the front of the vehicle. Two pilots stood by each vehicle.

Lily set her horse beside Reeves who had been waiting in front of the group of scouts.

"Black Striders!" Volk shouted across the group, "And soldiers of Earth. We are going north beyond the gates to where we will find the North Wind and its leader Boreas. While this ride will only last a day of travel, many perils can be faced.

"The unceasing cold will always accompany us like our shadows. We may be greeted by scouts and guards of the North Wind. But worse, we may almost certainly face the groups known as Storm Riders that travel across the snow. We have been fortunate enough to be given vehicles of flight by Commander Nolan and Commander Lin to scout the snow. A red flare will be shot across the sky if Storm Riders are spotted. If you think you see the flare, do not hesitate in sending word to the rest of us.

"This ride will be dangerous and I don't expect all of us to return to where we stand today. That is why I stand among you ready to put my own life aside. But this mission is necessary. If we cut Boreas off from his fortress, he will have nowhere to run should he fail. This war will end in flames and snow at the North Pole.

"When the vehicles are in the air, we ride north," Volk finished.

Lily walked over to Pane. He put a hand on her shoulder. "Have you ever been beyond the gates?" Lily asked.

Pane nodded. "Stay warm, stay safe," he said. Lily walked back to her horse and mounted upon it.

She heard the hum of engines behind her. She looked up and saw the vehicles were in the air. Each one rose out above the snow and left into the endless night north of the gates.

The group of Black Striders began to ride north. Lily joined Volk and Reeves who were at the front of the column. The horses were at a trot as they rode through the area between the gates. The north wall began to loom above them.

The gates opened above them. She heard gears move in the wall as the metal barrier in front of her lifted open. And the trot came to a dash as the horses galloped from the wall.

They rode west along the mountains that ran parallel with the gates. All Lily heard was the gallop of the horse hooves in the thick snow, as they rode. She looked along the mountains in the clear night. They jutted out into the night sky, their white tips piercing into the space of the stars. She wondered if the points she looked at were where she, herself, had trekked all those years ago.

"Can anyone cross above those mountains?" Lily asked Volk after they had rode a few miles.

"No Storm Riders attempt to travel south anymore," Volk answered. "Either that or we are terrible at our jobs. I often send scouts along the path we are traveling, and none in the past few years have spotted a single rider."

"Why is that?" Lily asked.

"For a start, the mountain trek is hard," Volk answered. "There is no game to hunt, no plants to forage. The natural paths are often steep or too narrow for their wolves to travel. And they'd be lucky if there weren't storms that descend upon them. They could take a step, believing to step again, but, instead, fall into an abyss. The worst part is the cold, however. Try imagining these nights, but a few thousand feet higher in elevation. No wood to start a fire, either. I haven't even traveled more than half a day's walk there."

Lily didn't need to imagine it. She knew how it felt. The cold, the wind, the feeling of hopelessness. She never wanted to feel it ever again.

"The second part is the lack of settlements. There is no point for them to cross, if all of the villages just south of the mountains are abandoned. Over the years of Death's chaos, many would choose to abandon their own homes and villages they have lived in for years, rather than choose to chance a confrontation with Death."

His horse slowed to a trot, and Lily's horse did the same. The column behind followed suit. "It was easier doing my job as well," Volk said. "With towns an hour's travel from the gates all I needed to do is travel, talk to people who I have sworn to protect, drink away in a tavern with a few of my dearest friends. It was better then. I wish you could have been able to see Alveran decades ago."

Lily didn't have anything to say to that. Part of her wanted to imagine what it had been like all those years ago. But, another part knew that many of the people she would've imagined would have been killed by Death.

The column traveled west onward. She looked into the night sky and twice she saw the vehicles swoop by the group, as they scouted and looked onward. She wondered what the column would look like from above. They traveled by fire light of the torch bearers and she knew that the group would be illuminated by just the few dozen who carried the torches. As they traveled, however, she saw no red flare that streaked the sky. Part of her wanted to see a red flare, just for them to know they had been found.

After nearly two hours of travel, the group broke north toward Crows' Hill. As they broke away from the mountains that had once loomed over them, Lily saw that the light of the sun was beginning to reach the north, as the day reached its middle. Over the horizon beyond the mountains, orange and yellow light shown like a dawn that lasted forever stood out into the snow. Only, it would last just a few hours.

Lily would have thought it beautiful if the mission hadn't been so dire. The snow plains were laid in front of them all, to the north. The only vantage she had in the tundra was the mountains growing fainter behind her that were lit up by the sun. She was glad, however, to be rid of the mountains. They had made her remember too many bad memories and made her question what her childhood would have been like without her father taking her to Death's Landing.

Soon, the group felt a wind come upon them. It was cold against Lily's forehead and cheeks. She moved her scarf up to protect herself from the wind. It wasn't a harsh wind, but it kicked up the loose snow as they rode.

"Reeves, should we stop here for lunch?" Volk asked. The world was flat where they stopped. The enemy would certainly be able to see them but they would see the enemy all the same.

Reeves signed an answer to Volk. Volk nodded and dismounted. "We'll stay here an hour," Volk shouted to the column. "Get your horses fed and watered and feed yourselves after. Lieutenant Commander Reeves will assign your watch shifts."

Lily dismounted and fed her horse the feed given to her. She melted snow in a bucket that was passed from rider to rider for the water for the horses. She, herself, was given to watch the last fifteen minutes of the break, to watch the northeast by Reeves. The only movement she saw was one of the vehicles going north before circling the group and flying back south. She saw a murder of crows fly by in the emptiness.

The group rode on, as the hour finished. Soon the group came upon the lake that was a few miles long that they would pass. It was frozen into ice and the wind kicked loose snow around the lake. Off in the distance, at the other side of the lake, hills sloped and ran across the plain. Something dark and gray jutted out of the tallest hill. She tried to squint hard to see what it was, but she was unable to tell.

Volk held up his hand to stop the column. He dismounted and walked to the lake's edge, to pick up a stone larger than the size of his fist. He handed it to Reeves. "You have a better throw than I," Volk said as he handed the stone to him.

Reeves launched the stone into the air and it landed nearly ten meters away from them on the ice. Lily heard a crack as the stone thudded along the frozen surface. Reeves signed off something to Volk, and he nodded.

"Stay to the edge of the lake," Volk said. The group followed his steps, precisely. Lily was always wary of every crack she heard, but, fortunately, no cracks appeared beneath her or anyone else.

Lily was soon able to see the structure of stone that she had seen earlier. It was one large tower and keep that was surrounded by a stone wall twenty feet high with watchtowers that added another fifteen feet to its height. The tower itself was nearly a hundred feet high at its uppermost point. She knew it to be Crows' Hill, without a second guess.

The sun's light began to falter as they finished crossing the frozen lake. She could feel the eyes of many in the column looking upon the fortress that loomed above them. The stars began to shine in the north of the sky as the horses began to trot up the hill.

Volk halted the group. "Reeves, pick two dozen men and watch over the rest of the column," Volk said. He dismounted and drew out his long sword. "Lily, you're with me. We don't know if the fortress is occupied."

Lily dismounted and drew out her own sword. She conjured a disc in front of her other hand. It was the only green in miles.

Lily followed Volk and knew that the two dozen behind her did the same. As the group came upon the wall of the fortress, they found the gates swept open. Volk entered the quiet first, and she followed.

Volk put a single finger to his mouth and motioned for them to encircle the fortress. Lily walked in the opposite direction as Volk. She saw, as they walked, that the tower was connected to the wall by an archway at each of the four ninety degree marks. She walked underneath the arch and found the stables against the wall.

Lily motioned for some of the people to check the stables. She walked on, as the group that had checked the stables shook their heads. As she saw Volk and his group come to face her, she knew that Crows' Hill was empty.

Volk sighed and put his sword in its sheath. "Someone, light the braziers," he said.

Chapter Ten:
A Deal with the Demons

Boreas watched the snow storm descend upon the walls. The wind and snow battered against the walls with intense force. The flames of the braziers danced in the storm as the wind relented upon them.

In front of him were great crates of weapons, provisions and furs to be given to the storm riders. Storm Riders lacked steel so he often made gifts with swords, spearheads, axe heads, mail, and other armor items. Food supplies, as well as spices, were also given. Those weren't as easy to get because he had to send his followers to markets, but some followers, gracious to his cause, had provided the crates' provisions.

He had five clans of the Storm Riders backing him. The other dozen or so were too small for any help from him or were too hateful of the south to trust him. Paid by his gifts, they often moved to territories that suited his plans, including the attack on the Gates of the Storm nearly a month and a half ago. He had to often remember their social reactions to each other and their gift preferences as well. The Cold Men and Red Winds hated the Night Riders, and the Night Riders hated the Storm Arrows, and so on. The Night Riders, Red Winds and Cold Men enjoyed steel over other goods, while the White Ravens enjoyed furs, spices, and provisions. Boreas had the list in his mind and always kept repeating it.

Boreas watched the last crate carried in front of him. They had been loaded onto a sled that Boreas would move using his magic. The sled was made of metal bars that were nearly twelve feet long. The crates were tied together by multiple cords of rope. Just short of a dozen crates were piled on and the uppermost stood nearly two feet above his head. Beside it was a second sled with the same number of crates.

Corvus and Ariadne appeared with Quentin Johansson. Corvus trudged through the snow with his dual edged spear. Quentin was in a woolen cloak that clung close to his body and made him look out of place when next to Corvus and Ariadne in lighter clothes.

"Lord Boreas," Quentin shouted, bowing his head. The wind sent his hair in a flurry around his head and face. "I hope you know which crates are which."

"Remind me," Boreas said.

"I put a red tape at the corner of the weapons, a blue next to the furs, and a yellow next to the provisions," Quentin answered.

"Thank you, will the World Engine be ready soon?" Boreas asked.

"My husband and I are certain it can travel around this world," Quentin answered. "However, I doubt it can make travel to other worlds like Haranae. A few more days, perhaps. I am sure it will be done in three days, maybe forty-eight hours."

Boreas nodded. "Keep working on it."

As Quentin left to the comfort of the fortress, Corvus and Ariadne joined Boreas. "May I speak a question?" Ariadne asked him.

"You have never questioned my orders before," Boreas said, "Which means this question is important. I will answer truthfully and you may ask."

"Why must my son stay behind?" Ariadne asked. "He should be with his parents when we get the Reality Stone and create the Annihilation Wave."

Boreas looked to Corvus. He could tell Corvus felt the same behind his cold eyes. "I do not trust Avertree," Boreas answered. "Nor can I leave Aethor or the Johannsons to watch him. It had to be Percival."

Ariadne stared at Boreas, but nodded.

Boreas conjured a portal in front of them. Corvus and Ariadne walked through followed by Boreas. He pulled the sled through but had to expand the portal so that all fit through. When the first sled was beside them, Corvus pulled the second sled through.

They stood out on an open, snow-covered valley. It would still be dark in the valley for another few hours before the sun would rise, so the stars dotted the clear sky. The Storm Rider encampment nearly covered the last mile of the valley. Tents made of hides and furs jutted up beside cook fires that lit up the night. Banners flew on different parts of the encampment. He could not tell by the colors where the tribes had been set up, despite the distance. He couldn't tell if he saw the white crescent of a moon surrounded by black of the Night Riders or the white bird of the White Ravens. The encampment was as close as Boreas would find to a city beyond the Gates of the Storm.

A horn blew from the encampment, and Boreas saw three riders coming toward them. Boreas could tell who they were, even from afar. Unlike most Storm Rider clans, the White Ravens rode on large elk rather than the giant wolves that most did.

The three riders halted twenty feet from Boreas. The three were all in coats of furs and hides, but Boreas could also see the white feathers around the hoods. While both of the side riders had the olive skin and long black hair of many beyond the gates, the middle rider was different. His hair was short and a mix of brown and gray and his skin was lightly tanned.

The middle rider dismounted and walked toward them. "It's good to see you again, Boreas," Willem said smiling. He was the translator for the Storm Riders.

"And you, as well," Boreas said. "What is the word throughout the camps of my summoning?"

"Not good," Willem answered, "I am certain that all clans were not happy to be summoned on such short notice." He looked over toward the two sleds. "With that in mind, I see that these are the largest gifts in quantity that you have given in months. I expect they will be able to accept that."

Boreas walked back with Willem while the other two riders brought his elk back to the encampment. "I hope your demands are not large," Willem said.

"That is why there are a large amount of gifts," Boreas answered. "I want some clans to move to Death's Landing. Immediately."

"That dead ruin?" Willem looked perplexed. "Why?" They entered the encampment. The light of the cook fires filled his eyes and the smells of the cooking meat filled his nose. To his left were the White Ravens where the riders escorted the Willem's elk back and to his right were the Red Winds a group with banners of red streaks of wind blowing snow. They were the smallest group of the five.

"I think it best if I tell the heads of the clans at the same time as well as you," Boreas said. His eyes darted around him. People covered in furs moved aside for them to pass. Whispers of a language foreign to him traveled through the encampment as Boreas, Corvus, and Ariadne walked through. "I don't want it to spread through the encampment. Whispers are deadly and they can spread like wildfire in dry brush."

"Fortunately for you, most of them have never seen a wildfire," Willem replied.

They came upon the center of the encampment and the pavilion, where the five clan heads will meet. It was a large, circular tent covered in hides supported by poles. The five banners of each of the clans hung on poles that stood in the snow. Four guards holding spears stood at the entrance to the pavilion: two from the White Ravens, one from the Cold Men, and one from the Red Winds. They stepped aside as they saw the four of them.

Willem entered first, followed by Boreas. Corvus and Ariadne followed but left the sleds for the guards to watch. In front of them were the five heads of the clans that followed him at a table. Boreas knew, however, that he needed to make sure that the Raven's Eye, the Head of the White Ravens, was the person he needed to persuade. The Raven's Eye was a big man, with a white beard and long white hair tied back. If he could persuade the Raven's Eye, he knew that the Storm Arrows and the Night Riders would follow. Some of the clans despised each other, but everyone revered him.

Willem sat at a seat away from the table. Boreas turned towards the five heads. "My friends, long it has been, over two months since I saw you last," Boreas began. "Thank you for joining me. I have a few requests for you that must be done quickly and decisively."

The Head of the Red Winds clan, a small man with a quick temper spoke first in a foreign language. Boreas knew him and the Head of the Cold Men, a thin balding man with a long nose and pointed beard would be hard to convince.

Willem translated for him. "We are not your followers at your gatherings. You tell us something you desire us to do, and we collect a payment from you."

Boreas looked toward the Head of the Red Winds. "Payments," Boreas began. "Of course." He looked toward Corvus and motioned for him to get a crate. Corvus walked outside and moments later he walked back into the pavilion with a crate in both hands. He set it on the floor and unlatched the top. Two rows of a dozen spearheads lined the top. Boreas knew that below the bottom were another four dozen spearheads. He picked one up, walked over and stabbed the table with it. "Here is your damn payment."

Willem translated, and the Head of the Red Winds laughed. He pulled it out of the table and pressed his fingertip to the point. He spoke again but this time with a smile on his face. "Good metal," he translated. "What are your requests?"

"I believe that a large group of Black Striders are going to attempt to cross through the snow to my fortress," Boreas answered. "I do not ask you to guard my fortress like swords for sale. I ask for you to leave for Death's Landing, miles from here. I believe they will cross nearby and it will be our time to strike."

The Head of the Night Riders, an aggressive girl with crooked teeth and long black hair spoke. "You would ask us to leave our lands for a desolation of stone and other Sorcerer garbage?" Willem translated.

"There are game trails in the Forests of the Ghosts nearby, and I do not ask you to tend to the fortress," Boreas answered. "I only ask you to hold the lands in and around it. And those who go hunting can patrol the forest as well."

Boreas could tell everyone but the Head of the Cold Men were beginning to be swayed. He spoke up in a raspy voice and Willem translated. "You ask a lot. How long would we leave? Fish are having their annual migration for our harvest. Why should we risk our annual supply of food for you?"

Boreas smiled. "I only ask two or three of you to go to Death's Landing. You may stay in your lands as long as you follow my other demands. I want all Black Striders found to be brought to my fortress if possible. I don't desire slaughter. No cutting of tongues, no slitting of throats. If need be, then I will allow you to kill them, but only then. Especially any pale girl with dark hair and blue eyes; keep her safe."

"What is special about the girl?" Willem translated for The Head of the Night Riders.

"The fate to which I am bound may rest upon her responses," Boreas answered. "Which means that she may very well determine your own fate."

The Raven's Eye stood up. All eyes turned to him. "You…" he began in English. "Ask… much of us. Why should we… help you?"

Boreas pointed to the south. "That is the enemy," Boreas said, "If they are able to set up outposts across the lands, many of you will lose what your clans have fought for for so long. They will back you into a corner of the lands and take everything. I ask your help often for my own goals, but my goals are parallel with your own. If that is the case then we must prevail together."

Willem translated for the Heads. Most of them were nodding in approval. The Raven's Eye took out a longsword of steel from a sheathe at his back that Boreas himself had given him. He laid it out on the table. This time Willem translated. "I will command my men and elk to travel. Tell us where you want each of us to travel."

Boreas told them. He wanted The Cold Men and one other tribe which ended up being the Red Winds by majority vote to stay in their lands. The White Ravens, the Night Riders, and Storm Arrows would all travel to Death's Landing, albeit by different routes. The White Ravens would travel directly there while the Night Riders and Storm Arrows would loop south to try and catch the Black Striders. No harm would come to any of the Black Striders that didn't take up a sword, although they were all reluctant to accept that last part of the plan.

The Heads left the pavilion except for the Raven's Eye. "I would rather not… speak in southern words," he said. The Raven's Eye looked at Willem and he translated for him. "When do you think this war will end?"

"Soon," Boreas answered. "Soon, no more blood will be spilt on either side. The world will be a better place in that time."

The Raven's Eye nodded and walked through the snow toward his troops.

"It's been a long time since I have been in an actual shelter," Willem said.

"Enjoy it," Boreas said, "I fear that a battle may occur in your stay."

"What is the name of the girl?" Willem asked. "Don't think of me as one who will make jokes about it. I am trying to keep her safe, that is all. I doubt anyone but the Raven's Eye will be kind to striders. And frequently, so-called accidents will occur with the other clans involving any captured striders."

Boreas looked at him. He saw that he did mean it. "Her name is Lily," Boreas answered. "Safe travels my friend."

"I can't say the same because you are almost certainly going to fight," Willem said, "But in my heart, I hope all the same."

Boreas walked out of the encampment with Corvus and Ariadne beside him. "The meeting went well," he told them.

"Next time, I think it would be better not to threaten them with a spearhead," Corvus said.

"I don't expect there to be a next time," Boreas responded, "I think what we've started will soon end." He conjured a portal. They left the encampment.

Chapter Eleven:
The Forest of the Ghosts

Crows' Hill was small compared to the Gates of the Storm. While it jutted into the sky nearly at a hundred and fifty feet, Lily could walk the walls in three minutes. Crows' Hill was named for the crows that perched on the top of the fortress. Parts of the peak had turned white from the bird droppings over the years.

Lily enjoyed the quiet of her watch of the surrounding area. If it wasn't for the cold, she might have even enjoyed the watch itself. She was in a bundle of her cloaks and her scarf was wrapped around her face. She was huddled close to the braziers, watching the small dancing flames and the hills and stars around her.

A Black Strider walked up to her. "Commander Volk wants to see you," she told Lily. She was small, with curly brown hair, and her cheeks were rosy from the cold.

"I doubt there will be anything during your shift," Lily said.

"I hope not," she said quietly, "I can't be so sure about traveling tomorrow." Volk and Pane confirmed that the group would leave tomorrow with the weather clear.

"Have you been north of here before?" Lily asked her.

"No," the girl answered, "No one has that hasn't left service, or we would have used a portal to here instead. I am barely even old enough to have joined, but my parents wanted me to join." She looked at Lily and blushed. "I'm sorry, I shouldn't be telling you my life story."

"It's alright," Lily said, "Will you be going tomorrow as well?" Lily asked.

"Yeah," the girl answered, "My name is Anita." She held out a gloved hand and Lily shook it.

"Lily," Lily responded, "I'll see you tomorrow, then." Lily walked the wall. She turned to one of the bridges that connected the wall to the main tower. There were only a few dozen Black Striders at Crows' Hill, and the fortress was desolate of voices. The soldiers from Earth had all been taken by portal back to the Gates of the Storm. That left only the Black Striders who were preparing for the journey tomorrow, those left to watch the walls, and the few who were let into the command room, herself included.

Lily passed just one Black Strider on her way up to the command room. Most rooms of the fortress hadn't been opened in years, despite their arrival.

The top two levels, the watch tower and the command room were the only ones used in the upper half of Crows' Hill.

Lily entered the command room after climbing the stairs. Volk, Pane, Nolan, and Lin all sat on the stone benches that encircled the stone table that was left behind. The room was, otherwise, barren. Commander Reeves was watching over the gates in Volk's absence.

"We have news from the Gates of the Storm," Pane said.

Lily could tell by the way he said it that it wasn't good. She sat herself on the bench beside him. "What happened?" she asked.

"The groups came back from their decoy scouting," Volk began. "All groups came back unharmed, but one. The group swung too far north and was met by an entire clan of Storm Riders. We have no idea what they were doing but they descended upon the group."

"How many were lost?" Lily asked.

"Fourteen missing or killed," Commander Lin answered, "Two made it back to the gates, one with an arrow in his thigh and the other tied to the back of the first with his shoulder halfway cut off."

"Are they still alive?" Lily asked quietly.

"We can hope they will stay alive," Volk answered. "I knew them both. Good men, I hate that my word has sent them this close to their graves."

Lily nodded. It was a grim detail she couldn't get out of her head. The rest of the meeting was spent finalizing the route of the trip. It would take nearly two days to reach the Fangs of the Stone. This time Volk would not lead the mission; Lily and Reeves would.

The meeting was dismissed after that. Lily went to the Gates of the Storm with Pane through a portal. She went back to her room. She cleaned back the ashes from the fire before and lit another fire. She fell asleep by the fireside.

...

Lily stood in the ruins of the tower she stood in. It was night and the horde of demons were barely discernible, as they charged upon the city from the mist that surrounded the ruined city. Lily began conjuring discs and shooting beams of energy from them. Whatever she and the other soldiers did was in vain. Hours passed as the horde descended. The black beasts kept coming forward. They encircled the tower foundation and began to destroy it. She did everything she could to stop them but with each she killed, another replaced it.

She felt a groan beneath her. The tower fell forward with her in it. She slammed against the wall as the tower collapsed into the floor.

Lily didn't tumble upon the city streets. The ground she fell upon was layered with a white mineral. She brushed off the mineral powder that stuck to her hand. She stepped back as she saw that the ground beneath was a blood red crystal.

She stood up. It was near sunrise, as the yellow light lit the waning night sky. She was on a cliff overlooking the ruins of the city.

Two figures stood in front of her. One wore a midnight blue and silver North Wind cloak while the other wore a mahogany colored plating. Lily, however, was startled by their faces or lack thereof. They were both hidden behind faceless black masks. They took their masks off at the same time, mirroring the other.

She didn't see their faces, even after they took off their masks. The figure in the North Wind cloak revealed a pale white mask behind the black, while the other figure was in a red mask.

The hum that had haunted her dreams for so long came back to her. The purple shockwave followed, sending the white mineral ground covering in her face. She fell back feet away from where she had stood. The cliffside groaned and the crimson crystals cracked beneath her. The cliff collapsed with her on top.

...

Lily woke up. She could tell that she would be needed soon. The fire had gone to cinders. She dressed in black, once more, before wrapping both her cloaks around her. She attached her sword belt and sword to her waist. She walked out of the gates to the south end, before conjuring a portal to Crows' Hill.

The whole time, she thought of two things: the dream and the dead scouts. She had no idea what the dream meant. The dream was strange to her. She knew that it occured on the Titan-world, but that was all she knew. She had no clue what the two masked figures meant.

The dead scouts were another issue. She would be venturing into miles of northern territory that no one had traveled in years, with thousands of enemies around her. She could be another name, another face to lie on the snow with blood around her.

The group at Crows' Hill was already preparing to leave. Nearly a dozen had already saddled their horses and were waiting at the entrance with lit torches. She walked toward the stables for her horse. She led the horse back outside. It trotted beside her, with each step a thump in the snow.

Reeves was among the few who were already there. He stood forever silent beside racks of quivers and bows. He was handing them out to the Black Striders who were trickling in beside her.

Lily walked up with her horse beside her and took a quiver from him. She slung it and a bow around her back. He signed to her. She didn't know what it meant. Unlike Volk, she didn't understand sign language.

"I'm sorry I..." she started but she was cut off.

"He says we are leaving in ten," a voice said behind her. Lily looked around and saw Anita wrapped in an overlarge cloak.

Lily looked around and saw Reeves nod before he signed something else. Anita nodded as Reeves left to the stables.

Lily turned to her. "What did he say?"

"I'll be riding in the front with both of you to translate," Anita answered. She walked up to the racks and grabbed a quiver and bow.

Soon the group left with Lily, Reeves, and Anita at the front. It was much more different than riding from the gates. They had always rode beside the mountains but now the only point of view was from the fading braziers from Crows' Hill. After a few minutes Reeves broke ahead in front of the group and stayed twenty feet from the rest.

"When did you learn sign language?" Lily asked Anita.

"I learned sign language in school, a year ago," Anita answered.

Lily turned toward her. "How old are you?" Lily asked. "Eighteen?" Anita nodded. "Why would your parents have you serve at eighteen? Wouldn't your parents have wanted you to carry on in school?"

"My parents and siblings all served," Anita answered. "My father: a city watch commander, my mother a Black Strider, my two sisters and brother were all guards. I, being the youngest, had to follow suit. They told me to become a Black Strider because I could do other duties rather than just scout. But, I am only here because the gates were attacked by the North Wind weeks ago."

"I am sorry," Lily said, "I know how it feels for your parents wanting you to follow them, rather than take a separate course."

"May I ask who it was?" Anita asked.

"My father," Lily said, "Death." She could tell Anita was shocked to hear it. "He wanted me to destroy Earth and follow in his footsteps of annihilation and destruction if he was slain."

"I think you beat my parental issues," Anita whispered. Lily wondered if she should tell her that her father was alive. But she didn't want to worry her about the Death as well as the Storm Riders. The dead scouts came to her head once more. She tried hard not to linger on the dead.

The group continued on for another few hours as the sun rose just barely over the southern horizon against their backs. Reeves came back just to confirm directions with Lily before he rode back in front of them.

Soon, the group stopped by a hot spring. Steam rose from it, and Lily could feel the heat even a few feet from the water. There were a few dozen scattered across the few miles of land. Lily checked with Reeves on the course. They were heading in the right direction.

Reeves dismounted and signed something to Anita. "We are stopping here," she told the people behind her. "Get a bucket to give your horse a mix of snowmelt and spring water." She watched as Reeves signed off another message. "Feed the horses some grain, then feed yourselves. No fires and we leave at midday."

Lily began collecting snowmelt while Anita got spring water. They watched as the snow melted when it came in contact with the water. They fed both the horses. Neither of them drew watches, so they sat beside a hot spring eating lunch.

"What clans of Storm Riders will we come upon?" Anita asked. "I know that there are eighteen known groups of them from a book."

"We only need to watch for a few," Lily said, "The White Ravens are the largest group. But, others are just twice the size of our group. Don't worry about them. You are a sorcerer and can conjure things at your will. If you can't outfight them, then outsmart them. They have spent their lives never reading or learning the simplest about healing or strategy."

Anita looked at her, worried. "Yeah, but they have arrows and other weapons. Any stray one can hit my neck or head and I'd be dead."

"I won't let that happen," Lily said.

They rode off after the hour finished. Soon, the hot springs were out of sight behind them as they continued through the sloping hills of the tundra. After an hour of riding, Lily saw a faint firelight a mile ahead. Reeves fell back into the group after he saw it.

As they came closer, Lily saw that they were two torches set into the snow. They illuminated two shadows unmoving in the snow between them. Reeves halted the formation with his hand. The riders stopped behind them. He pointed at Lily, Anita and two riders to follow. He drew his sword and dismounted.

Lily dismounted behind him and drew her own sword. She caught up with Reeves and so did the two riders and Anita.

Lily saw the two shadows more closely, and it was nauseating. She heard one of the riders swear behind her and Anita gasp. They were dead. Their flesh was a pale milk-white contradicting the black they wore. The corpses were leaning back from a spear from their stomach, to their back, into the snow. Sewn into their cloaks was a red banner with gusts of wind blowing snow.

"Who the hell would do this?" One of the riders asked.

"The Red Winds," Anita whispered. Lily saw her eyes averting from the corpses. "This must be their territory."

Lily turned back to Reeves. He walked up to the corpse and gently pulled him from the spear. He set the body down into the snow. He took off the red banner which had been poorly sewn onto the cloak and threw it into the snow. He did the same with the second corpse.

"I recognize him," the second rider behind them said, "He's been missing for weeks. Never knew him by name though."

"Why haven't the animals gotten to them?" Anita asked.

Reeves patted down the bodies and pulled out a small pale herb from each of the corpses. He sniffed one and threw it away into the snow a few feet from them. Reeves looked toward Anita and said something to her in sign.

Anita looked toward the two riders. "He wants you to take two sleds from our supplies and bring the bodies back to Crows' Hill," Anita said, "Make sure there aren't any of the herbs left. They are highly poisonous that's why the animals were kept at bay."

Reeves walked back to his horse and mounted again. Anita could feel the eyes of the riders behind her as the two riders pulled the corpses back. The sun's few hours of light came to an end as they began to ride on.

After another hour through the tundra, Lily saw a great pale mass stretch out in front of them. Thin, pale trees, nearly white as snow stood silent in front of the column of riders. Lily knew what it was the instant she saw it. They had come upon The Forest of the Ghosts. And, somewhere to the eastern edge was Death's Landing.

The group soon came upon the edge of the trees. As they trotted through the forest, Lily realized that the forest was correctly named. The shadows cast by the moon felt like there was always something creeping by, whether because of the leafless branches or a shadow being cast from a cloud. The silence sent chills through her, the only sound being what the horses or the riders made.

After at least a half an hour of travel, the ground began to slope up slightly. They began to trod up and down a hill range. Riding up and down the slopes was hard for the horses. They had trouble riding down the hills due to the heavy snow. Any large cavity in the ground below and the horse may tumble over. Any sheet of snow looser than that of around it and the horse would slip forward. At least three times a horse behind her fell or slipped on the snow.

Despite the terrain, they managed on. At one point, the group came over a high ridge. Lily could see at least a mile around them before the darkness around her obstructed the rest of her view. The pale trees covered the whole length of her vision. Ahead was a much rockier hill that was crowned with one large tree, which was gnarled and twisted. It was slightly darker than the rest of the trees around, and much wider.

"Is that... ?" Anita began to ask.

"Petrified," Lily finished. It was exactly like The Grim Hollow, a tree that was part of a ghost story that was in the crystal woods by the Capital. Except, she knew that the ghost story had some truth to it, and she had been briefly attacked by it herself. "It's dangerous. We should move away from the tree. I never knew there were others."

Reeves nodded and he began to lead them to the right. Though Lily knew not all of the people in the column knew of the story, she doubted anyone in the column had desired to go near it. It stood eerily in the darkness, it's sharp leafless branches would definitely have looked like claws in the moonlight if someone was directly underneath it. Soon the tree disappeared from under vision behind the rest of the trees.

The column continued along the ridges and hills for most likely another mile. They soon came upon flat ground.

After a few minutes, once more in the forest, they came upon an area where the trees were much sparser. Reeves dismounted from his horse and signed toward Anita.

"We camp here, no fires," she told the riders behind her. "We don't know who or what lurks in these woods."

The riders dismounted. A group of them tied up the horses. Lily and Anita both drew watches for two hours near midnight, so they had the rest of the waning afternoon to rest. They ate after they tended their horses. They had the rest of the afternoon to sleep.

Lily brushed snow away from the foot of a tree before propping herself against it. She wrapped her cloak around her shoulders. Anita sat at a tree a few feet in front of her. Lily could tell she was anxious. She had her sword laid out against the snow and with every sound her head darted to and from, always going to it.

Anita glanced up at Lily, after she had jolted from the hoot of a snowy owl that landed a few trees away from them. "I'm sorry if I seem too worried and scared," Anita whispered.

"I am, as well," Lily said. She glanced at Anita's sword. "Have you ever used a real edge before?"

Anita shook her head in response. "I only trained once or twice with a blunted one," she answered, "They decided I would be better with other jobs, after they watched my performance."

Lily stood up and plucked two branches from the tree she was under. She gave one to Anita. "Let me help you," Lily said.

Anita brushed the snow off her and held up the branch like a sword. "Is this how I hold it?" she asked. Lily looked at her. She was too tense and she made herself too much of a target.

"Relax," Lily said. She rotated Anita's body and pressed her shoulders down. "Now it will be harder for me to hit you."

They did their dance. When Lily told Anita where she would hit, she was always able to block but when she didn't she always tensed up again. Soon, they even had a few other Black Striders join them. After an hour, the small group disbanded.

Lily tried to find sleep in the few hours before midnight but she was unable to. Anita came to wake her to their watch. She could tell she was anxious despite their training.

The outer edge of their encampment was an eerie silence. Little moved in the snow around them. A gentle snowfall arrived upon them, clouding most of the moon's light.

"Why do you think it is called the Forest of the Ghosts?" Anita asked.

"Why do we call anything with such terrifying names?" Lily asked. "Perhaps, to be remembered. I know I'll remember the stillness of our watch for days."

"I know I will, as well," Anita whispered. A breeze came by chilling Lily's bones. She tried to wrap her cloak closer to her body. The snowfall was brief. It passed within an hour. The only sounds she heard was a murder of crows flying in the distance. She nearly fell asleep in the quiet, before Anita woke her up. "I saw something moving out there," Anita whispered.

"Don't point," Lily whispered, "Tell me where."

"Five trees down to my right," Anita answered, "Behind the brush, about twenty feet away."

Lily looked. She saw a shadow move behind the brush. She wouldn't have noticed it if she hadn't been told. In the tangle of shadows, she saw one more streak move among the rest. She stood up and slowly unsheathed her sword.

"Follow me," Lily whispered. "Swords out, keep your eyes open."

She slowly moved closer to the grey brush. The brush rustled and she held out her sword. An elk's head appeared from the brush with a few leaves in its mouth.

She relaxed her sword and turned around toward Anita. "Nothing to be afraid of," Lily whispered.

But all Anita did was gasp. Lily turned around just in time to see the shaft of wood hit her across her forehead. She heard a scream behind her, as her body fell back into the snow.

Chapter Twelve:
Death's Landing

Images and sounds came to her head through the night. Clashes of steel and people crying out as they lay dying in the snow. Riders of both elk and horse came running by. Then her world began to move. She was out of the snow, yet still in the forest. The leafless branches still loomed above her with their shadows trying to grasp her under the moonlight. Then they were out of the forest. A black fortress loomed above her. The walls were bathed in orange light but not the inside. And she was among an encampment of thousands.

Lily woke up to someone pressing a bandage along her forehead. Her vision was foggy but soon adjusted. He didn't look like a Storm Rider. He had no olive skin and his hair was a mix of brown and gray rather than black. "Relax," he whispered, "You took a hard hit to your head."

"What happened?" Lily asked groggily. She tried moving her arms but they were bound in front of her. She was at a small table in a tent made of animal skins.

The man sat in front of her. "The Storm Riders found your group a third of the way through the Forest of the Ghosts. A battle erupted and because you aren't beside people in black I think you know how the battle ended."

Guilt swept through her. She had always told Anita to be safe but in the end, they had been attacked. "Are my friends safe?" Lily asked.

"I wasn't there," the man said, "I can't assume any made it out but we took half of them prisoner. The other half ran or lay in snow the color of crimson."

"Is there a small, young girl with brown hair among your captives?" Lily asked.

The man gave her a saddened look. "If she was your friend, I am truly sorry," he said, "I hope that perhaps your friend wasn't a fighter and she may have run off. Most of those that fought were injured or killed. If you may excuse me, I must inform my leader of your condition."

He stood up. "Who's your leader?" Lily asked.

"My leader is the Raven's Eye, the Head of the White Ravens," the man answered, "And my name is Willem." He left the tent with her bound. She was left with her to think of the guilt she had. She saw only a glimmer of a chance that Anita escaped but she hoped it true. Being captured by the White Ravens, however, was another issue. Her father had taught her of some of the Storm Rider clans but the White Ravens were the ones he had mentioned most often. They were the largest clan, but they weren't the cruelest either.

Willem came back into the tent around ten minutes later. "The Heads of the Clans have been informed of you, and will meet you, shortly," Willem said upon his arrival.

"Heads?" Lily asked. "When have multiple clans been working in unison?"

"Since Lord Boreas has brought them together," Willem answered. "I assume you know of him considering your group came to attack him." He sat back down into his seat.

The news was not good. If Boreas had a whole army of unified Storm Riders, then that was ill news to all. "Why are they meeting me, specifically?" Lily asked.

"Lord Boreas gave a command to all of the groups to leave all Black Striders unharmed," Willem answered. "But he also gave a description of someone he wanted protected and transported to his fortress. You met this description."

The meeting was either to be held by Storm Riders or the North Wind. Lily knew immediately which to choose. "I am the girl he described," she gave in response.

"He told me the name of the girl," Willem said, "So I must ask you. What is your name? And do not lie, or you will wish that you hadn't."

"Lily," she answered.

Willem took a sigh. "So, you are her," he whispered, "What is your relationship with Boreas?"

"It is complicated," Lily answered. "You aren't one of them, are you?"

"A Storm Rider?" Willem asked. "Yes. But not by blood or birth, but by language and marriage."

"How?" Lily asked.

"Do you really want to listen?" Willem asked.

Lily held up her bound hands. "I have nothing else to do."

"Well," Willem began, "I was born south of the gates in a nearby village. A hundred berry farmers, few soldiers. Most of these villages are abandoned today, over past fears. It was when Death's battles were beginning. The Storm Riders, back then, would send small groups through passes over the mountains. They raided my village, when I was a boy. I wasn't in the fighting, so, rather than being slain, I was taken to be hostage as a servant."

"As a slave?" Lily asked.

"In a manner of speaking," Willem said, "Yes, a slave."

"Why isn't your tongue cut out then?" Lily asked. "A commander at the Black Striders had his when he was taken captive."

"Reeves," Willem whispered. "Ben Reeves and I grew up together. We were both taken that same day. When we were taken, I began to grasp the language on those mountains. I was able to understand phrases, and even speak a few. We got through the mountains and I was taken to the Raven's Eye with the rest of the captives.

"He was young then, he just got his reign. But, unlike most of the clan heads, he was unusually cunning, albeit kind and honorable. Had he been born south of the wall, he may have been one of the finest men in the decade. So, when he found out I could speak the language, he gave me a choice: be taught by him and other people and become a translator, or become a servant with my tongue cut.

Being a kid, I had little codes to keep so I accepted his offer."

"What about Reeves?" Lily asked.

"I begged the Raven's Eye to allow Reeves to take the same offer," Willem said, "He allowed it, to my surprise, but to my further surprise, Reeves refused. He got his tongue cut. But Reeves escaped. I saw him do it. I remember seeing him disappear through the snow away. I assume he came upon the Gates of the Storm and trained to be a Black Strider."

"Why haven't you tried to escape?" Lily asked. "You could easily slip out in the night and teleport to your old village."

"The Raven's Eye gave me everything," Willem whispered. "I can't go against a man like that. He gave me my life and he gave me freedom. Storm Riders have few laws, but one of the few is that you are classified a citizen if you can speak their language." He paused before speaking again. "And I can't use magic anymore."

"How is that possible?" Lily asked.

"Storm Riders hate magic, even the Raven's Eye has little tolerance for it," Willem whispered, "So when I made my choice, I began drinking a tea that suppresses magic. Once a day for two moon cycles. And I couldn't make a portal if I wanted to."

"Will the other Black Striders have to drink it?" Lily asked. She would feel even more guilt if she was carted off to see Boreas, while they lost their ability to use magic.

"No, Boreas would be furious even then," Willem answered. It gave her a little relief but not much. She would rather them all sent to Boreas, not just herself.

"You said by language and marriage," Lily said.

"Indeed," Willem said, "I am married. A girl who hadn't eaten for two days had stolen some food for her and her sister. She was caught and given two choices: death or loss of tongue. I said that was too harsh, so the Raven's Eye said marriage to make my place here official because not everyone agrees with the language laws. And five years later, I speak to you with a son."

Two Storm Riders entered the tent. They both carried spears with a metal head at the tip. Lily knew Boreas must have given them to the groups. They began to confer with Willem.

Willem nodded and stood up. "The Heads of the Clans will speak to you now," he said.

Lily stood up. One of the Storm Riders took her by the shoulder and led her out.

Death's Landing loomed above her. The black fortress loomed above her like a shadow without its host. No lights were alight inside, but the walls were lit and she saw some silent watchers staring out into the snow.

Memories she believed she had forgotten came back to her. The lone tree where Death plucked a blue flower from its branch and put it in her hair upon their arrival to the fortress. Death teaching her astronomy in the observatory above her. Death teaching her how to shoot a bow and arrow. And the night she found out she would cause The End and her running away into the snow. She remembered everything.

The outside was cold, for it was still night and she was grateful she was in her cloak still. Cookfires were being set which made her believe it was dawn a hundred miles south. But, it wasn't a peaceful walk through the encampment. She was given angry looks by many of the people, and some shouted at her in a foreign language.

"Do I want what they are saying to be translated?" Lily asked.

"If you do, you'll run back at them with a knife in your hands," Willem said.

Lily thought she was being led into the fortress, but she wasn't. Instead, she was taken in front of the entrance hall, where a pavilion stood. In front of the pavilion stood three banners. The White Ravens stood in the center, with the crescent moon of the Night Riders to the left, and three arrows of the Storm Arrows to the right. She remembered Death teaching her those banners.

"Inside, speak little of magic," Willem said, "They do not enjoy the talk of it."

Inside the pavilion were three Heads of the Clans. The Raven's Eye was unmistakable, compared to the other two. He commanded respect with his large body and long gray hair. A woman with black hair sat at his side, while a man with short dark hair sat at his opposite.

The woman beside the Raven's Eye spoke first. She and the man beside the Raven's Eye conversed with Willem before nodding. The Raven's

Eye kept quiet, staring at her before Willem translated a question for him.

"Why did Boreas ask for you to be brought to him, specifically?" Willem translated. "He knew there would be Black Striders and asked for you to be taken to him."

Lily looked to the Raven's Eye. "It is hard to explain," she answered, "And I don't even know myself. There is a connection between the two of us, something that hasn't been explained. He is my enemy, yes, but he isn't evil."

Willem translated and the Raven' Eye spoke again. "How did he know that there would be Black Striders?"

Lily had tried to avoid answering it the first time, heeding Willem's advice but it didn't work. She had to answer this time. "I can see the future in dreams," she answered.

The Raven's Eye spoke once more. "Can you see mine? Ours? Boreas's? Or just you own?" Willem translated for him.

"Just mine and Boreas's," Lily answered.

The group began to confer once more with each other. Soon, Willem whispered to her, "You leave for his fortress now."

Lily didn't know how to feel. On the one hand, she wouldn't be in the hands of Storm Riders, a group who hated Sorcerers. On the other hand, she was going right to Boreas. When they were out of the pavilion, Lily asked if the other captives would come.

"No," Willem answered, "They would leave in a week. It is a quicker ride there with a smaller group." He led her back to the tent she had stayed in earlier. Lily waited while Willem prepared the group for travel.

An hour later, Willem came back to bring her. Lily walked through Death's Landing one final time. The fortress loomed into the sky that was forever night. A long shadow would've been cast from its peak if the moon or sun was out. She looked south and there was a faint light in the sky.

Much of the camp had already left the fortress. "Where is everyone?" Lily asked. Nearly half of the cook fires were out and she saw barely any faces.

"They have gone hunting, checking their traps or foraging," Willem answered, "They have to feed themselves for the next few days, after all."

"I didn't see any traps when we came through the forest," Lily said.

"That would defeat the purpose, if a deer can see a net, or a squirrel a snare," Willem said.

Lily wondered how many traps she could've passed on her travel through the Forest of the Ghosts. She doubted many or they would have set off one or two.

They exited the walls of the fortress and came upon the outer area. Storm Rider tents covered the few hundred feet away from the wall but in much sparser density. Many of the animals were set in pens around the walls. Elks that stood taller than men stood on one side while wolves the size of bears stood to her right. She knew that she preferred the elks on sight.

The Raven's Eye was giving orders to half a dozen Storm Riders who would be escorting her to the north pole. He nodded to Willem when they arrived, but paid little mind to her. He left after he finished.

"Have you ever ridden an elk before?" Willem asked. He led her to an elk already saddled.

"Same concept as a horse?" Lily asked.

"Pretty much," Willem answered, "But, watch out for the antlers."

She mounted onto the elk and took the reins in her bound hands. They ached from being tied in rope for hours but she knew she shouldn't complain.

Soon, the eight of them were riding forward, away from Death's Landing. *If this was what the dream meant about Death's Landing, then it wasn't so bad*, she thought to herself. But she also knew that her father and Boreas awaited her at the north pole. That gave her little hope.

Chapter Thirteen:
Out of Chaos, Serenity

The sun set over the horizon giving the land an orange glow to match the golden prairie. The lake turned gold and anything at its banks cast long shadows along with the few pale trees on the grassland that grew small, murky green leaves on their branches. Flocks of birds with long legs, white feathers, and golden underbellies flocked the shores to fish small brown fish. The land was peaceful.

Lee looked across the land to the jungle. It loomed hundreds of feet above the long grass that grew in the plain a dozen miles away.

"We'll see any of those beasts coming a mile away," Peter said. He threw his spear into the water. They were trying to catch the same fish that the long-legged birds were. They hadn't expected the rain to come and had been underprepared with supplies so the two of them had carved spears from wood and tried fishing. He pulled out his spear from the mud and water.

"Doesn't mean we can't be vigilant," Lee said. He spotted a fish in the ripples and waited before throwing his spear. It caught its side and stayed in its belly. Lee pulled back the spear. He held it up for Peter to see. It flopped in the golden light before finally stopping. "I have caught three more fish than you."

"Yeah, three caught against zero caught," Peter said. "I am not made for this." He must have seen another fish because he threw the spear into the water.

"What are you made for exactly?" Lee asked.

Peter wiped his glasses which had been sprayed by water. He pulled up his spear without a fish. "Reading," he groaned.

"Technically you survived the battle of the meadow two years ago," Lee said, "I think you can spear a fish."

"Technically I was stabbed during the battle," Peter replied.

"Afterward," Lee said. Lee waded up the shallow water and put the fish on the bank next to the other two he had caught. He put the spear into the sand. "How much farther do you think we have?" Lee asked.

"Hopefully the drone charges in the night and we can get to the Reality Stone tomorrow," Peter answered. "But I don't think I'll give you solace in telling you that I don't know." He waded into the water a little farther before waiting in the shallows.

Lee took out his knife and began to cut the fish. "The stone and blade are certainly strange," Lee said.

"In what way?" Peter asked, not moving his head as he looked in the water. "They are most often opposites of the other."

"I wasn't on Torfaa, the dead world, but Pane filled me in," Lee said, "How would you describe the opening to Torfaa? Alive?"

"No, dead," Peter said, "And the flowers here were alive. Just like opposites."

"And the inside of it?" Lee asked. "How did that feel?"

"Cold," Peter answered. "But silent and calm."

"And this is calm as well, is it not?" Lee asked.

Peter turned his head looking away from the water. "I have a feeling you have had a realization I have not."

"If the stone and the blade are two sides of a coin they must have the same purpose," Lee said. "And that purpose they have is to change. Out of order, they breed chaos, and out of chaos, they make serenity. The pattern may continue forever if the universe kept ticking."

Peter waded out of the water and put his spear next to Lee's. "An interesting theory," Peter said, "And I wouldn't be surprised if it was true." He began to cut up one of the fishes as Lee finished the first and moved to the last.

Lee looked over to the bag beside Peter. It looked heavier than when it was the day before and there was a bulge that came from it. "What's in the bag?" Lee asked.

Peter looked over and flipped the top off the bag. Lee saw three of the seed pods from the jungle. "I don't expect to come back here," Peter answered, "So I thought it would be best to bring a part of this world over to another. Much like what happened with magic coming to your own world."

"Do you expect them to grow?" Lee asked.

"I hope they do," Peter answered, "But they might not if the conditions aren't right." He flipped the top of the bag back over. "Why are you here and not with the Black Striders?" Peter asked.

Lee looked up at Peter. It was hard for him to say why. "Lily saw me die," he whispered.

"In the north?" Peter asked after setting his knife down.

"Time is inevitable," Lee said, "You can slow it down, speed it up but time cannot be stopped. When Lily sees something in her dreams it has always come true. If we didn't know an event even existed, we would know or if we didn't know a place to be it always held true. Time is a river. You can throw pebbles and stones into it, you can block it up, but the course never changes."

"The dreams often exaggerate or adjust details," Peter said. "But if you think the river flow can't change then why are you here?"

"I want to make my last breath worth it," Lee said. "I think that would be here, not with the Black Striders." He finished cutting the last fish and so had Peter. They packed it and left the lake side. "I once stayed on Earth. I always thought I would die there when I chose. Perhaps when I was older. I loved the prairies there, and I wanted to have my last days there."

"We could make that happen," Peter said.

Lee brushed his fingertips against the long grass. "Nothing can make that happen."

"Does anyone else know about this?" Peter asked. "And should we tell the others?"

"Sage," Lee said. "But, even you didn't figure this out. No offense to her, but if you couldn't, she won't. And, it would be worse if we tell them. Even you tried to get me to leave, and you're not the most compassionate."

"Are you calling me heartless?" Peter asked.

"Less than Graves," Lee joked.

They remained silent as they walked on. "You really are going to die, aren't you?"

Lee said it all in a nod. He was going to die.

...

Sage looked across the prairie. The long grass rustled below them from a faint breeze and so did the small green leaves of the tree above her. It was peaceful on the hilltop, beneath the lone tree.

The lake gleamed gold beneath the sunset. She saw Peter and Lee come in and out of view while trying to catch fish. Graves had gone somewhere to forage, despite everyone's protests for him to stay put. Sage had set up a fire with stray branches and kindling she had found. She was watching John. While she had slept for a few hours after the encounter with the two beasts, he had slept the whole time since then.

"It's a beautiful place," John said. Sage looked at him propped against the tree with a bandage over his head. His eyes were open, surveying the area, and he smiled at her. "I didn't get to see it after we walked through the portal."

"We thought the same about the jungle," Sage said. She looked around. "I wouldn't be surprised if a lion or two appeared from the brushes."

"Perhaps, I should amend my statement to it's a peaceful place," John replied, "I doubt lions appear in peaceful places."

She smiled and moved over next to him. "How do you feel?" she asked.

"Good enough to make jokes, although I doubt I could walk down to the lake and back," John answered. He looked at her. "How do you feel?"

"What do you mean?" Sage asked.

"We were nearly both killed by the beasts," John answered.

"I never got to say it," Sage began, "But, thank you." She paused. "For saving my life. And everything else you've done for me. If you hadn't been there, I certainly wouldn't be here."

"What I did," John began, "Wasn't enough. We could've been killed. You could've died, and I would never forgive myself dead or alive."

"It was enough," Sage said, "Because I am here with you." She held his hand in hers.

"I really do care for you," John whispered, "More than you could know." He leaned forward and brushed his lips against hers.

"I know," Sage whispered as she kissed him back.

That night, the golden light of the sunset soon gave away to blue. It was a deep blue, not the light blue of the sky. It flooded half the sky from the horizon and she saw the brightest point miles away.

"I do believe the worst is behind us," Sage whispered as the embers of the fire began to flicker out in the night.

"I believe it is," John said.

The Reality Stone was still there. Boreas hadn't found it yet. Tomorrow they still had a chance to make things right. And, for once, the world was at peace.

Chapter Fourteen:
The Last of the Riders

Pane looked along the snowy hills that sloped in the night. The sun had set at Crows' Hill hours ago, but it would be hours until midnight would come. He had to see a portal at the entrance for so long, informing him that the riders had made it to the Fangs of Stone. That hadn't happened yet, and it should have been hours ago.

The night before, Pane had assumed the worst when two riders came back from their direction with two bodies on sleds. He had been relieved when they said that Lieutenant Commander Reeves had ordered them to bring the bodies back. He was now on surveillance by choice at a watchtower at the wall.

"Are you still thinking about the bodies?" Volk asked him.

Pane looked toward Volk. "You always have to prepare for the worst with this stuff," Pane answered, "And, any few minutes from now, we can see more bodies hauled up to this hill. My daughter could be among them."

"General, I live here," Volk said, "I know the worst. Your daughter is strong. She'll be safe. What's the news about the Reality Stone?"

"Thanks for reminding me about the joy upon Haranae," Pane sarcastically said. He took out the pager Peter had given him and set it upon the stone railing of the watchtower. "Peter paged in a few hours ago. When he had first sent a page to me two days ago about being delayed by rain, I didn't assume the worst. But they were attacked by some beasts of the jungle hours ago."

"Did anyone die?" Volk asked.

Pane shook his head. "They all elected to stay so I don't assume the complete worst. Peter just now sent that they see blue in the sky. They'll have it tomorrow."

Volk's attention suddenly shifted. "Riders," he whispered.

Pane looked out into the night and saw the black shadows galloping along the hills. There were two horses. But, behind them were nearly three dozen pale shapes larger than horses bounding through the snow and they were closing in upon them.

"Wolves," Pane whispered, "The Storm Riders are closing in upon them." He looked toward Volk.

"Sound the alarm," Volk whispered. He looked toward the opposite watchtower of the entrance. "Sound the alarm!" he shouted.

The bells started to ring, as Pane and Volk began to travel toward the space between the two watchtowers. They descended down a flight of stairs and entered the space between the two. They passed two archers going up into the watchtower with two others behind them. Pane looked at the two riders being chased down by the Storm Riders. They were riding fast but the wolves behind them were catching up.

"They must've been riding for at least an hour," Pane said. Half a dozen archers had come to the Gates and stood next to small braziers. Behind them were others holding arrows with towels around the arrowhead. They had been put into a flammable liquid and the holders were trying to avoid touching the lower half of the arrow.

Commander Volk soon had the archers in position. There were six archers above the gate and four in the watchtowers. The archers held the arrowheads into the braziers and the towel ignited. "Nock!" Volk shouted. "Draw! Loose!"

Ten arrows launched into the air at the Storm Riders. The spits of fire shot overhead of the returning riders before falling at the two dozen Storm Riders. Two fell and a wolf tumbled through the snow with a flaming arrow at its neck.

Arrows came in return by the Storm Riders, but they all fell into the snow around the wall. Pane had only been able to tell by the poofs of snow that came. In the night, the shafts of wood flying through the air were nearly invisible without the fire.

A volley of fire arrows returned at the Storm Riders. A wolf was struck down, but the group was nearing Crows' Hill with the riders. They had only stopped two wolves and at best four riders. Pane made up his mind.

He unsheathed his sword. "I am going to hold the gate for the riders to pass through!" he shouted at Volk. He ran behind the archers and their companions and passed two more coming upon the space. "You two are with me, to let the riders pass through," he told them. They slung their bows onto their backs and unsheathed their own swords.

They came upon the snowy courtyard as the gate was slowly being opened by a group at each of the sides. "When the two riders are through, close and bar the gates, with or without me in," he ordered them. They gave him shocked looks first, but nodded. "I'll make a portal to the other side when I get back in."

The three of them entered the snow outside the walls. He looked up and saw another volley of fire arrows fly into the snow. The riders had nearly come upon the fortress, when a horse tumbled through the snow with the rider. The other horse didn't stop, as it came upon the gate. Pane broke off into a run to help the other rider. As he looked at the rider that had crossed by his side, he saw that there were not one, but two riding on the horse.

The rider behind jumped off and tumbled into the snow beside him. The hood of his cloak fell off his head and Lieutenant Commander Reeves was beside him. He unslung his bow, and motioned for Pane to help the fallen rider.

Pane nodded and began running as best he could through the snow. He was left forever with a limp from the specters all those years ago. While he had desired for his fighting days to end years ago, he knew that the fallen rider also might be Lily. The two behind him began to fire arrows with Reeves. Pane was nearly a hundred feet from the fallen rider, when the remainder of the Storm Riders began to come upon him. Only three riders were still coming at the rider, half were dead and the rest had retreated back to where the arrows couldn't reach. Pane felt arrows whistle by him, and saw fiery arrows overhead hurtle toward the wolves.

He had managed to get to the rider, when a wolf descended upon him. He lunged out of the way and he saw a glimmer of light as an arrowhead caught it by the throat.

A rider swung a club with a six inch long stone at his chest. He stepped backwards and slashed his sword, cutting off the stone and a few inches of wood before putting the sword through the rider's chest.

A spear whistled by Pane and caught his arm. The man who had thrown it grinned before an arrow sank into his back. He coughed up blood briefly before falling forward into the snow.

Pane's arm was bleeding freely, when the final rider came upon him with an axe of metal that gleamed when a fire arrow's light passed into its reflection. Boreas had certainly given it to him or people in his clan. The rider had finally managed to reach Pane, and swung his axe down where Pane had been moments ago. They slashed at each other until Pane's sword cut into his chest. He groaned and sent another swing that was far from where Pane was. Pane cut the man down and snow turned crimson.

He touched his wound just as a volley of arrows from the Storm Riders came upon him. He leapt behind the dead horse for cover as the volley landed into the snow. He heards arrows collide against the horse flesh that was his cover. He looked towards the rider but it wasn't Lily and he knew immediately he was dead. His legs were crushed under the horse and his head was bashed in from a rock he had landed upon. Another volley descended upon Pane as he fell through a portal he created. There was no one to help, so he used a portal.

He fell into the snow, with Reeves helping him up. They walked through the gates as they closed behind him. "Dead," was all Pane said.

Volk came running over to him. "Someone grab a healer," he told the archers that had run with Pane out through the gates. "And, someone get Commander Lin and Commander Nolan." He looked toward Reeves. "Are you the last of them?"

Reeves nodded but signed something toward Volk. He walked off to help the other rider who had rode with him. Pane barely had time to take in his grief before Volk came up to him.

"He says that half of the group was taken captive, including Lily," Volk whispered.

Pane clenched his jaw and looked at the other rider who was dismounting her horse. She was small with an overly large cloak and rosy cheeks. Reeves walked her to them. "What's your name?" Pane asked her.

"Anita, General," she answered.

"Anita, I am going to need you to go with Reeves and General Pane to the top of the tower to tell us what happened," Volk said. He walked off as a healer came by to look at Pane's wound.'

The four of them walked the flight of stairs into the command room. The healer washed and bound the wound. It was three inches long that went along his arm. He didn't have any of the healing potion that closed wounds, so it was bandaged. Anita sat herself down and was rubbing her hands together by the fire. The healer asked her and Reeves some questions, but they were unharmed minus the cold.

"Cold is something that is a permanence here," the healer said before leaving. The healer handed the three of them a drink, which helped them ward off the cold, before they left the room in silence.

"What happened to my daughter?" Pane asked.

Reeves signed something, most likely that Pane had taken care of Lily as a child to Anita, and she nodded.

"We stayed in the Forest of the Ghosts during nightfall. I was the first to see them, and Lily and I investigated," Anita answered, "We thought, at first, we were safe because all we saw was an elk, but it was the White Ravens. They ride elks, after all. She was hit in the head by the shaft of an axe and fell into the snow. I screamed and alerted the camp. The rest of them attacked. The man who hit her laughed, as I was backed into a tree. But, he didn't see me draw my sword." She looked down to her gloves which were red with blood. She didn't need to say the rest.

"Reeves pulled me away from Lily when a few of the Storm Riders came upon us," She continued, "With a few others, we managed to escape. We watched them encircle the remaining fighters and a man spoke to them, that they could surrender. There were about a hundred of them, most on elk, so the group surrendered. Lily and a few others were pulled away by sleds."

Pane nodded, as Volk entered the room with Nolan and Lin, and Anita and Reeves stood up as they entered, and sat down when they did.

"I think we want to hear exactly what happened," Volk said.

Anita nodded. "We were riding north in the time we expected. We passed through the Red Winds territory, came upon the Forest of the Ghosts, and made camp there during the nightfall. It was about midnight when they came. Men covered in furs, riding elk."

"The White Ravens," Volk interrupted. "It's bad enough that he has other tribes working for him in separate locations, let alone them."

"I am not sure they are working in separate locations," Anita whispered, "They were working together."

"With who?" Volk asked.

"Many of the people that hadn't fallen were taken captive," Anita began again. "Reeves, myself, and three others managed to escape when the others were surrounded. We watched as the group surrounded our own. Someone spoke to them, and they laid down their arms. The five of us went south, and we found four of our horses that had run from the chaos. We were able to escape from the Forest of the Ghosts, and began to cross the snow south. The Red Winds surprised us a little over an hour ago, killing two of us. Those who chased us were those who you fought, just now."

"So, are you saying that the Red Winds and White Ravens coordinated this?" Lin asked.

"The White Ravens weren't in their territory," Volk said, "They are one of few who we know, for sure, where they populate. They were certainly working for Boreas."

"So are the Red Winds," Pane entered, "One of the men I fought had an axe made out of steel. It had to be given to his clan by Boreas."

"Boreas planned this too well for us," Nolan said, "He has his whole fortress, nearly impossible to get to. We can't get to it from land. Our vehicles won't be able to fly through the snow storm at the North Pole, either." He looked toward Pane and Volk. "What do we do?"

Pane turned toward Volk. "Do you trust everyone in this room?"

Volk looked across the room. He stopped going over everyone, and nodded. "What do you intend to say?"

"Everything," Pane said. He looked over to make sure the door was closed. He told them of the Crimson Blade and the Reality Stone. He told them how Boreas had been able to acquire the Crimson Blade, and that if Boreas was to get the stone, he could create the Annihilation Wave. He also said that they had begun to set up a base at the Titan-world to protect the stone. Everyone but Reeves had their mouths open by the time Pane and Volk finished speaking.

"So, we have a genocidal maniac resurrected from the dead, and Boreas, who wants who the hell knows what, with an army of his anti-government, anarchist cult behind him who are both looking for two singularities that control the universe," Nolan whispered.

"Do we know what they will try to do with the Annihilation Wave?"Anita asked.

Pane and Volk both looked at each other and shook their heads. "We need to go to the Titan-world," Volk said, "The time has come. We need to make the Reality Stone the top priority if they obtain it tomorrow."

"There isn't anything else we can do," Pane agreed, "I'll tell General Anders. I gave him notice to begin preparations before we left. We'll direct our resources to protect the Capital, the Last City, and what we hold in the north, as well as any spare resources to the Titan-world."

"Reeves, you'll go in my place," Volk said, "Anita, you'll translate for him. I'll hold the gates and Crows' Hill the best I can. Nolan, Lin, I want one of you to go to the Titan-world, as well, and bring some of your soldiers. I can expect one hell of a fight to come to you."

Lin and Nolan looked at each other. "I'll go," Lin said.

"We'll leave tomorrow," Pane said, "Tell your men the truth, however. That we don't think we'll get to Boreas's fortress, but we believe that protecting an object of immense power will help us succeed."

The meeting finished after they determined how many to send to the Titan-world. Two in three of Lin's force would go, as well as a third of Nolan's.

None of the few remaining Black Striders would go, however. There were far too few remaining, and they would be spread out far too thin.

Pane left Crows' Hill. He conjured a portal in the snow, and the Last City stood at the other end. A snowfall blocked the night sky from being visible overhead. The golden city was quiet in the cloudy night, except for the wind that came with the snowfall. He walked down the hill where his portal had been conjured, and entered the city.

Many of the residents had left for obscure villages with populations of no more than a hundred people, where a distant family member lived to be away from the violence. He wondered what it would be like, to not know all of the conflicts to occur, to not have any part in the game with the North Wind.

Pane walked through the spires, toward the palace. Guards stood aside, as he entered the palace, but he didn't go to Anders first. He took the stairs up into a room that he had seen only a few times.

He had entered the Chamber of Whispers. It was dark, without any windows, and the only light originated from lanterns which hung from the walls. He walked over to an old man who sat at a desk. He took out from his robes a small roll of paper he had written on before he left Crows' Hill. He set it down on the desk.

The man finished writing down something before even bothering looking up. "General Pane," he laughed, "You always come here for the worst of times. I wonder what is in the message today."

"You don't wonder," Pane said, "That is why the Chamber of Whispers was founded. To keep whispers safe."

"Indeed, I do not," the man smiled. "Whenever someone brings me messages in the middle of the night, I fear that something terrible has occurred or will occur. Dark skies, dark words." He looked at the rolled up paper in his hand. "Who is the intended recipient?"

Pane looked at the paper. "James Fonsesca," was all he said before leaving the chamber.

Chapter Fifteen:
Dark Skies, Dark Words

The room was dark and few shadows entered into the room from the cloudy sky. Fonsesca watched as the snowfall drifted down upon the silent city. Few lights came from the spires upon his street. The scene would have even been peaceful if he hadn't known why the residents had all abandoned the city.

He took another drink from the bottle in his hand. Many like it were scattered across the floor. He hadn't been able to sleep tonight like most nights, so he went back to drinking. His dreams were plagued by the same person over and over again. The two faces of Death he saw near every night. Aethor said he gave him mercy two years ago, when he spared his life but killed his friends. But, it was the cruelest irony and trick of all. He hadn't killed him but, instead, had haunted him.

Before Death had been resurrected, his nightmares had mostly been kept at bay but with him resurrected, it had changed him. The nightmares followed him like a shadow.

A knock came from the floors below him. He went back to the window and saw someone standing in the snowfall. His first thought went to the North Wind. *He could be here to kill me*, he thought to himself, *any moment he could break the doorknob he had fixed days earlier and come up the stairs or wait for me with a knife at the side of the door.*

The last visitors he had were Peter and John, days earlier. They had tried to help him a second time, but they failed. He helped them with setting up the two drones, which Peter and Pane would use in searching for the Reality Stone. He wouldn't, however, go with them. Not if the crossroads could lead to Death.

He tried to see if it was anyone he recognized. Fonsesca couldn't recognize him. He wasn't any of the known North Wind followers, for sure. And, it was only one person. He looked along the street and saw no one hiding in the shadows. If it came to a fight, there was a decent chance he would overpower the person. *But then again*, Fonsesca thought to himself, *Death could change his face into a human's. It could be him down there.*

Curiosity overcame his paranoia. He took another drink, finished the bottle, and walked over to his bedside drawer. He opened the top shelf and took the gun from it. He loaded it and took off the safety.

He always preferred the weapons of decades earlier; he never knew why, but he did.

Fonsesca opened the door of his room and descended down the stairs. He needed the railing to support himself. He hoped his aim would be good, if he needed it. "I probably won't even be a challenge for him," he whispered to himself.

He set one last safety for him if it came to a fight. He took a knife from the kitchen and set it on the table closest to the entrance.

Fonsesca put his gun barrel against the doorway. All it would take was for him to move his arm slightly inward and it would be over. He unlocked the lock and waited briefly. Nothing happened, so he opened the door.

Fonsesca was met by the cold, and stared at no one he knew. The man's face was covered in shadows and snow covered half of his dark hair from the minutes outside. "What bird is black behind white?" The man asked.

Fonsesca stared at the man. *What kind of riddle is that?* He asked himself. The man didn't blink or do anything. He glanced at the gun beside the doorway. He wouldn't need it. "Piss off, poet," he growled and slammed the door.

He walked beside the table and picked up the knife. He glanced at the door but it stayed still. He put the knife back among the others in the kitchen.

"What kind of message was that?" Fonsesca asked himself. He glanced once more at the door. He realized then. It was no message, but rather a code and he was supposed to complete it. "One of Pane's codes," he whispered.

He moved back over to the door, fumbled with the lock and opened it. The messenger gave a blank stare back at him, still as a statue. More snow had fallen in his hair making it look nearly white. "What bird is black behind white?" The messenger asked once more.

"A crow disguised as a dove," Fonsesca answered.

The messenger continued his blank stare. "And why is a crow disguised as a dove?" The messenger asked.

"To gain something it cannot, a crow," Fonsesca answered.

The messenger remained motionless for the moment. He held out a rolled piece of paper in his hand. "Message from General Pane," He said. He handed it to him. That was all he said, before walking away through the snow, one more quiet shadow in the night.

Fonsesca looked over it. He looked across the street and at the windows of the spires nearby. Of the few that remained in the street, no one stared at him. He shut the door behind him.

He rotated the scroll in his hand. *If Pane has asked for me again, something has gone wrong*, Fonsesca thought to himself. He broke the seal and opened it.

I am sorry to tell you like this
but Lily has been captured in the

north. She went north with a group of Black Striders. We don't know her condition at the moment other than that she was captured.

Lee and the others have made their way to the Reality Stone. They will acquire it tomorrow. With that said, we will be moving our forces to the Titan-world. I haven't told them of Lily's capture yet. I know what condition you are in, and drinking yourself to the grave will not help destroy your demons. If there is anything left of the man I knew just weeks ago, then come with us. We can make this right, where all of our conflicts began.

Fonsesca clenched his jaw and threw the piece of paper onto the table. "She's been captured twice before," he whispered. "She'll make it through." But he knew that lying to himself wouldn't help. Something about this time was different. If Storm Riders had caught her she would be treated like all the others caught. If she was lucky enough to have been caught by one under Boreas's payment, then she would be sent straight toward Boreas and her father.

He picked up the paper from the other end of the table and walked back upstairs clinging to the railing for every step. He started a fire in the fireplace. The single log began to ignite, and will soon meet with the other ashes below it. He looked at the paper and tossed it into the fire.

He walked over to the table and picked up the bottle he had been drinking earlier, but found it empty. He opened another. Something caught his eye in the reflection of the bottle caused by the fire light. A stranger was staring right back at him. He was gaunt and unshaven, his hair a tangled mess and his eyes had shadows below them.

He looked behind himself and saw no one. It was himself in the reflection. "Will I drink myself to the grave?" he asked the reflection staring back at him. The reflection stared back as he stared at it.

He set the bottle down, undrunk.

Chapter Sixteen:
The Last Dawn Before the New

Boreas heard a knock at his door. He looked away from the fire he had been staring at and turned toward the door. "Come in," he said.

Quentin Johannson opened the door. "Lord Boreas," he said bowing his head before smiling, "My husband says the world engine is repaired and ready."

Boreas smiled. "Thank you," he said, "Give Ray my thanks as well. Call forward a meeting at dawn."

Quentin bowed his head and closed the door. Boreas stood up and walked out of his room. The fortress was quiet, despite that it would be changed forever. With the Reality Stone, Boreas will be able to get the justice he deserved, and so much more.

He walked the hallways and stairwells, and came upon the top of the fortress. The wind whipped his hair across his face and the cold bit at his skin. Snow and wind pelted his body in the storm causing him to cling to the side of the walkway.

Boreas knew he would be up here. Aethor looked across the fortress down below. "I thought I would find you up here," Boreas shouted over the wind.

"If you thought you would, then you have a strange perception of me," Aethor shouted back. Boreas walked beside him upon the railing. "You have news or you wouldn't have come. What is it?"

"The world engine is ready," Boreas said, "Your daughter may be in the jungle, you know that don't you?"

"And?" Aethor asked. "We'll burn that barrier when we get there."

"It won't be that easy," Boreas said, "It never is. I don't think she'll come willingly."

"Years ago when she left," Aethor said, "I let her leave. What's done is done. I am not going to control her and confine her to her room for the rest of her life."

"Yes, you let her leave," Boreas told him, "And yet just after she left, you were defeated. I don't think it was the soldiers that stopped you or the man that put the blood curse on you, but the confliction of her leaving. And you, not her, were the one confined; not to your room but a desolation, the Titan-world."

"That was one of the many reasons," Aethor growled. "Since we are looking back on the past, what made you stop fighting years back?"

Boreas looked toward him. He had to stop, or it could have torn apart the world. "Years ago, the North Wind was gathering hundreds of followers. But, I didn't want to attack them multiple times. I wanted to wait, gather more followers and do one swift strike. A coup, most likely. But a group of my men wanted to attack immediately."

"And they betrayed you, divided the North Wind in half, and destroyed those that remained?" Aethor asked.

"Yes," Boreas said. He looked upon the courtyard below. He remembered the battle well and the slaughter that came with it. "That's where the fight happened. When the fighting was done, we survived. But the North Wind was destroyed. Everyone who fought on their side was killed; we lost so many, as well. I killed the man that started it, all myself. He was the last to survive; the last to die."

"What was his name?" Aethor asked.

"Dead men don't need names," Boreas growled, "And this man shouldn't be remembered." He paused, and they both stared at the courtyard below, empty in the night. "So when the fighting finished and I killed him, I sent the others home. What we started was done. It died in the courtyard."

"My plans died two years ago, not when Lily defeated me on Earth, but in the courtyard when I performed The End," Aethor said, "I have lived for centuries now, much of that time spent as the last of my people. I spent much of that fighting each world, until each was purged of humanity. I succeeded on three of the seven, my kind adding a fourth to that tally. I should have just kept fighting, not been clever, and been quick about it; the opposite of you."

The two of them remained silent, once again. Boreas looked toward the ramparts and saw the guards change next to the braziers in the wall. They would be the few not to hear him speak. Dawn was upon them.

"So here we are, two men who have failed once, I even twice, with our goals given one last chance," Aethor whispered.

"Some world," Boreas said. "Before we leave, I need to tell the North Wind that the time has come. I will be in the hall." He began to walk back toward the inside. "You are welcome to join us."

"I have heard enough monologues to last a lifetime," Aethor said, "A fair few of them from my own mouth."

"Very well," Boreas said, "Get yourself ready from the jungle."

Boreas walked away from the top of the fortress and walked down the halls. After minutes, he came upon the hall. It was overcrowded with his followers, many sat down around the stone round tables, others stood along the walls. Those who sat all stood up, as he came into the hall.

He walked through the hall toward the center of the hall. At the opposite end stood the high table, where Corvus, Ariadne, Percival, and Avertree sat around it. Aethor's chair was vacant. He stopped in the middle of the room.

"My brothers, my sisters, my friends," Boreas began, "Dawn has begun down south across our world. While we can't see it, it is there. And, it is the last dawn in the universe, as we know. Today is the day we change the path our worlds have been set upon." His audience whispered, and he briefly let them, before he continued.

"I must be honest with you, now, and it is time you know the truth. Nearly two months ago, I went searching for an object of immense power: the Crimson Blade." He took it out of his cloak. He let the viewers whisper, as it floated, giving off its faint red light. "This however is only half of a whole. The Reality Stone is the second of the two. I intend to find it today. With the two, we will be able to create an event known as the Annihilation Wave. And with the Annihilation Wave, we will be able to take down our enemies who we have banded together to fight. Those that have oppressed all of us, the corrupt who take hold of our world and chain our decisions out of greed and power. This is the enemy we have joined together to fight. Ready yourselves, because, together, we will succeed."

The hall remained silent until those around him broke into applause. Boreas smiled and caught the Crimson Blade floating in the air. He walked over to the high table. Corvus and Ariadne stood up, as he approached, and left their seats to join his side. "Follow my orders well," Boreas said to Avertree.

Avertree gave a sly smile, which worried Boreas. "Of course, I will," he said. Boreas looked toward Percival sitting beside Avertree. Percival gave him a near unnoticeable nod.

Boreas, Corvus, and Ariadne left the hall. Many had already vacated it for their duties. The three of them walked through the courtyard. Boreas watched the blue flames of the braziers flicker to life and fall, as they came by and left. He walked through the archway beneath the wall directly into the storm. Wind and snow battered his body and sent his cloak flying around him.

Quentin and Ray Johannson stood, facing spikes that jutted through land and snow in the miles that stood in front of them. They turned to face the three of them. In Quentin's hand was the lockbox with the Annihilation Detectors. He took out the wrist pad and handed one to Boreas, then Ariadne, and Corvus.

"Thank you," Boreas said. He looked at his detector and turned it on. He saw the arrow where he stood on the screen and the dot that was at the arrow that signified the Crimson Blade.

"Be victorious, Lord Boreas," Quentin said beneath his cloak. He shook hands with him.

Boreas turned toward Ray. "When you are ready," he said.

Ray smiled. He took out a controller and pressed a button on it. The ground shook beneath them. Snow started to shake around them and a hum began to go through the air. In front of them, a massive patch of snow began to collapse on itself.

Boreas looked at the cavity and saw the world engine float in the air. The slow spinning hull at the center of the craft caused a vortex of snow. They watched the world engine rise into the air before stopping.

"Safe travels," Ray said, as he and Quentin walked off through the snow.

Boreas looked back and saw Aethor coming toward them. He stopped at their side. "Are you ready?" Boreas asked them. The three of them nodded. "Lets go get the stone." He conjured a portal and they entered the world engine.

Chapter Seventeen:
The Tree Over the Prairie

Sage woke up at dawn sleeping beside John. The sky was a variation of reds, oranges, and yellows and all across the horizon it was clear of clouds. The group ate breakfast in silence. Hopefully, it was their last day on the planet.

John was able to stand, but not well. His pace was slow around the hillside camp and he was overly cautious of navigating rocks. As the sky turned blue, they finished cleaning the camp. Peter was already sending the drone to where they had seen the deep blue light in the night sky.

Sage watched the plains in front of them. The long grass rustled and swayed in the faint breeze, and light reflected off of the lake. In the time, Sage, John, and Lee watched the land through binoculars. They spotted a herd of large, brown-furred creatures with thick matted fur and two curling horns at the back of its head. They watched as the herd grazed on grass, as they traveled to a watering hole a few miles away. They joined the same birds they saw at sunset last night along the reeds.

Lee left to pick up Graves, who was brooding by the lake, alone, when Peter said the drone would arrive soon.

"I wonder what else is out there," John said.

"We could spend months here and we would barely scratch the surface of the jungle," Sage said.

"I'd spend those months with you," John whispered.

Sage smiled. "So would I."

It was nearing midday when Peter became startled by the screen he was looking at. "Lee, you might want to make a portal," Peter whispered.

Lee walked over to the screen. His eyes went wide. Sage went over to see but Lee held out his hand. "You might want to see this in your own eyes first," Lee said.

Sage went back and slung her bags over her shoulder. She helped John carry his and even slung one of his onto her back. Lee conjured a portal and walked through. Much of the picture was the blue of the sky. She helped John through, and was immediately baffled by the view.

The five of them were on a flat space of dirt and rocks. The plateau held a view of miles and miles of the grasslands below. Clouds covered the sky miles away to the horizon. But that was only half of it. Behind them was the greatest tree she had ever seen. It sprouted hundreds of feet into the sky and the canopy spanned over the whole plateau, and much beyond. The leaves changed as her eyes looked out, rippling from light to dark greens. Thousands, potentially millions of flowering plants hung from the branches changing from purples to blues to yellows. Dozens of species of birds nested among the branches that hung above them.

"I am lost of words," John whispered.

"We all are," Peter said. She looked and saw him placing the drone back into its place.

Even Graves was baffled although briefly. "Let's get the stone before it's too late," he said.

"About that," Lee said, "Where could it be?" Sage scanned the tree. She didn't see the deep blue she had seen last night.

"It could be in a hollow somewhere up the trunk, beneath the roots or somewhere in the branches," John said, "How could we find it? At worst, we'll have to wait until the night."

Sage looked below the tree but saw something odd. Roots that sprouted out from the ground had rings of flowers grow that spanned around the tree at those points. They weren't, however, regular flowers, because different types grew on the same branch. It was similar to what had grown all the way at the border of the jungle. Peter had noticed as well. "It's in the roots," she said.

"How do you know?" Graves asked.

"They are the same as the border of the jungle and desert," she explained, "There are different flowers in the same plant. It has to be in the roots."

"There must be a cavity below," Peter said.

The five of them began to walk toward the great tree. Sage looked at each ring of flowers as she stepped over them, trying not to damage any of the flowers. There were seven rings they stepped over. Some a few feet wide, one only a few inches. Many had three or four different flowers growing on each ring, some different in shape, others in color or size.

As they crossed over the last ring, the tree loomed above her. She touched the root and smiled. The tree was so wide that her whole vision was off the tree and the looming canopy. She looked into the canopy, as a hum went through the air. The thousands of birds above all flew away in the same direction at once. Sage knew who had come.

They all looked at one another. "He's here," Lee whispered. Sage looked into the clouds and saw the world engine burst through. It hurtled over the prairie toward the tree. "Circle the tree and find the entrance," Lee said. He drew his sword.

"What are you doing?" John asked. "You're not going to fight him?"

"No, but I'll certainly hold him," Lee argued.

"I'll hold him back Lee," Graves said unsheathing his broadsword. "You go get the stone."

Lee shook his head.

Peter looked at him with his face twisted into a frown. "Is this it?" He asked Lee. "Is this what you think is the end?"

Lee looked toward the world engine hurtling toward them, the hum getting louder with the second. It had nearly bounded from the clouds to the tree in just the minute. "Not much of a better end," Lee said, "But only if you got the stone away from here."

Peter looked to the ground. "There is no point in arguing," Peter whispered. He clutched Lee's shoulder and nodded.

Lee nodded and pushed Peter away. "Go," Lee said. "Go!" He shouted. He ran off jumping over the rings of flowers toward the world engine which was at the edge of the canopy.

"We need to search the area," Graves said, "Quickly!"

They began to run around the tree, searching for the cavity to the Reality Stone. The world engine was soon out of view by the hulking mass of the tree. Briefly, as she ran by, she saw darkness beneath a root larger than her body. She thought it was a shadow but when she turned back toward it she saw it was the entrance.

"Over here!" she shouted. She pushed dirt aside as she tried to expand the cavity. Soon, all four of them were pushing the dirt away from the root until the cavity was large enough for them to go under with their packs.

She went into the cavity first and the others followed, Graves last. They were in an eerie darkness. Peter lit a flare and bathed the tunnel in red light. She walked through the passage beneath the tree until she came upon a small room. At the center of the room was a hole in the ground. A deep blue light came from it.

She walked over to the hole and they all peered through it. At the bottom of the whole was a basin where the light came from.

"There it is," Peter whispered. They jumped into the hole one by one until they surrounded the basin.

Although Sage had seen the Crimson Blade briefly, the Reality Stone unlike the Crimson Blade fit its name well. It was small and could fit in her hand. It had ridges that ran around it parallel to the poles it was floating on. The stone itself was a deep blue glass-like color, much like the ocean.

"Before we touch it," John whispered, "Didn't we think the last one would be a bomb?"

Sage looked from John to Peter to Graves. "We did think that," Graves whispered.

"I don't think this one should concern us," Peter said, "This one isn't made out of antimatter."

They looked at each other. "I am not touching it," John said, "Graves you're the Sorcerer it definitely won't react if it's you."

"No he has to make a portal back," Peter argued.

"Enough bickering," Sage whispered. Her heart pounded as she said it. "I'll do it."

They looked toward her but no one argued. John handed her a cloth and she went forward to grab it. She soon felt the stone in her hand. Nothing happened.

She smiled toward them just as she heard dirt moving from the entrance of the tunnel above. Graves conjured a portal to the Spectral Boundary as she heard the people running toward the hole above. Her stomach turned. She knew the worse had come as they moved toward the room. *Lee had failed*, she thought to herself. She sensed the others knew as well.

They left through the portal just before they came through from above.

...

Lee ran toward the world engine, sword in hand. He jumped over the seven rings of flowers until they ended. There was about fifty feet from him and the cliff of the plateau. He summoned a disc in front of his other hand. The world engine was directly next to the canopy causing the different shaded leaves to rattle.

Red light came from the ship and fell feet away from the edge of the plateau. Four people emerged from the light. Boreas in his North Wind cloak led them followed by Aethor in a mahogany colored armor, Corvus with his dual edged spear, and Ariadne.

"Lee, where are the others?" Boreas asked. "It doesn't have to come to fighting. We can end this without violence."

"They'll be gone before you can stand by the tree," Lee shouted. The disc above his hand disappeared in a cloud of sparks and he drew one of his pistols. He fired at Boreas until he ran out of bullets. In a flash, he had drawn the Crimson Blade. Red matter warped around it making a shield blocking all of the shots he had fired.

"Corvus, Ariadne, find the stone," Boreas commanded. The shield in front of him changed into a scimitar. Aethor made a sword appear from jet black matter. Corvus and Ariadne ran to his right and toward the tree.

All Lee could do was hope that they had already found the stone. Lee conjured a disc and threw it at Boreas. He let it fall upon his scimitar spraying him in sparks. Aethor already came upon Lee. He slashed at Lee. Lee did the best he could to block but he saw Aethor's blade cut slightly into his own with each attack. Lee conjured a shaft of sparks and threw it at Aethor's body. It hit him in the chest and caused him to fall over. He knew, however, that it did no harm to him.

Boreas came at him with his scimitar. Lee leapt to the side. He didn't want the Crimson Blade to come into contact with his own sword. If Aethor's could cut part of the way, the blade could snap it in half.

Lee tried thrusting his sword at Boreas's chest, but he knew it backfired. Boreas moved aside and brought the scimitar to Lee's leg. Pain flew through it, and he collapsed on the knee. Blood was already coming from where it had cut through his leg. He gasped.

All Lee could do was stop Aethor's sword from connecting with his head. He blocked the attack and rolled to his side, gritting his teeth as he rolled on his knee. His back was now to the prairie and Boreas and Aethor were between him and the tree.

Boreas already had a disc conjured as Lee stood up. It hit Lee square in the chest causing him to fall backward. He immediately felt the pain of a rib or two break as he was hit. He tried to support himself with his sword and coughed blood upon the ground. He looked toward his opponents.

"Lee," Boreas said, "We don't have to fight like this. I saw you die in my dream but that doesn't mean you have to. Lay down your weapon. We can get you to a healer in time."

"You saw me die in your dream," Lee said. He raised his sword, pain killing his leg. "It will happen. That is how it works." He conjured a disc over his hand and threw it at Aethor.

Aethor lazily brushed it aside with his sword.

Boreas walked forward toward him. "If I could explain why I have done everything then you will know that this is not necessary."

"Yes it is," Lee whispered. He swung at Boreas. Boreas moved to the side and bashed his chest with the hilt of the scimitar.

Lee tumbled backward and fell chest first into the dirt causing him more pain. He coughed up more blood. His sword skittered near the edge of the plateau. He crawled through the dirt toward it. He picked it up just in time to turn around and see Aethor's sword come down upon him. Lee held up his own but it snapped from the impact with the black sword.

Lee cried out as the sword drove itself into his left shoulder. Pools of blood were forming in two places on the ground. He gasped as he looked up toward the canopy. Aethor held his sword above him but didn't attack. He withdrew as Boreas came to him.

"Are you sure you want to do this?" Boreas asked.

Lee breathed heavily before slowly lifting his body up. He tried to stab Boreas with the broken blade. Boreas blocked it with the flat edge of the blade causing it to fly from his hand.

Lee coughed up more blood onto the ground. He was losing too much. Even if Boreas was telling the truth, it wouldn't matter.

Corvus and Ariadne had already turned up to Boreas. They had no prisoners or weren't carrying the stone. *They had left*, he thought to himself. *At least this was worth it*.

"They made a portal just as we came upon the room," Ariadne said.

Boreas tried to mask his anger, but he did not hide it well. It was a few seconds before he spoke again. "You fought well, Lee," Boreas whispered.

Lee looked at him. "If you are going to kill me," he whispered, "Make it quick."

"That will be done," Boreas said. He gave Lee a smile as if he was sorry. *Perhaps he had been serious about letting me stay alive*, Lee thought. It didn't matter anymore.

Lee looked out toward the prairie below him. He was on the edge of the plateau and could see it all below him. He saw the grass rustle in unison with one another in the faint wind and the water beds shine in the midday sun. He closed his eyes. Lee held the image in his mind. Death came quick.

Chapter Eighteen:
The Abandoned City

The travel through the Spectral Boundary went by slowly. Sage thought of leaving Lee behind as they traveled. Lee had been old but, to her, he always seemed like a survivor. Now he was almost certainly gone.

The ground came to her eyes. It was followed by cold and a stretched out image. Then the snow and the Last City. The city's golden spires gleamed in the light that came and passed through the veil of the clouds.

She pushed herself off of the snow and immediately wished for warmer clothing. She blew into her hands giving her a slight warmth. She looked toward the other four of them. All of them were sullen. She looked at the Reality Stone wrapped in cloth, still in her hand.

"Keep that hidden," Graves said, "We don't know if there are any of Boreas's spies nearby."

Sage wrapped the stone tightly in the cloth and tucked it into her fist. The four of them walked toward the city walls. Sage kept by John, watching his gait with each step.

A pair of guards awaited their arrival. "Commander Graves," one of the guards said, "Where is Commander Lee?"

Graves frowned and waited briefly before answering. "Dead," was all he answered.

The guards blinked at him, but nodded. "Very well," the other guard spoke, "We are to escort you to the Titan-world."

They looked at Graves and he nodded. The four of them followed their two escorts. The city was empty, except for the guards. The only people in the streets were pairs of guards running to their intended destinations.

"Has General Pane ordered a lockdown of the city?" Graves asked.

"Yes," one of the guards answered, "He expects an imminent attack from the North Wind. He has not released the intelligence to that." Sage could take a guess why. They would have had the stone before Boreas and expected him to attack.

They entered the palace. The portal at the center of the entrance room was the portal powered by the Luminous Creek with blue sparks at its ring. Floating blue, pink, and white lights hovered like fireflies overhead.

The portal at the center of the room showed a picture Sage had never seen before. It stood at the front of blackened ruins of a city full of golden spires. The ground was white with a covering of snow. Above the city were jagged cliffs with a thin pale white covering, but, underneath, she could tell it was crimson. This was the Titan-world.

The guards waited for the four of them to walk through before they followed. Graves walked through first. Sage followed, taking her first step into a new world. Overhead, gray clouds cast thunder for the world to see. She looked to the ground and picked up a handful of the covering she thought had been snow. It was a mineral laid out across the ground like sand or snow. Where she had taken the handful, a crimson spot of a reflective stone stood uncovered.

"It looks like blood," Sage whispered. She set the handful of the mineral back down above the patch.

They began to walk through the barren city. Much of the entrance was spires reduced to ash and rubble but, as they continued, the spires began to form complete shapes. The inner half of the city had been abandoned, not destroyed.

The group came upon what once may have been the palace. Guards stood in front of it and moved away as they came forward. The doors of the palace opened. Pane walked forward followed by three people who she had never seen before, two of whom were in the black of the Black Striders. The third was in an army of Earth uniform. She saw a face, however, who she had not expected. Fonsesca followed the other four. His hair had grown out even further since she had last seen him, and he was slightly more gaunt and pale, but, otherwise, he looked normal.

Pane sighed. "You need to come with us, quickly." He looked toward the guards beside him. "Put the city on lockdown. No guard leaves unless already assigned to." The guards left them. He looked back toward them. "Follow us."

Sage, John, Peter, and Graves made no word to the rest of them. Sage looked at Fonsesca and gave him a small smile. He nodded and pushed her along.

The whole group walked through the door. The large room was circular and the decorations along the wall would have once been beautiful if they hadn't been faded and started crumbling. They entered one of two doors that were in the room. They walked through the passageway into a massive cavern in the ground. Sounds of metal work filled their ears as they entered the walkway. Machines that resembled dragonflies stood in rows below them. They had two narrow wings on each side and they were colored in a deep blue or teal. The four of them stared agape at the rows below. There were at least a hundred of them.

The group walked up a flight of stairs and entered a room. An old, faded map of the city was outstretched on a table. Sunlight entered the room through the side of the room from a large window that overlooked the city.

"Where is Lee?" Pane asked as he entered behind them. Sage looked to John and Peter. None of them spoke which gave him the answer.

"Boreas arrived as we had," Graves whispered, "He bought us time. Whatever he did, we are here because of it." Graves turned to Sage. "Show him."

Sage unwrapped the cloth that was clutched in her hand. She set the Reality Stone on the table. It glowed a soft blue light across the room.

The five of them stared at it. "Is that it?" Fonsesca asked.

"Yes," John answered.

"Lee knew he would die," Peter whispered. "It was in one of Lily's dreams, Lee had said. And that was why he went with us instead of with you." He looked toward the two Black Striders.

Sage thought of Lee's death. It had been her who had pressured Lily into telling others. Lily had been the one who was against it, but Sage had convinced her to tell Pane. Her stomach turned. If she hadn't convinced Lily then Lee may still be alive. A worse idea went through her mind, but it was cut short before planting itself in her head.

"We have something, we need to tell you," Pane said abruptly.

The idea she had just thought began to sprout. Lily was captured by Storm Riders, who were working under Boreas. Lily had seen herself in her dreams, dying at the fortress after being captured. The thought bloomed in her mind. *Lily was going to die.*

Chapter Nineteen:
The Other Option

The night was terribly cold. As the group taking Lily to the north pole moved closer to the storm, they were met with bitter onslaughts of cold winds. They had left the Forest of the Ghosts in the late afternoon and now were heading toward Boreas at the North Pole.

Soon, snow began to descend upon them in ferocious gales. Twice Lily had nearly fallen from the elk she rode on from a strong gail. The group soon came up to a hill where a small cave was being hidden away in the snow. "We should set camp for the night here," Willem shouted from his elk. The half dozen Storm Riders dismounted from their elks and began to tie the elks up.

Lily dismounted from her elk and fell into the snow. She entered the cave. It was no more than a dozen feet deep but the wind wouldn't affect them in it. It blew away from the entrance, not into it.

"Don't take this personally, but I am going to need to tie your legs," Willem said.

Lily sat down against the far end of the cave wall as he tied up her legs at the ankle. The half dozen of her escorts began to tend to the elks, while Willem began to make a fire with wood and kindling he had found a few hours ago at the end of the Forest of the Ghosts. He ran a flint across the back of a small knife, to make sparks. The kindling caught after thirty seconds and Willem added the logs to the fire. The other Storm Riders soon joined him, and they began laughing and talking in the night.

Lily stayed silent through much of it. She didn't want to provoke them in any way. She didn't want to find out how intolerant of Sorcerers they were, beyond the stories told by Willem. After being given a meal of a salted jerky, Lily soon tried to sleep away her captivity.

...

A mist began to crawl across the land before the ruins. The demon onslaught soon broke through. The ruined city was soon befell by the black mass of creatures. On her tower, Lily soon began to conjure shapes of sparks, one after another, whether it be a disc flung at a group or a shaft at one.

But the horde kept on coming, and the long night continued to relent her. The strange noise that haunted her sounded through the air. The demons stopped the attack as the faint purple light grew larger in the sky. The shockwave hit the city.

She heard a groan go through the tower. It began to crack and the tower began to shatter. The tower buckled and Lily fell forward into the wall. She closed her eyes and fell into the horde of the demons.

She expected the tearing and clawing of the demons, but she didn't find it. The night was still, quiet. She opened her eyes. She was under a tree, lying in the grass. A lone tree, it's leaves and branches were still. Lily looked into the night sky. A crescent moon loomed over her. She recognized the moon and tree, but not the landscape. It was a meadow. Grass and patches of flowers grew in the landscape. Snow covered mountains miles away jutted into the sky. It was familiar, but empty. Something grave was missing from the landscape.

...

It was still the night when Lily woke up. The blizzard still relented outside. The six Storm Riders and Willem were all by the fire. They were all staring at her. Their gaze broke when she looked at them.

"You talked and muttered in your sleep," Willem explained, "Does that happen often?"

Lily nodded.

"Troubling memories?" Willem asked.

"Troubling future," Lily answered. She looked toward the storm. It wasn't the battle that worried her. It was the part afterward. She recognized the meadow, but couldn't tell where it was. A howl went through the wind. More responded after it. "Wolves?" Lily asked. "Or riders?"

Willem looked out into the winds and snow. "Wolves," he answered. He looked at some of the riders and began to speak in their tongue. Two of them moved out toward the cave's edge and pulled the elks into the back of the cave. "I would not enjoy running into wolves when we travel," he said, "There are at least a dozen in that pack."

"Have you ever been surrounded by wolves?" Lily asked.

"Not by the packs you speak of," Willem said.

The group left in the morning, despite the continuing storm. Lily looked out into the storm to find any shadows of a hunting pack, but found none. Still, they were not the worst of her fears. They would enter the ice spikes soon and, by midday, they would be at the fortress.

After an hour, they came upon the boundary of the ice spikes. The spikes were jagged and jutted dozens of feet into the air. She could tell some of the points were still sharp.

"How were they formed?" Lily asked.

"The Storm Riders say their Gods," Willem answered, "But I doubt the reasoning behind it. I was never a godly man. My guess is just stronger ice."

Lily looked at the spikes as they walked through them. *Perhaps a glacier was once here*, she thought to herself. She guessed that a glacier stopped moving and was eroded away by the storm. She knew that the blizzard survived for months on end, before winding down and increasing later. The ice that was left was just stronger.

The group followed a narrow path that she knew some had been through before. In the harsh wind and cold, she saw no markers in the path. It all looked the same to her. The group must have been riding for a few hours when she saw a faint light in the distance before an ice spike passed in front of it. She knew what it meant. She was at the Fortress of the North Wind.

The group followed the path further for a few minutes, before the walls loomed in front of them. The last of the ice spikes disappeared on her sides, as they came upon the clearing in front of the wall.

The eight of them waited for a few minutes before a group in midnight blue cloaks came in front of their party. She expected to see Boreas or her father at its head, but was shocked to find Percival walking forward. He gave the slightest glance at her before turning his eyes to Willem.

Willem dismounted from his elk and walked forward to him. They shook hands and exchanged a few words. Percival nodded in the end and thanked him. Percival told one of the people behind him something, who then ran off into the fortress.

Willem walked forward and mounted back onto his elk. "This is where we part," he said to Lily. He nodded as she dismounted from her elk. Two of the people behind Percival each took her arm.

Percival just stared, as she came forward. He looked to the two people who had Lily by her arms. "She can walk herself," he said. It was hard to hear in the blizzard so it came out only as a whisper but they let her go.

Percival and her walked side by side into the fortress. She noticed a long mark across his forehead. It had been when she had made him fall at the cliffs two months ago. She had made him hit his head on the rocks. She hadn't noticed it at the catacombs in the dark.

The others dispersed as they entered the courtyard. Braziers full of blue flames flickered to life and out as they walked by them.

"Is my father here?" Lily asked.

"No," Percival answered. Instead of taking her through two large doors where the straight path led, he took her to the right and they walked along the side of the fortress. "He is searching for the Reality Stone with Boreas."

"Boreas isn't here?" Lily asked.

"No, he is not," Percival answered.

"Are your parents in charge then?" Lily asked.

Percival didn't answer directly this time. "Why did you come?" Percival asked. He led her through a small door that was the entrance to a stairwell. They began to walk up a circular stairwell.

"I came here to stop Boreas and my father," Lily answered.

"I knew that," Percival said, "What I meant was, why didn't you try to overpower them while coming here? If you had been able to get far enough away there was no way they wouldn't have been able to track you."

"I was bound against seven of them," Lily answered. "If I had been able to subdue them long enough to escape I was still bound. I couldn't conjure anything, or even conjure a portal. I would have been left running in the snow with the wolves, hoping I wouldn't be caught by someone much worse than the Raven's Eye."

The stairwell stopped in front of them. "And now you are at the wolves' den," he said. He opened the door. A dozen North Wind stood in front of her all with spears, but in front of them was someone far worse than the dozen combined. Avertree gave her a mocking smile.

"Look who finally decided to drop by," Avertree mocked, "When Boreas said that Black Striders would head north, I wasn't surprised, but I never expected you. Come along now, daughter of Death, your trial awaits you."

"Trial?" Lily asked shocked. She had been expecting to be thrown into a cell until Boreas and her father arrived.

"Oh, you'll love it," Avertree mocked again, "But it's not really a trial. It'll just be me shouting at you, until I tell you what I'll do to you."

"I should have done more than just punch you the last time I saw you," Lily sneered.

"I think you do," Avertree said, "But, this time you are tied up, and if you try I'll have my guards kill you."

"Your guards?" Lily asked.

Avertree made a quick glance to Percival who was on Lily's left before answering, "North Wind, they and Percival will be here to protect me in the event you, as you put it, do more than just try to punch me."

They came upon a room. Lanterns hung at both sides of the door. Two of Avertree's guards opened it. Avertree walked in followed by Lily and Percival.

Lily's stomach turned, as she was shocked to see the room. She had seen it twice in her dreams; once when Lee died, the other time when she did. Lanterns hung or were placed on small holders at the sides of the dark room giving only a faint light. A long table was at the end of the room.The guards didn't follow them in.

Avertree seemed to notice. He looked toward Lily. "Could you have seen this room in your dreams, I wonder," he said. He studied her face. "You did, didn't you? Do you know what will happen?" Lily didn't answer. Avertree looked to Percival. "Tie her legs down." Avertree sat down at the middle of the table.

Lily went down on her knees. She was too busy noticing the stark similarities to the scene in her dreams to care that Percival was tying her with a rope at her ankles. When he finished, Percival moved to the side of the room.

Avertree looked to Percival. "Before we begin Percival, I'd like you to cut the act," Avertree said, "I know Boreas told you to spy on me." Lily looked toward Percival. He stared at Avertree. "Before I tell you what I will, I would like to ask you not to draw your sword, because, when I finish, I will have convinced you, otherwise." Percival again just stared. "I am taking control of the North Wind," he said bluntly.

Percival drew his sword without hesitation. Avertree rolled his eyes. "Why exactly should you be in control of the North Wind?" Percival asked. He held up the sword pointing at Avertree.

"The other option," Avertree answered. It was a vague answer Lily didn't understand but it had something to do with her, because Percival and Avertree both glanced at her.

"What are you talking about?" Lily asked.

"Why you aren't on Haranae right now, but here instead," Percival whispered.

This time, Avertree didn't mock or taunt her in any way. "Boreas's morals brought all of us where we are now," Avertree began, "And they are why he is unfit to lead the North Wind. To get the Reality Stone, Boreas needed someone who was at least part Titan in order to enter the jungle. That left no one known, apart from you, the daughter of Death. And rather than kidnapping you, he chose to revive the very man who swore himself to destroy all humanity but the last of us. He chose to resurrect a genocidal murderer who will kill billions if uncontained instead of one girl. In no way can a man like that be fit to rule the North Wind."

Lily let his words wash over her. Boreas had chosen not to kidnap her and, instead, chose to resurrect her father. Even from her stand point, she thought it was poor judgement. Boreas had never attacked, unless provoked or if it was his justice, but even the other option sounded better.

Avertree looked toward Percival. "I know you chose to be neutral in that decision. You knew it was a bad one but you didn't say anything. Are you with me or not?"

Percival looked down at his sword. He lowered it and put it in its sheath. "In," he answered. "If he comes back with the Reality Stone, how do we stop him?"

Avertree looked toward Lily. "We kill her," he answered.

Lily's stomach turned and she looked toward Percival. He didn't even glance at her this time. "Why?" he asked.

"Two days ago," Avertree began, "I sent kidnappers to her house. I was surprised when they came back and told me she wasn't there. I had sent for her to be kidnapped, so that we could use her as leverage in an exchange we would have made when

Boreas returned. I would hang her from the walls if he didn't hand over the blade and the stone. Knowing her father would have been there, I am sure the end result would be as I hoped. But my case for why I should lead if Boreas had resurrected Death wouldn't work, unless people see Death. When he sees her body already dead, I am sure he would turn into his Titan-form."

Lily gasped and looked over at Percival. He looked from Avertree to her and nodded. "That would work," he said heartlessly.

Avertree smiled and pulled out a knife. He walked over to Lily.

Percival broke him off. "Let me do it," he said, taking out his sword. "Do you remember on the cliffs, when you hit me with a disc and I fell upon the rocks? You nearly killed me with those rocks. I still have the scar." He pointed with his free hand to his forehead. "I should do it."

Avertree put the knife away. He sat down at his chair again. "The things we do for revenge," he said.

Lily looked over to Percival. "You don't have to do this," she pleaded with him. "You know you don't. You are better than this." She could feel tears go down her cheek.

Percival stared at her eyes. "No, I'm not," he whispered. "If it is any consolation, this is for the greater good." She tried to break the ropes at her wrist but she knew it wouldn't happen.

Lily turned back toward Avertree. She could see the faintest of smiles on his face. He didn't call

Percival away. Percival pressed his hand into her shoulder and put the point of the blade at her back.

Lily closed her eyes. What she had seen in her dreams was happening. She couldn't change that. The worst part of it was her promise to Sage. She knew what would happen here, and Lily had promised her she'd be safe. Percival removed the point of the blade from her back. Lily took her last breath.

But Lily breathed again. She didn't feel anything done. She felt her wrists loosen. She looked toward Percival and he gave her a small smile. "But, she also chose to let me live," he said.

He dropped the blade from his hand and already conjured a shaft of sparks in his hand. Before Avertree could even stand up, the shaft flew at him and flipped him out of his chair. He cried out.

The doors opened as the guards came in. Percival was already conjuring to fight. Lily picked up the blade and began to cut the restraints at her legs. Percival was already fighting off the guards. He already incapicitated one and was avoiding two with spears.

Lily finished cutting off the ropes just in time to see the back end of a spear swinging at her head. She moved back and avoided the pole. She jumped up and met a thrust with the pointed end with the sword. She caught the head of the spear with the pommel and pulled it away from the man's grasp. She conjured a disc and shot a beam of light from it. The guard flew back and was incapacitated.

She saw that two of the guards now had her back to the wall with spears. She looked over and saw Percival had knocked unconscious another two but was still fighting off three with the broken shaft of a spear and a sword he had taken from one of them.

Lily felt the glow of a lantern against her face. She looked briefly and saw it on a metal holder. She picked it up and threw it at the guard to her right. His cloak lit on fire as some of the liquid inside of the lantern touched his clothes. He frantically tried to put it out. The other guard thrusted his spear at her. She conjured a disc upon the middle of the shaft as she moved out of the way. The wood shattered and she brought the back of her own spear against his head. He crumpled to the floor. The guard who she had lit on fire had managed to take off the burning clothes but had looked up just in time to see Lily bring the shaft to his head.

Lily looked at Percival. The last of them had his sword inches from Percival's neck. Percival had both of his arms against the man's trying to keep away the sword. Lily rotated the spear in her hand and looked for an opening. She threw it at the man's shoulder that was holding the sword. He screamed as it pierced his armor and shoulder. The guard dropped his sword. Percival pushed his arm away and rammed his elbow into the guard's temple. He fell to the floor.

Lily walked over to Percival. "Thank you," she whispered. She looked at his arm and saw a gash bleeding freely. She tore off part of the fabric of one of the guard's cloaks and handed it to him.

Percival took it. "Thanks," he said as he began to press and tie it around the gash.

Lily looked at the unconscious bodies around them. There were only nine of them. "Three of the guards are missing," she said.

She handed Percival his sword back. Percival looked around counting them just as a screech went through the air. Someone had triggered the alarms. Percival picked up a sword from one of the unconscious guards and handed it to her. "I can get you a way out," he said.

They exited the room and heard the clanging off armor from the direction opposite they had come. Percival led her through the same hallway as before. He opened the door to the walkway and they were met by hails of snow and wind. At the other side of the walkway where the stairwell was, two guards appeared. Both had their spears raised toward them.

Lily looked behind her and saw the six guards that they had heard coming cut them off. She and Percival were surrounded.

Lily conjured a disc in front of her and shot a beam into one of the two guards in front of the stairwell. He flew back into the door. The other guard thrusted his spear at her. The walkway was too narrow. She felt a sharp pain in her leg as the spearhead nicked her thigh. She was pulled forward as the spear was pulled back. The spear had pierced itself into her cloak and had pulled her forward.

She fell onto the stone as the spear tore itself away from the fabric. She rolled away as the spear tried to pierce her on the floor. She stood up and conjured a shaft of sparks bringing it down upon the middle of the spear. The wood snapped in half, clattering the front of the spear onto the floor. The guard brought his sword out but too slowly. She brought the shaft across his face. The guard was knocked back and fell over the walkway.

Percival was still fighting the last two of the six guards. Lily threw the shaft at one of the guards and he fell to the floor. The other guard looked toward her but too long because Percival brought a disc against the back of his head. He slumped to the floor.

Lily looked at the cut on her leg. It wasn't deep. She tore off a strip of one of the fallen guard's cloak and wrapped it around her to stop the bleeding.

Percival walked over to her. "Can you walk?" he asked. Lily stepped forward and nodded. "We have to get you to the other side of the wall. Then you can get a portal out of here." He led her through the stairwell. They soon entered the main courtyard.

The fortress was in chaos. People were running across the courtyard. Many didn't know what caused the alarm. Lily and Percival began to run across the yard. She pushed passed a pair of people who were running in the opposite direction. They ran to the entrance of the wall through the path toward the main hall. Braziers lit and flickered out as they ran through.

Just fifty feet before they came upon the entrance, bolts of energy flew at them from the wall. Lily lunged behind a brazier as they flew toward her.

Chips of stone fell on her as they pierced the front of the brazier.

Lily conjured a disc of sparks and threw it in the opposite direction of the wall. She moved her arm and turned it around like a boomerang. She poked her head above the brazier and directed it at one of the people firing at her. She hit him across the head as he poked out his head to fire.

She turned to Percival who was a brazier behind her on the opposite side. He conjured a beam of energy from a disc he had conjured. "Cover me!" she shouted toward him.

He nodded as she moved forward. She saw beams of energy fly by her as she ran forward. She ran forward to the brazier closest to the wall. She conjured a disc and whispered "Ignysfire." The disc burst into flames. She stretched the tendrils of flames and flung them at the wall. The side of the wall exploded in flames and shards of stones. The guards who had been shooting at her scattered.

Percival ran up to her. Lily ducked behind the brazier just in time as a beam of energy flew passed them. She looked over and saw Avertree clutching his shoulder a few hundred feet away leading at least a dozen guards. To the other side she saw another dozen coming at them.

Percival responded by spending a beam of energy at the group before ducking on the opposite side of the brazier. "I can't fight off that many!" He shouted over the wind and snow.

Lily looked up as they advanced toward them. "Come with me," Lily said. "I'll tell Pane what you did."

Lightning blasted away the other brazier sending stone across the snow. Other bolts and beams of energy flew at them. "Do I have much of a choice?" Percival asked.

Lily conjured a shield of energy in the middle of the path and they ran forward. She heard the shield break into a shower of sparks behind her as energy chipped the stone at the wall. Soon they were on the other side of the wall.

The wind howled as she conjured a portal in front of them. They jumped through.

Chapter Twenty:
The Gallow of the Spider

Boreas emerged from the arc of red light. Aethor, Corvus, and Ariadne followed him. He already knew something was wrong when he had looked over the fortress from the view of the world engine. And he didn't need anything else to anger him. He had been minutes late to the Reality Stone, and now he didn't know it's location, and he knew that the only means of getting it would be a full scale assault.

Boreas had seen at least a dozen guards along the entrance and saw the back end of the wall above the gate destroyed. At least another two dozen were waiting in the courtyard below. There was also a congregation of a few people upon the ramparts along with a structure that had not been there before.

The four of them walked through the wind and snow toward the wall. All of the guards stared at him armed with bows. They were waiting for him, and not in the way he wanted.

He walked in through the entrance and came to see Avertree standing in front of the two dozen guards. Avertree had his arm in a sling and his other near a sword. Percival wasn't among them.

The guards surrounded the four and raised their spears. The guards closed the gap as the group moved closer to Avertree. They were in the middle of a wall of spearheads.

"I believe this doesn't need much explanation," Avertree threatened, "Give me the stone and the blade and you will live."

"Where is Percival?" Boreas asked not caring about the threat..

"I would like to ask you the same," Avertree said, "He did some rather interesting things an hour ago."

"Such as?" Ariadne asked. "If you harmed my son I will personally slit your throat." Corvus, beside her, raised his dual edged spear.

"Well, he tried to assist in helping the escape of your daughter," Avertree smiled looking at Aethor. "But, I think you will be glad to know that he escaped."

"My daughter wasn't here," Aethor said.

"Oh, yes, she was," Avertree corrected, "She was taken captive by Storm Riders and sent here for you Boreas. Had she come here just hours earlier or later, she would have been far more fortunate. But, she still is here in the fortress."

He motioned to the structure he had seen earlier on the ramparts. The structure was a pole of wood with another shaft propped perpendicular. At the end was a rope with a dark haired girl tied by the neck. Lily was awaiting to be hung at the gallows.

"I have killed many people in all my life," Aethor said, "Few times have I remotely enjoyed it. But, I tell you what I will do to you, I am going to enjoy very much."

"Silence him Boreas, or I will," Avertree threatened.

"No, I think we are all in agreement here," Boreas sneered, "It is a terrible thing to use a parent's children against them, and you have used everyone's children who stand here."

"I haven't used yours," Avertree said. He smiled. "As far as I remember, yours died nearly twenty years ago as an infant in a terror attack. How could I have possibly used your children against you."

"When this is over, and I am ready to kill you, I'll tell you why," Boreas sneered, "And I'll tell you this, you will die today, and you will die in agony."

"Such kind words," Avertree whispered, "Maybe, I won't let you live. But, I will let her." He looked up again to the gallow. "So I give you the choice, retain the stone and blade, or her."

"We don't have the stone," Boreas said.

Avertree looked surprised by that. "Now, that is a pity," he whispered, "I don't think you can say you don't have the blade. I will accept that trade."

Boreas looked from Ariadne to Corvus. Both were tensed up waiting for the fight to begin. He looked over to Aethor who was waiting for his answer. Boreas knew what Aethor wanted him to do: to hand it over. Boreas took out the Crimson Blade from his clothes. It gleamed a faint crimson in the snow storm.

"A wise choice," Avertree said.

"Do you know what the blade can do?" Boreas asked.

"No, but I think I will learn just as quickly as you," Avertree answered. He held out his good hand.

Boreas held out the one with the Crimson Blade. He didn't want to play Avertree's game. It had already gone so well for Avertree. But, the last part wouldn't be completed because he wouldn't play by the rules.

"Clearly, you do not," Boreas smiled. A red light came from the blade. A sphere centered around the blade began to expand around them until it covered the whole courtyard. And Boreas wasn't surrounded by just the wall of spearmen. Everyone was shocked at the sight. Hundreds of shades stood around them.

"The shades around us were all men and women torn apart by a man like you," Boreas sneered, "And this courtyard was where they died because of that rift." He looked up towards the ramparts. There was a second girl beside the first.

One was a shade, the other was the corpse. But the shade's image was clear to him. And neither were of Lily. "If you thought I was foolish and naive enough to believe you would keep her alive, then you gravely misstepped. And worst of all, you killed an innocent, not even your enemy, not for the gains of everyone around you, but for yourself."

Avertree looked to the ground and snarled. "This was only going to end with five lives lost," he said, "I guess there will be more."

"Yours will be among them," Boreas sneered, "I will spare those who drop their weapons now. If he promised you wealth, you will find none. If he promised you power, you won't find any in death. You will gain nothing by standing against me, but a painful death and a headstone." No one dropped their weapons. He looked to the others who were ready to fight. "Go," he whispered.

Boreas conjured a weapon with the Crimson Blade. A blade formed from red matter that formed around the handle of the blade. He looked toward Avertree who was already behind his wall of spears. The spearmen moved forward. Boreas cut through their spears with ease. Swords were drawn by the spearmen.

The massacre began. Boreas weaved through the incoming attacks, snapping the sword of the first man to attack him, before cutting along the man's stomach. Another raised his sword to strike, exposing his stomach. The Crimson Blade stretched and impaled the man before he could lower his sword.

Three came toward him next. One still had his spear and threw it at Boreas. Boreas moved to the side, and met a sword from the second of them. He moved past a strike from the third, and entered into the shimmer.

The world became colorless and Boreas moved as an invisible ghost. Before they could do anything, Boreas had already cut the throats of the first two. Had he not been in the shimmer, all he would have seen was the opening off their throats, followed by a seeping crimson liquid. The last of the three began swinging wildly at the snow, oblivious to his location. Boreas moved by the swinging sword and with a stroke, cut through armor and flesh.

Boreas exited the shimmer and turned toward the others. The wall was in ruins where the archers had been. Aethor just stabbed his last foe and only one remained. Corvus struck the last of them through the knee with his spear. He pleaded to live but his head was pulled back by Ariadne and was given a knife across the throat.

The ground around them was more red than white. Crimson stains were thrown everywhere in the white canvas of the snow, as two dozen dead bodies remained of Avertree's guards.

Boreas looked over to Avertree, who had stepped away from the violence. He was looking at the massacre and his eyes met Boreas. Without hesitation, he began to run away from the courtyard toward the main hall. Boreas motioned for the other three to follow him.

The four of them walked toward the main hall. Avertree moved through the circular tables toward the exit. He was cut off, however. Onlookers began to stream into the hall blocking the exits. Boreas passed through the entrance of the hall and stopped.

"Move out of the way," Avertree sneered toward them. They all moved forward and now the hall was full, nearly half of Boreas's supporters were among them. "Move out of the way!" Avertree pulled out a gun and held it out against them. He moved his arm around waiting for one to move. None did.

Avertree turned toward the four of them. "He is Death!" Avertree shouted at them pointing at Aethor. "Death has been in disguise among us this whole time. Boreas resurrected him! I am trying to save you all. I am your leader! Anyone who stands against me is betraying the North Wind and humanity itself."

No one moved, once more. Avertree pointed his gun at a group of people blocking the exit closest to him. He pulled the trigger. People in the hall screamed but no one felt a thing. The bolt of energy stopped feet away from the girl it would have hit. Aethor had his hand outstretched, and the bolt fizzled away.

A second shot rang through the air but it didn't come from Avertree, but toward him. The bolt of energy streaked across his stomach. Unable to catch himself with only one hand, he fell to the floor and cried out.

Boreas looked toward where the shot had come from. Quentin Johannson moved through the crowd. "Lord Boreas," Quentin said, bowing his head. Boreas nodded towards him and began to walk through the table toward Avertree.

Avertree turned around and tried to pull the gun toward him. Boreas pinned his arm against the floor, and Avertree dropped the gun.

Boreas glared at him. "The North Wind can't betray you because you betrayed it," he said, "Avertree, you are a snake and a coward. You have no intention of helping the people around you, unless it benefits you. Your spiders are gone and you are surrounded by those you have angered. What did you intend to do with the blade and stone? Do exactly what I had intended for the North Wind to do? No. You probably thought of the opposite. Ruling everyone with absolute authority, beyond that of a president or a dictator or a king, but of a God. It must have sounded so simple and sweet in your mind. But, that was just a fantasy. As most ideas are and will always be."

"So are yours," Avertree whispered, "A fantasy."

Boreas smiled. "I haven't given you one last justice yet," Boreas whispered, "I said that when the time came and I was ready to kill you, I would tell you how you used my daughter against me." He knelt down beside Avertree. "But, I'll tell you now because I am ready to let you die." He whispered the words into his ear and Avertree didn't say a word. He had no words to say to what Boreas had said.

Boreas looked toward Aethor, Corvus, and Ariadne. He turned back toward Avertree. "Death may not come quick," he whispered. Boreas picked up the gun off the floor and walked over to Aethor. He set the gun down on the table.

"He threatened to hang your daughter," Boreas whispered, "Even if it wasn't her, he did the worst to you." He paused. "You should be the one to do it."

Aethor looked down toward Avertree a few feet away from him. "Give him the mercy he would have given to my daughter," he answered. Boreas looked at him and nodded.

Aethor pulled Avertree up and walked him out of the hall. The hall began to follow them out. Boreas looked at Quentin, as he came by. "What happened when I was away?" Boreas asked him.

"Rumors aren't always the truth," Quentin said, "But, word is that a girl was carried in by Storm Riders. Percival helped her out, but a fight occurred. He got out, but she didn't."

"She escaped," Boreas said, "Avertree used a double."

"Avertree then confined everyone in their rooms," Quentin said, "But, Avertree didn't have the men to do it so no one really followed through with it once we heard the world engine."

The two of them walked with the rest of the hundreds following Avertree. They walked up a stairway before they came upon the blizzard outside.

Boreas pushed through the crowd and walked up with Aethor and Avertree. As they came on the turn before the gallow, Avertree began to realize where Aethor was taking him. He attempted to push away from Aethor but was unable.

The gallow was not a welcome sight. The girl was propped against a smaller pole behind her. The guards Boreas had seen around her were no longer there. From afar, she did resemble Lily. She had the same dark hair and pale skin, but she was shorter than Lily.

The group stopped and looked at her. She didn't move in the storm. Behind Boreas, he heard some gasp upon seeing her and murmur prayers.

Boreas walked forward toward her. She had a bruise and cut that had formed across her face. She had put up a fight. He took the noose off of her neck and untied her from the post that kept her upright. Her back was covered in blood from a stab. Boreas glared at Avertree. He set her onto the ground and took out the Crimson Blade and held it over her. A red light formed from the blade.

The onlookers were shocked as the girl's eyes opened and she began to breath. Boreas looked up to Quentin. "Get her to a healer," Boreas said.

Quentin was too shocked to say anything, but nodded. He helped the girl up and took her away.

Boreas looked over to Aethor and motioned for him to bring Avertree. Aethor brought Avertree to the gallows, put the noose around his neck, and propped him on top of the box.

"I call this justice," Boreas said. "For treason, attempting a coup, and the murder of an innocent, I sentence you to die. Do you have any final words?"

"I should have killed you when you walked in," Avertree said.

"Yes, you should have," Boreas said.

Aethor kicked the box from underneath him. The noose tightened around his neck and it felt like a long time before Avertree stopped clawing at his neck. Soon, he hung limp in the wind.

Boreas looked toward the onlookers. "I failed you," Boreas said, "I trusted a man I shouldn't have, and this is where we are because of it. He is one of the many men we try to fight against, all of us together. I was unable to obtain the Reality Stone, but I promised you that today's dawn would be the last dawn before the new. Will you follow me for one last time?"

Boreas looked at the group of hundreds. Many more had come into the courtyard to listen. He was speaking to most of his followers now, many hundreds, maybe even a few thousand.

Ariadne knelt down. "I will follow you to the end," she said.

Corvus knelt down beside her. "I have for most of my life," Corvus said, "I don't want to break that now." Soon, the onlookers began to kneel one by one. Boreas was surrounded by kneeling figures. Aethor was one of the few who didn't but gave him a nod.

"Be ready for the dawn," Boreas said, "It will be a long night but in the end, we will see the sun rise upon a better universe. Anyone who doesn't want to fight, will not. But, I ask those of you who do to do your best, because our world depends on it."

The group kneeling began to cheer for him, before they dispersed. Boreas looked to Corvus and Ariadne. "Corvus, look to our spies and find out where they are keeping the Reality Stone," Boreas ordered, "I want to know by nightfall. Ariadne, tell Dr. Johannson in the armory: every man and woman who wants to fight will be armed by means of Alveran or Earth. Those who can, will work in the world engine. Every little gadget that is ready for combat will be used."

They nodded and walked off. Boreas looked over toward the courtyard. It is crowded and chaotic, but everyone was avoiding the bodies from the massacre. Aethor walked up toward him. "Did you know it wasn't my daughter?" he asked.

"I took a guess it was a bluff," Boreas answered, "But, he didn't know what the Crimson Blade was used for." He looked toward Avertree. "I hope the girl didn't suffer as much as he did."

"She wasn't hung," Aethor whispered.

Boreas looked back to the massacre in the courtyard. He held the Crimson Blade up. The blade glowed red once more and the bodies disappeared. "Where will you go at the end of this?"

"A dead world," Aethor answered, "I succeeded in three worlds all those years ago. Each led to different outcomes. Torfaa has the wall of mist created by the Crimson Blade being there for a long period of time. Another was torn apart from the fight. It will grow back but not for hundreds of years. The third was exactly as I intended, and I will go there. What will you do?"

"I don't know," Boreas whispered, "Some part of me never thought this would work. I'll figure it out when we get there. We should prepare for the battle." He left the ramparts in silence.

Chapter Twenty One:
Night Falls

Lily looked across the basin. It had been nearly an hour since she and Percival had left the fortress. The abandoned city of the Titan-world stood against the cliff, but she knew it wasn't abandoned. It was preparing for war. Dozens of guards were at the city lines, some of whom were manning turrets for the world engine. It would be a deadly fight, without a doubt.

The two of them had gone to the Last City, to find that the soldiers were abandoning it for this world. It hadn't been hard for them to overhear where everyone had gone.

She turned toward Percival. He was looking at her. "Are you sure you want to do this?" Lily asked him.

"It's either this or run away," Percival answered, "My life is in your hands."

Lily conjured a portal and walked through. Percival followed. They were a few dozen feet away from the city lines. She had seen this city once before. In a dream, she had walked through it and in another dream she saw the aftermath of a destruction, a skeleton. But, the skeleton of the city now was alive and ready to fight.

Lily walked forward and Percival followed. The two of them were met by guards and metal. Four of them who were watching the entrance raised their spears toward the two of them. She knew they would recognize Percival immediately.

"Drop your weapons!" The lead guard shouted. Lily looked over to Percival and nodded. He took off his sword belt and dropped it against the mineral. He held his hands in the air. Lily did the same.

Two of the guards walked around them and took their flank. The other two walked at each of their sides at the end. "Move forward!" One of the guards behind them shouted.

The two of them walked forward through the city. She looked at each of the spires as they cast long shadows across the walkway. Sunset had come early on this planet.

They soon came upon the palace where more guards recognized Percival. To Lily's surprise, no one had recognized her yet. They walked into the palace. The two of them were flanked and surrounded by eight guards now.

They stopped in the middle of the room. The two of them waited with their escorts beside them. Lily recognized the room from Death's memories. She looked to the end of the room with the circular pads. She knew that they could be traveled upon to the upper levels. She wondered if Pane knew that.

One of the doors opened at the edge of the room. First filed in Lieutenant Commander Reeves, with his hand close to his sword, followed by Anita, Commander Lin, Commander Graves, and Pane. Their mouths all dropped when they saw her.

"Lower your weapons," Pane whispered. He limped toward her and hugged her first. "We thought you were dead," he whispered, "When Reeves came back we assumed the worst."

They let go of each other. Lily looked toward Anita besides Reeves. Both of them made it out. She walked over to Anita and hugged her. "Who else made it out?" she asked. Lily looked over to Reeves.

"Just us," Anita answered, "Half of us were captured with you. A few made it out with us but we were ambushed. I am glad to see you are safe."

"How are you still here?" Graves asked. He looked over to Percival but seemed to get his answer. "Why should we trust you?"

"He's the reason I am still alive," Lily answered. "I wouldn't be here if it wasn't for him."

Pane looked to the group of guards behind Percival. "Go back to your posts," he told them. They lowered their spears and one of the guards handed Pane Percival's and Lily's swords before they walked off. He looked away from Percival to Anita. "Anita, go bring Lily upstairs. We will talk about this later."

Lily walked away with Anita. Anita led Lily through the door from where they had come, and Lily found herself in a massive hangar. Below were dozens of flying crafts, which had a strange resemblance to dragonflies. She wondered if there were dragonflies once in this world. She had once seen them in Death's memories fly around the city before. Workers were running around them preparing them for flight. She saw a bright blue flame burst into life and disappear at one of the work tables and at the end of the hangar was a lone dragonfly that was slowly hovering above the ground with its wings buzzing to life.

"Can we fly them?" Lily asked her.

"General Pane says we can," Anita answered, "They are built to follow people's intentions."

"What do you mean?" Lily asked.

"He says they fly based on how a person wants them to fly when they are in the dragonfly," Anita answered. "But, he only wants people who know how to fly to use them in combat."

They continued on, walking along the walkway. "When did you come here?" Lily asked.

"Yesterday morning," Anita answered, "We had left Alveran in the night. The days are weird here. The planet is tilted on its axis and we only have ten daylight hours but eighteen night hours. I think the sunset of Alveran and here match today."

"Where are we going?" Lily asked.

"Your sister," Anita answered, "They came back today with the Reality Stone."

"We have the Reality Stone?" Lily asked. At least there was the one chance they had. If Boreas hadn't brought it back to the North WInd, then he or Avertree wouldn't have it as easy when they attacked.

"It's in a vault at the top of the hangar," Anita said. She pointed toward the top of the cavern at the opposite side. The walkway ended near the top of the cavern where there was a vault. Two panels of metal joined together. Lily could tell there was at least two inches of heavy metal in the locked doors.

The two of them came upon a door. Anita opened the door for Lily and they walked in. A window showed the sunset that flooded into the room. She heard a glass shatter to her side. She looked over and saw Peter standing at the side of the room, who had dropped his glass. Three people were at the table that spread across the room. Lily looked first toward Sage. Sage's eyes were red and her lip quivered when she saw Lily.

Sage stood up and burst into tears. She ran into Lily's arms. "I thought you were going to die," Sage whispered.

"As did I," Lily whispered. She looked at her and brushed away Sage's tears. "But part of me knew I would come back."

"How?" Sage asked.

"Because I promised my sister I would come back to her," Lily answered.

Lily let go of her and looked at the table. John and Fonsesca had stood up from their seats. John walked up to her and hugged her. Fonsesca came after him. "I came when I heard you were taken captive," he whispered.

"And, now, you're here," Lily whispered. She let go of him and looked over to Peter. She hugged him as well without a protest this time. She let go of him. "Where's Lee?"

Peter looked down to the floor. "He didn't make it," he answered. "Died getting us the Reality Stone."

Lily sighed heavily and looked out the window. She felt guilt go through her body. "It was my fault," Lily whispered, "I was the one who told him to go to Haranae."

"What you saw in your dream was going to happen, no matter what," Sage said, "We could only change where it happened."

"Then why is she still here?" John asked. "If that logic works and what Sage said is true, shouldn't she have died?"

"In your dream, did you ever feel yourself truly be killed?" Peter asked.

Lily thought it over. She had always thought she had died in the dream but it ended before she had been struck. She never felt it. "I never felt myself die," Lily answered.

"You never were," Peter said. "You were going to be in the position you were in but you never were. The logic isn't defeated and you are still here."

Just then Percival walked into the room followed by Graves, Pane, and Reeves. Graves and Pane were arguing over something when they walked in. Pane looked over to Lily. "Tell us what happened," Pane said.

They sat down at the table, all except Percival who stood at the end of the table. She knew this would decide Percival's fate, but she didn't change anything to the story. She told them what happened after the Forest of the Ghosts. She spoke of where she was taken to Death's Landing before traveling to the north pole. Percival looked down when she got to the part about the fight at the fortress of the North Wind.

When she finished Pane looked back to Percival. "Do you vouch for him?" Pane asked. Lily nodded. "What do you want, Percival?"

"Before Boreas left, he told me to watch Avertree," Percival answered, "If Avertree succeeds in taking the blade from Boreas, he will come with everything he has; without mercy. I can't stand by in a world like that."

"And if Boreas comes?" Graves asked. "What will you do then?" Lily knew Percival was against Boreas coming.

"Commander Graves, do you expect me to say, simply, that I would fight beside you without hesitation?" Percival asked. "If so, then you are wrong. I will fight for whoever I think is right in the end. That is why Lily is here. As am I."

"And, you think we are the better cause?" Pane asked.

"Avertree may be a lot of things, but he is intelligent enough to know Boreas has made mistakes," Percival answered, "He made one when he revived Death and another when he left you in the cave on the dead world. None of this would have happened, if you hadn't escaped that cave." Percival looked over to Lily. "Boreas based many decisions on what has happened in the dreams between the two of you. Have you seen anything in your dreams that hasn't."

Lily thought it over. "I have dreamt of a battle here twice," Lily answered, "Before I arrived at the fortress of the North Wind, I saw it happen."

Everyone turned to Percival. "Boreas promised everyone that today's dawn would be the last dawn before the new," he answered, "He's not a man to break promises. He'll attack at latest by nightfall."

"We have been preparing for this," Pane said, "Is there anything else, Lily, that you've seen?"

Lily thought it over. Some parts of their dreams were so strange that she doubted they would come true. But, she remembered one thing about the very first dream she had. She, at first, thought it had been only to accompany the dream to terrify her. But, The End stood out to her in this instance.

"Did Boreas ever tell you what he truly wanted?" Lily asked.

Percival didn't answer at first. He looked to the floor and answered, "No."

"What are you hinting at?" John asked.

"Before my father was revived, we believed Boreas was after the blood matter in his body to create The End," Lily answered.

"He needed Death to allow him to pass through into the jungle," Percival answered.

"No," Lily answered, "Boreas needed the Reality Stone. With blood matter, what's done can only be done once. It killed my father and Boreas isn't even that strong." She paused thinking about her dreams. The pieces of the puzzle were all coming together. She had seen the Annihilation Wave in her dream. The shockwave in the sky she had seen so many times was that. Worst of all, she had seen the outcome. In her last dream, she saw something she hoped she never would. It haunted her as a child, and it haunts her now. Humanity was gone on Earth. "He needed the Reality Stone to create the Annihilation Wave. He told me what happened to him. He lost his sister because of Alveran, and he lost his wife and child because of Earth. And "

"Are you suggesting he'll wipe out everyone except his followers?" Pane asked.

"I have hated Boreas for so many years, and even I am not sure he would go to that extent," Graves whispered.

"Would someone with morals to not kidnap you really be that hellbent on destroying humanity?" Percival asked. "Why would he, a human, do that?"

"The Assassin was human and he served Death to his end," Peter said, "And he was a psychopath worse than most. The only good he ever did was get Lily out of the cave on the dead world."

"Look," Lily said, "I have seen The End and I have seen the Annihilation Wave. You asked me what else I have seen in my dreams and that is it. Percival, I am sorry, but the man you've followed your whole life is going to murder billions. He has joined Death in this."

Percival looked to the floor. One by one, the group began to realize what it meant. A hum went through the air. Lily stood up from her seat and looked outside. She walked over to the window. The sun had nearly completely set in the sky and only the end of the circle was visible. A beam of red shot through the air and a shadow covered the edge of the sun. The world engine had arrived at the opposite end of the basin. Arcs of red light began to shoot down from the world engine.

Lily looked to Percival, who was walking up to the window. "Can you tell who it is?" Lily asked him.

"There's mist," Percival answered. Lily looked out and saw a mist beginning to form over at the other end of the basin. The arcs of red light looked like red lightning as they flashed into existence. "Avertree is dead."

"This is Boreas's endgame," Pane whispered, "Whatever has happened before now, ends here." He looked toward Percival. "Are you in or out?"

"In," Percival answered. He looked to Lily and nodded.

"We need to shoot down the world engine," Pane said, "Fonsesca, Commander Lin, go tell the pilots. If we take it down with the dragonflies, we may have a chance. Reeves, Graves, get a dozen men and guard the stone. I want everyone ready for battle. Don't kill anyone unless it's a kill or be killed scenario. If you see Boreas or Aethor though…" he trailed off. Everyone knew what he meant. "The long night has come and we will see the dawn. I promise you that."

Chapter Twenty Two:
The Overview

With the arrival of the world engine, the base had gone into chaos. Pane had given the orders, but that didn't stop the hysteria, as Lily entered the hangar. She looked at the dragonfly that she stood beside. She, Peter, John, Sage, and Fonsesca had all gone into the hangar.

The blue metal was sleek and smooth and the cockpit above was colored in a darkened glass. She looked toward the two wings on the side she was one. Below them were thrusters designed to move the dragonfly to the side without moving it forward or backward. At the bottom of the dragonfly were four clamps that were once used for clamping to the side of cliffs. At the end was a 'stinger' that was used for mining. The plan was to use the 'stinger' as a plasma cutter on the hull of the world engine to cripple it.

"Dragonflies don't have stingers, right?" John asked.

"A different world, they may have had different inspiration," Peter answered.

Lily looked toward Fonsesca behind her. "Are you sure you want to fly this?" Lily asked. "You never have before." Being one of the few people from Earth, apart from the few who had come with Commander Lin, Fonsesca was one of the few who had ever flown in the sky before.

"Only dead men have flown it before," Fonsesca answered, "And there is always a first time for everything." He took his helmet into his arms. "Pane says it is safe."

"And, have we ever done something genuinely safe for Pane?" Peter asked.

Fonsesca looked toward the ground. "Fair enough," he said. He looked toward Peter. He held out his hand, and Peter shook it. "Stay safe during the battle, my friends." He walked over from the group toward Lily. "I'll be safe."

Lily nodded. Fonsesca climbed the ladder into the cockpit. Another pilot went over to him and began to talk to him about the controls. Lily heard the pilot tell him about how his intentions moved the craft although she didn't understand much of it. Foncesca nodded, and the glass around him began to close.

The four of them walked away from Foncesca and the dragonfly. They left the lowest level of the hangar and began to walk along the walkway above. Lily looked below and saw dozens of pilots running around the hangar, some of them waving toward friends, others shouting orders to other people.

They walked along two flights of stairs, and came upon the second highest walkway. She looked toward the highest, about forty feet away. She saw Graves and Reeves giving orders to a dozen men, all of whom were clad in the golden armor of the Last City and armed with spears and swords. She knew that any one of those spears can blast a beam of energy that could severely burn someone, she herself having been hit by one two years ago.

Peter led the group out of the hangar into a narrow hallway carved into the stone of the cliff. Lily didn't know where they were going, but Pane had told them to walk through the passage. The light was very faint, and it was hard to make out the stairs as they walked into the darker recesses. Soon, however, the hallway ended and Peter opened a door.

The four of them filed outside. They were in a small ravine in the cliffs behind the city. There was a single file path that continued along the ravine, which eventually led into the open. The walls of the ravine were blood red and were covered in a fine covering of the white mineral. To Lily, it looked like flour on a red pastry, rather than the same mineral. The four of them walked the narrow path into the open.

The skies were dark and clouds were rolling over the sky. Off in the distance, she heard thunder and she saw a flash of lightning miles out. The other half of the sky was filled with a thousand stars before being covered by the thunder clouds.

Beside the end of the pathway were two mounds of the mineral. There was a headstone marked at the end of them. They were graves.

"Whose do you think they are?" Lily asked.

"Pane said he found the skeletons of them, when he first came here," John whispered, "He must have buried them here." The four of them walked away from the graves.

Pane and Percival were at the edge of the cliffs. They were looking at the city. The world engine hadn't attacked the city, yet, for reasons unknown. Lily looked along the city and saw a dozen turrets scattered along the ruins of spires covered in tarps. A mile away from the city, the looming mist had grown and ended. It covered miles of the basin the city stood in. The world engine loomed above.

"What should we expect from those in the mist?" Pane asked Percival.

"Boreas has grown in numbers since two weeks ago, but he hasn't surprised you this time," Percival answered, "I doubt he has the supplies for all of Boreas' supporters to attack with him."

"What supplies does he have?" Peter asked.

Percival and Pane turned to face Peter. "One of Boreas's followers was a scientist from Earth," Percival answered, "He and his husband worked on items and gadgets for Boreas. He was primarily working on helping Boreas find the Reality Stone. Boreas never expected to come short of finding it. I don't know what else he was making for Boreas apart from weapons with the rest of the engineers."

"What types of weapons?" Pane asked.

"Nothing more than what we are armed with," Percival answered.

Lily wondered how much Pane trusted Percival. He had allowed him to observe and take note of their defenses, but Pane was always good at figuring out liars. After all, Pane had been the one to figure out Avertree was working for Boreas.

Pane, however, must have trusted him enough to put him with Lily and Anita on a spire. When Boreas moved forward to attack the city, the three of them, as well as Peter, John, and Sage would wait at one of the ruined spires and try to impede their attack, just like some of Lily's dreams.

Pane would first send a signal by starting the bells in a ruined tower near the edge of the city, which would signal them to attack.

A rumble went through the cliffs. Lily walked up toward the edge of the cliff. To the right of the palace, a concealed opening began to crack open. The dragonflies began to buzz to life as the swarm began to leave the hangar below them.

The swarm flew out of the city. Lily wondered what the North Wind thought of the swarm, as it began to fly over the space between the city and them. As they flew over, the North Wind answered.

Flashes of light came from the mist as the dragonflies began to light up the night in orange fire.

Chapter Twenty Three:
Sting of the Dragonflies

The swarm flew over the space between the city and the mist. Fonsesca would have thought the sight almost peaceful if the situation wasn't so dire. He was surprised how quiet each dragonfly was. It wasn't until there were many flying when someone could hear them from far away.

The dragonfly was easy to control but, nonetheless, he was nervous when flying it. Most of the flying came down to two control pads at either side of his arm which supposedly were controlled by his intentions. He wondered how it worked but it didn't matter because he was already in the air without any problems. In the middle were the controls for the stinger. It was a control stick with the buttons for clamping onto the world engine and for igniting the stinger. A black screen was in front of the controls where it received an image from a camera next to the stinger.

Fonsesca looked over to his right. A storm was rolling in, and flashes of lightning lit up the dark clouds.

Fonsesca turned on his intercom in his helmet. "Commander Lin, should we worry about the lightning?" Fonsesca asked.

"We should be more worried about what lies in front of us," she responded through the intercom.

Fonsesca looked toward the world engine, which loomed in front of them. The swarm passed over the end of the mist. Fonsesca sat up and looked down below, into the mist. He could barely see anything through the mist. Flashes of light came around him.

At first, he thought it was lightning, but he saw the storm was still a few miles away. He turned on his intercom just as the dragonfly in front of him burst into flames. Fonsesca swore as he evaded the flaming wreck just in time. He looked toward the world engine. It hadn't attacked the swarm. He realized where the blast of energy had come. He looked down and saw more flashes come from the mist, illuminating the mist briefly.

The intercom went hectic and he tried to tune it out. In front of him, he saw two more dragonflies burst into flames as energy pierced through their bodies and ignited them into flames. A third was clipped in the wing and spun around frantically, before flying toward the right of the mist. Fonsesca passed over it before he could see what happened to it afterwards.

Fonsesca adjusted his dragonfly higher so that it was closer to the height of the world engine. A bright light flashed around him. He jumped in his seat, but the dragonfly still flew and he wasn't set aflame. It was only lightning. He looked and saw the edge of the storm was right over them.

He saw another dragonfly burst into flames below him. Despite the ground fire from below, his attention was to the world engine. Most of the swarm was getting close to the world engine and the frequency of the attacks from the ground were less. But that's when the turrets of the world engine began to attack the dragonflies.

Blue blasts of energy shot from the sides of the world engine toward the swarm. Fonsesca avoided a blast toward his direction just in time. Briefly, his vision was blinded by the blast, but it soon adjusted. Around him, dragonflies were being blasted into shells alight with blue flames instead of the orange that the ground weapons had caused.

Fonsesca heard Commander Lin's voice over the intercom. "Fly for the turrets and aim your stingers there!" She shouted. "It doesn't matter if we damage the hull, if it still fires on us."

Fonsesca lined his dragonfly up with an originating source location of the blasts on the world engine. Toward the bottom left side of the hull was a flashing light which led to one of the blasts flying into the swarm.

Fonsesca was hundreds of feet from his target turret, when he avoided one last blast of energy. He hovered next to the turret. He heard the buzz of the wings to his side because he had stopped flying. The turret was covered in black sheets of metal, and at the front of the turret was a barrel which was as wide as his shoulder width and had a faint blue glow. The glow became brighter.

A blinding flash of light came from the turret again. Fonsesca looked away to where the blast of energy went. He saw it fly through the last of the storm into the open air. It struck the ground in between the city and the world engine in an explosion of blue fire and the mineral covering.

He moved the dragonfly slowly over to the turret. He moved one of his hands slowly toward the control stick. The screen next to the control stick lit up. He saw the image below. There was a long piece of metal a meter wide and as long as the dragonfly that made for an easy spot to clamp down upon.

Fonsesca tilted the dragonfly up, so the front didn't ram into the turret. He slowly moved the dragonfly forward until it was just a few feet away. It was terrifying to feel the dragonfly not moving in the air. On Earth, when flying in a police car or drone, he had never been still in the air. Part of him expected the dragonfly to drop to the ground as a stone and turn into a flaming wreck.

He moved the two clamps toward the piece of metal and slowly moved the two sides of the clamp over it. He pressed a trigger on the control stick. He heard a hiss of air pressure and the clamp crushed into the metal. The wings around him went silent. He moved the stinger above the clamps onto an area directly in the middle of the turret. He looked at the barrel of the turret. It was glowing brighter again. He shielded his eyes, as another blinding flash of light came.

Fonsesca ignited the torch. A blast of blue flames seared out from the stinger. He moved it closer and saw the flames searing into the middle. The camera dimmed as the stinger cut into the metal showering the dragonfly and the turret in sparks.

He looked toward the front of the barrel, and saw it still glowing, waiting to fire at another dragonfly that came into view. He looked toward the camera. The stinger had cut through at least a few feet of metal. He looked closely and saw what he wanted. The inside of the turret was igniting into orange flames. The glow at the end of the turret had stopped. It was crippled.

Fonsesca smiled. He turned off the stinger. The blue flames stopped in the camera. He let go of the world engine. The dragonfly wings buzzed to life. He moved away from the turret to an empty space.

No more than half of the dragonflies were still flying and there were another dozen turrets that gave off the same faint, blue light. Fonsesca looked for another turret to cripple, and saw there was another one still alight a few hundred feet above him which had just fired a blast of energy at an approaching dragonfly. He looked across the sky, as the blast missed and flew above the dragonfly.

At first, he thought another flash of lightning from the storm had streaked across the sky, but one hadn't. The light had come from the ground. The dragonfly jerked upward and Fonsesca knew immediately he had been hit from one of the turrets on the ground. Immediately after, he felt his stomach turn as he began to fall. The dragonfly began to spin violently as he fell.

He swore and looked toward the two wings on the left and saw the smoldering remains of them. He knew that if it had been a direct hit he would have been on fire, then and there. Fonsesca moved his hands toward the control pads and began to move them frantically.

The dragonfly's spin began to slow. He looked toward the ground which was coming startlingly closer to him. He was plummeting farther away from the mist as he moved forward. He tried to line himself up with the ground.

He jerked forward as he hit the ground. The dragonfly skittered along the ground like a skipping stone on a lake. It was a few seconds before the shower of the mineral covering on the ground fell still.

"At least, I am alive," Fonsesca whispered. He took off the straps around his body and began to hit the glass. After a few hits, it popped open. He breathed the fresh air. The dragonfly was a smoldering wreck and there were at least three fires.

The ground between the city and the mist was littered with the burning shells of the dragonflies. But,

225

it was unmistakable what he saw. The mist was creeping forward, and so were Boreas's forces.

Chapter Twenty Four:
Sweeping Mist

Lily looked from the world engine back to Pane. Most of the dragonflies had fallen in bursts of flames over the course of the last few minutes. The fires and lightning gave the only light in the basin covered in mist. The last third of the dragonflies were coming back to the city. The ground was littered with flaming shells.

Lily hoped Fonsesca was safe. He had come back to fight just after he had thought she was captured, and now he may be ashes on the ground.

"Can we check to see if Fonsesca is safe," Sage asked from behind her.

"Not until the last of the swarm returns," Pane answered. He looked over to Percival. "I thought you said they weren't armed with anything more than what we were."

Percival looked to the ground. "I didn't know he had turrets ready," he whispered, "Death must have told him about the dragonflies here, and he brought them along."

"Death didn't even know whether or not we could fly them," Peter said.

"Look, Boreas is bringing all his forces here, I know it," Percival warned, "If you truly believe that Boreas has intentions of destroying everyone but his followers, then you should aim the turrets along the edge of the city and on the spires to shoot everything to ashes and cinders."

"And do you think Boreas has that intention?" Pane asked.

Percival sighed. "Maybe," he whispered. He looked out toward the mist and the world engine. "I don't know what happened at the fortress after I helped Lily escape, but I knew how many Avertree had behind him. And Avertree is dead. However much they're supported, Boreas and Death are, individually, a threat to treat with paramount importance."

Lily looked back to the North Wind encampment out in the basin. She looked at the wreckage. She noticed one shell of flames right next to the mist. But it was enveloped by the mist just as she looked at it. She tensed. The mist was moving forward.

"They're moving forward," Lily whispered.

Everyone else looked over to the mist, as it creeped forward. "Get to the spire where you are positioned," Pane said. He looked toward Percival. "You as well. If you say Boreas and Aethor defeated Avertree, then we need everyone to slow him down."

"Where will you go?" Lily asked Pane.

"Defend," Pane whispered, "I thought my fighting days were over, but I'll still give whatever is left in me. When I send the signal, attack the forces."

Lily nodded. "Stay safe," she whispered.

Pane smiled. "And you," he whispered.

Lily smiled at him. She turned toward Percival, Sage, Peter, and John. "Let's go, he'll be in the city in half an hour, at the latest," she said. The five of them ran from the overlook on the cliffs. They followed their path back to the route they had come.

The five of them went past the graves and walked the narrow ravine path until they came upon the door. They walked through the tunnel and into the hangar, once more.

The overview of the hangar was a chaotic sight. The last of the dragonflies were returning to the ground and a dozen were already on the hanger floor. Dozens of other soldiers were running around the hangar in a frenzy. Lily looked over and saw Graves and Reeves in front of the vault with the Reality Stone, along with the dozen other guards who waited for the fighting to break into the city.

Reeves looked up to them. He nodded to them, as they looked overhead. Lily nodded back. At that moment, she wondered how Reeves would react if he knew that she knew about his past. She brushed the thought away, and walked with the rest of the group.

The five of them walked along the railing and went down flights of stairs, until they finally came upon the exit of the hangar. They walked along the tunnel to the entrance of the palace.

They walked through the room and into the open night air. Lily looked out through the city toward the basin. Through the main walkway, she could see the mist slowly creeping closer toward the city. Lightning flashed overhead and thunder rumbled, immediately afterward. They were right under the storm. She looked up and briefly thought snow was falling from the sky. She lifted her hand out and let it fall on her hand. It wasn't snow, it was the mineral that covered the rest of the world.

The five of them walked through the main walkway. Here, the city was silent. The previously ruined spires of the city came into view.

Peter, who was leading them, turned in toward a spire. It was blackened by the fire but was, otherwise, unharmed. It was three stories high and there were windows for action against the North Wind. Peter opened the door and walked inside.

The four of them followed him into it. It was dark inside, but lightning flashed giving the room a brief light. It was a single room with stairs circling the side. It was hard to tell what the room once was because the inside was blackened and the furniture that was left was burned to ashes. She heard someone behind her lock the door.

Lily held out her hand, as the light from the lightning was inadequate to light the room. The room was filled with green light by Lily's action. She walked toward the stairs and began to walk up. The next room was filled with the same blackened remains as the first. Lightning flashed in one of the blackened windows. Immediately, the sound of thunder rolled into the room.

They continued walking up the stairway. The last room had a lantern lit in the middle of it. There was a balcony opposite to the main walkway. The fire hadn't destroyed the top as bad, and there was what looked like a desk at the side of the room. Anita was waiting on a metal case, looking out the window that overviewed the street where they had come.

"Lily," she whispered. She looked toward the others who were filing into the room. "General Pane told me to give you these when the fighting starts." She stood up from the briefcase and brought it over. She unlatched the top of the case.

Lily looked inside and saw four handguns from Earth to the right and some weapons from Alveran. There were two knives to the right and two spears at the bottom. The spears glowed with a faint blue light.

"Can any of these kill someone?" Sage asked. She stepped away from the case.

Lily looked at the spears once more. She had been previously hit by one of the blasts of energy and it had left her in a bed for hours. "Not unless you hit them in the face," Lily answered. She took one of the knives and attached the sheath to her sword belt.

"If it's any consolation, some of them wouldn't hesitate to do the same," Percival said. He walked outside on the balcony and began to survey the area.

"Should we trust him?" Anita asked in a whisper. Lightning flashed once more and thunder rolled in.

Lily looked to Percival but he was still surveying the area. She nodded. "I trust him, as does Pane," she whispered. Anita nodded.

Lily moved over to the window. The wind was picking up and it blew her hair back. She covered her face, as the mineral blew at her. She looked out toward the end of the city. The world engine was only partially in her view. It hadn't attacked anything yet in the city. It stood meekly in the air above the basin. She looked toward the mist. None of the crashes were in sight and the mist would arrive at the turrets laid out at the edge of the city within minutes.

She turned toward the others. Percival had come back into the room and had picked up one of the spears. He was balancing it with his hands. Sage and John had sat down next to the balcony. "If anyone wants to leave, now is the time," Lily said. She looked from Anita, who was standing in a corner, to Sage. Lily didn't want anyone to get hurt and she knew that Anita had been in the north because she had been following orders, in the first place, and Sage only went where her sister did.

Sage stood up and walked over to her. She took Lily's hand in her own. "When you were captured and we were told, I cried and told myself, over and over, again you would come back," Sage whispered, "And, part of me knew you would always come back, because you promised me you would. And, you did. And, I want to stay with you. I don't want to run away from not knowing whether or not I would see you again. I am staying."

Lily wrapped her arms around Sage, and hugged her close. Lily wanted Sage to be safe but she knew Sage wouldn't leave her side, either.

Explosions broke out along the city edge, and the sounds made Lily jump. She let go of Sage and went to the window. The mist was upon the turrets that were laid out along the city edge. Blasts of

231

energy punched through the mist but the light was gone as quickly as it had entered. One by one, explosions began to light up the night as the turrets erupted into orange flames as the fight continued.

Lightning flashed and hit the ground near the edge of the city and, for a second, Lily thought it had been the storm above her. But, it wasn't lightning. A burst of energy flashed from the mist and blasted a turret apart.

"Boreas," Percival whispered, "He only taught a few people how to do that. He's in the mist coming for the stone."

"We have to stop him before he gets to the stone," Lily whispered.

As quickly as the fighting had started, the night went silent. And, the mist crept closer and entered the city.

"Will we be able to see through the mist when it comes?" Peter asked.

"We should be able to see their shapes," Percival answered, "I doubt we'll be able to see any distinction."

"Boreas will have the Crimson Blade with him," Lily said, "We'll be able to see that light."

"Just aim for the red light," John whispered, "That's not so hard."

The mist began to creep toward them. Lily looked toward the other spires around her. She briefly saw a face pop outside to look toward the mist in a window two spires to her right. The face disappeared moments later. Lily moved back inside.

"How close is it?" Anita asked.

"The mist is a few hundred feet out," Lily whispered, "Percival, where would Boreas be in the mist? Would he be in the shimmer?"

"He'd be in the street out there, I know it," Percival answered, "He'd want the clearest way to the Reality Stone. I don't know if he'd be in the shimmer. He promised his supporters he'd get the Reality Stone. I'd expect him to be with them, but, if he's trying to end humanity, he might enter during the chaos."

"Aiming for the red light isn't so simple," John whispered, "It never is."

Lily looked out the window again. She put her finger to her lips. "They are here," she whispered. She looked out the window again. Lightning flashed and she saw the shapes of figures walking through the mist. She saw no red light that meant Boreas.

Lightning flashed, and more thunder rolled in. She thought it was thunder, but it continued off in the distance. The bells had begun. Pane had signalled them to attack.

The fighting began. Blasts of energy shot from the windows of spires around her, punching holes into the mist. Shafts and discs, conjured by Sorcerers, were flung into the mist and broke into showers of sparks, as they collided with people and the ground. People below screamed and shouted, as they were pelted with attacks, but they began retaliating with their own attacks. Lily moved out of the way, so that she didn't get shot by the people below.

"Should we wait for Boreas?" she asked. She wasn't worried about them hearing below. They were occupied at the moment, even if by some miracle they heard.

"He might not even use The Crimson Blade if he thinks it'll attract trouble," Peter said.

"He'll use it when he needs to," Percival said, "If he's near the Reality Stone he might as well." He creeped out to the balcony and looked out. Lightning flashed and he looked back toward them. "There's no one behind us."

"Keep watch over there," Lily said to him.

Lily turned toward the window. She conjured a disc over her hand. She peaked her eyes over the window. She looked toward one of the figures who was now illuminated by the blue blasts of energy that fired from his weapon. She threw the disc through the window. It crashed into the figure in a shower of sparks.

She ducked her head back inside hoping no one saw her. She conjured another disc above her hands. She was about to poke her head out again when rubble flew from the window where her head would have been. Two more blasts of energy shot into the ceiling. As she looked at the ceiling, she realized why she was targeted. The disc had made green light which could be seen below. She moved over to the lantern in the middle of the room and put it to the side where the light was harder to see below. They were in near darkness, apart from the flashes of light that came from the battle and the storm.

Peter moved beside her with one of the guns in his hand. He quickly popped his head up. He breathed in and fired twice at the shapes below. He looked toward Sage, John, and Anita. "Get to the room below us," he said, "They won't know who to shoot at them if there are two people firing from two locations."

They got up and began to run down the stairs. Lily looked at Percival. "Are you sure there is no one out there?"

Percival looked up again. He moved his head back down after he checked. "Positive," he answered.

Lily walked over to Percival. Behind her, she heard Peter shoot into the street below. "Go watch over them downstairs," Lily whispered, "Please." He nodded, and filed down. Lily walked back over to the window. "How many are in the street?"

"I couldn't count them," Peter answered, "But, too many. They've begun to position themselves into groups moving forward. It's hard to see through the mist but it looks like the sorcerers are in the outside of the group to conjure shields while everyone else shoots from the inside."

"Has anyone started fighting them?" Lily asked.

"A few dozen toward the front of the mist," Peter answered again, "They might have been the guards at the front of the palace, or Pane may have sent them."

Lily conjured a disc over her hand. She knew the risk of them seeing the light but she took it. She popped her head out and the disc flew from her hand toward the people below. Peter had been right about their position. She saw the conjured shapes made by Sorcerers in the front of them, and people behind them were shooting at the windows. The disc she had thrown hit one of the shields conjured by the Sorcerers. The two shapes exploded into showers of sparks.

Lily ducked her head back inside just as blasts of energy came at her. The wall of the window chipped away some more, and there was a singed area around where the blasts hit.

Lily heard someone fire below. It was followed by a yelp that made her heart stop. Peter and Lily looked each other in the eyes. Someone had been hit. She bolted to the stairs and began walking down them. She nearly fell and tumbled, as she ran down the stairs.

Percival was by the window. He was rapidly conjuring beams of energy from a disc and blasts of energy were chipping against the window and the wall back at him. On the floor, John and Sage were looking down at Anita. Her clothes near her stomach had been burned even more black by a shot from the people below them.

Lily slid to the floor. "What happened?" She asked quickly.

"People had fired from below," Anita whispered, "One shot hit the window frame and part of it hit me."

Lily cut part of the fabric away with her knife and looked at where she had been hit. The burn was the size of a small orange. The burn was red and blistered, a contrast to the pale skin around it. It wasn't fatal.

"How bad is it?" Anita asked in a whisper.

"You'll be alright," Lily whispered. She looked toward Peter who was opposite to her. "Check if Pane gave us anything for this." Peter nodded and ran back up the stairs.

"Can she stand?" Percival asked. He had moved away from the window and dropped down with them.

"Why does she need to stand?" Lily asked. She was angry that he was asking her to walk just after being shot in the stomach. It would be better if she moved little until she was properly bandaged.

"Four people broke from the group," Percival whispered, "They are trying to break down the door. They'll be in here any second."

"We'll hold them before they can get to the stairs," Lily whispered, "Watch over her." She looked toward Sage and John. They nodded. Lily stood and Percival followed her. The two of them walked down the stairs.

As she looked through the room, she heard the group outside trying to break down the door. She turned to Percival but she didn't see him. He wasn't there.

"Just the shimmer," he whispered. She could tell he was to her left from where his words came. "Get beside the door out of their sight. When they break through, wait until they are all inside. Then close the door."

Lily nodded. She crept over to the side of the door, opposite of the door knob. They wouldn't be able to see her when they entered because the door would be in the way. Just as she came to beside it, she heard the door knob snap. The side of the door knob on their end dropped loose onto the floor. The door opened.

The first man came in. He looked around but didn't check where Lily was, behind the door. He was wary but moved forward. Three others followed and were all suspicious, but none of them checked behind the door. The first of them was a Sorcerer, and so was one other. The other two carried energy weapons from Earth. Lily closed the door behind them.

They all turned around and the two non-magics raised their weapons. Lily conjured a disc in front of her, just as one of the non-magics was hit in the face by Percival. He cried out, as Percival became visible in front of the group. Percival crushed the man's throat with his elbow and threw him against the wall. He was left coughing for air on the floor.

The confusion gave Lily enough time to attack the closest to her. The disc in front of her grew and a blast of energy shot from it toward a Sorcerer in front of her. He was blasted into the wall and fell unconscious to the floor.

Lily moved toward the other Sorcerer who had entered. He had already conjured a shaft of sparks and swung it across the room at Lily's head. Lily ducked out of the way, but he had already begun to attack Lily again. She was nearly hit along her stomach, except she moved out of the way. She threw her disc which she had already conjured at the man.

He blocked the disc with the shaft he had, and showers of sparks came over him as both disintegrated. He covered his face from the sparks, and Lily lunged toward him. Just as he moved his hand down, Lily brought her own fist to his nose. He stumbled back and blood began to drip from it. He moved forward and tried to punch her. He was off balance and threw the punch over her left shoulder. Lily caught his arm and brought his body forward. She brought her knee up and into his stomach. He cried out as the wind left him. She struck him across the head with her elbow. He fell to the floor.

Lily looked toward Percival. He kicked the man, who he had already dispatched earlier, in the head, while he was making a final effort toward the gun.

"Nice plan," she whispered. Percival nodded. He picked up the two non magics' guns. "Let's get back up there."

The two of them moved back up the stairs. Peter had begun pressing a bandage onto Anita while John had a gun trained on Lily and Percival as they came up. He lowered it. "Are they dead?" he asked.

"Unconscious," Lily whispered. She moved toward Anita. Her burn had been covered up. "How do you feel?"

"Better," she answered.

Percival had already moved back toward the window. He looked back toward Lily. "I saw him," he whispered. He pointed out into the battlefield.

Lily immediately knew who he meant. Percival had seen Boreas. "Are you sure?" She asked. She stood up and moved toward the window.

Chaos was the only force left on the battlefield. The mist had dissipated from the battlefield, and, now, the storm was upon them. Flurries of the mineral falling from the night sky, landing upon the forces. Both of the opposing forces had begun fighting each other on the streets. Boreas' forces had broken away from inside the spires and had begun fighting with the guards who had been left in the palace. It was strikingly similar to the battle at the Last City; there were few bodies she could see across the streets and most battles were determined by blows that left the other unconscious. There both seemed to be an unspoken agreement not to harm the other as much as possible.

Lily looked at where Percival pointed. It was unmistakable. Lily saw Boreas's pale hair as he moved forward with her father and Percival's parents. They were fighting their way toward the palace.

Lily looked toward Sage. She didn't want to leave her, but Sage had already cut her off before she could say anything. "Go, quickly," she whispered.

Lily gave a weak smile and nodded. "If anyone enters that door who isn't us, shoot them," she told Peter and John. Percival and Lily ran out of the room. They moved down the flight of stairs. None of the four bodies had moved since Lily and Percival had left them; the four were still knocked out.

Lily and Percival opened the door. It was chaos outside. The fighting had barely ceased since they had checked from the window and neither side was winning. Lily's hair whipped around from the storm.

"We can travel around and cut into the palace!" Percival shouted over the wind. The two of them ran behind the spire and began running toward the street behind it.

They nearly crossed into the street when Percival pulled her back. A flash of light came and a blast of energy struck the wall where she had been moments before. Lily conjured a disc over her hand and Percival did the same. They walked forward. There were three people at the end of the street with weapons raised at them. Four more Sorcerers came from the opposite side. They encircled them.

"Get to the palace," he said, "I'll hold them off." Lily was about to ask how when his disc enfolded and was cast into lightning. The seven around them gasped and were momentarily shocked. "Boreas taught me this," he said, "Go!"

Lily bolted toward the palace. She threw her disc at one of the non-magics and kept on running beyond them. She felt blasts of energy come at her but she heard the lightning Percival had conjured crackle and blast apart stone behind her.

She ran at the palace until she came toward the last spire. She was just a few dozen feet away from the doors of the entrance room when she turned around at the last spire. Lily briefly saw something come toward her head as she made the turn.

Pain traveled through her head and her hands hit the floor and mineral covering from the storm behind her. She fell to the floor dazed. Lily could feel blood coming down from her forehead. She looked up to see the object coming at her again.

Lily moved away just in time and did the only thing she could on the floor. She grabbed a handful of the mineral and threw it at her assailant's eyes. He cried out and Lily kicked him in the stomach.

She looked at the palace doors just at the right time to see that Boreas had managed to enter the palace, followed by her father, Corvus, and Ariadne.

She was about to run toward them when her assailant pulled her to the floor. She fell over and landed on the mineral covering. She turned toward the man just as he tried to punch her head. She moved out of the way and she struck his ribs with her elbow. She kicked the man again in the stomach. He fell backwards against the wall.

Lily stood up and looked toward the palace. Boreas had already entered and he was gone.

Chapter Twenty Five:
The Mask of the North Wind

Boreas entered the palace. He, Aethor, Corvus, and Ariadne were in the circular entrance room. Guards immediately ran up to them despite the chaos. A shaft conjured by a Sorcerer flew by his head, narrowly missing. Boreas looked to the guard who had thrown it at him. He conjured a disc and a beam of energy flew from it, hitting him in the chest. He flew back into the wall.

Another guard slashed at him with a sword. Boreas weaved out of the way as the guard let out a flurry of slashes. Boreas conjured a shaft of energy and brought to the guard's face who fell limp to the floor.

Boreas looked toward the others behind him. The three of them had already dispatched the rest of the guards. He looked toward Aethor. "Does this place bring back any memories?"

"Some," He answered, "Many of them I am not fond of."

"Watch the doors," Boreas ordered. He looked at his wrist. Boreas turned on the Annihilation Detector. The screen lit up. The red dot that signified the Crimson Blade was where he was. The blue dot was in the complex.

He looked toward Aethor again and showed him the detector. "Where would it be?" Boreas asked.

Aethor looked at it carefully. "The hangar," he answered, "Follow me." The four of them exited through one of the two doors in the circular entrance room and followed the hallway. They soon entered the hangar. The hangar was full of groups of the North Wind and the guards fighting against each other. Some Sorcerers were fighting in close quarters combat while others were fighting behind crates and dragonflies.

"Thank you, for warning about the dragonflies," Boreas said.

"Well I wouldn't have liked them to have aimed at the mist," Aethor said. He scanned the hangar and pointed out near the top. Boreas looked toward it. Out of the fighting and chaos were nearly two dozen men guarding sealed doors at the opposite side of the hangar. "The Reality Stone is in the vault."

The four of them began to run along the railing toward the vault, when they came upon an intersection. Nearly two dozen guards surrounded them. They came along the intersecting pathway and to the left side of them. The right was open to the four of them.

He looked to the three of them. "Get to the stone," Corvus said.

"We'll hold them off," Ariadne added.

Boreas nodded and bolted to his right. Blasts of energy flew by him and Aethor from the guards as they ran. He looked back up toward the vault. A man in the black of the Black Striders was watching Boreas and Aethor, as they ran toward the vault. All that was needed was for them to climb a single flight of stairs, which was in front of them in the opposite direction of the vault, and they would be in front of the guards at the vault.

He looked toward the Black Strider. Another man was beside him. Commander Graves stood coldly, looking down at them. He whispered something at the Black Strider. The Black Strider already had a bow out and was drawing an arrow.

Boreas pulled Aethor behind the stairs as the arrow soared toward the two of them. It would have struck Aethor's head between his eyes. Boreas watched as it clattered along the walkway two dozen feet away from him.

"They recognized us," Boreas said, "They didn't even need to see the blade."

"You know the moment we move out, he's going to shoot one of us," Aethor said.

Boreas nodded. He moved his hand into his robes and took out the Crimson Blade. It glowed a faint red light. "I guess it doesn't matter if he sees us," Boreas said, "They already know it's us." The Crimson Blade glowed red. Around the handle, red matter spun into a shield. "Follow me and, in your first chance, take out the Black Strider."

Aethor nodded toward him and Boreas moved into the open. Immediately, an arrow came and struck the shield where his head was behind. The arrow dropped to the floor. Behind him, Aethor blasted two beams from a disc he conjured. The two beams blasted by Boreas's head.

"Missed," Aethor grumbled, "He's agile." They walked forward, as conjured weapons from the other Sorcerers struck the shield, but none made a dent in it. Another arrow clattered to the floor as they made it to the stairs.

The red matter around the shield disappeared and moved to cover the open air around the stairway. Red matter formed along the Crimson Blade created a long narrow sword. Boreas looked toward Aethor. He had conjured a spear of ink black matter. "I'll stop the archer," Aethor said. He turned the back of his wrist to show a black knife concealed.

Boreas nodded. They ran up the stairs. An arrow whistled past his head as he came behind the red matter. Boreas saw the dark spear fly through the air and miss the Black Strider. He barely saw the knife fly but the Black Strider fell over the railing onto the set below.

Graves had already come to meet Boreas, first. He swung his broadsword at Boreas's chest. Boreas moved out of the way and blocked the next attack with the Crimson Blade. The broadsword stopped in the air, and a gouge had been bitten into it when the two weapons made contact. Graves slashed at him again. Boreas blocked the attack with the flat end of the blade pushing his movement toward the railing. Boreas held his leg out and Graves fell over.

Boreas looked toward Aethor who was single handedly fighting all the other guards. Already, six of them were along the floor. The vault was directly in front of Boreas, and so was what he wanted most behind the doors.

He held out the Crimson Blade. A blast of light came from it and the vault was destroyed before his eyes. In the back of the room was a blue light floating on a pedestal. He looked at the Annihilation Detector. It wasn't a trick, the Reality Stone was in front of him.

Boreas walked forward toward the stone. He walked through the broken vault doors and over the rubble. He held out the Crimson Blade. He held it in front of the Reality Stone and watched as an eye opened in the hilt.

He smiled just as a beam of light shot toward him. Boreas looked behind him just to see a beam of energy hit across his shoulder. Searing pain went through his shoulder and he flew to the edge of the room. He fell onto a pile of rubble.

The Crimson Blade fell to the floor a dozen feet away from him. Boreas looked at his shoulder. His clothes were blackened and he knew his shoulder was burnt. He looked toward his attacker.

Aethor stood at the entrance toward the room. He walked toward the Crimson Blade and picked it up from the floor. Boreas tried to move toward him. "Stay down," Aethor hissed.

The eye opened up on the Crimson Blade again, and the Reality Stone floated toward it. The two objects joined together and a violet light filled the room. Death had the Annihilation Wave.

Another figure came through the vault doors. Lily looked from Boreas to Aethor. Her face was of confusion. "Stop him!" Boreas gasped. Lily's expression went to shock, and she knew what was happening. Her eyes went wide. She conjured a disc and it flew toward Aethor.

In a flash of a deep blue light, the disc disappeared. The whole surrounding changed in an instant. Boreas' stomach turned and nausea went through him as his eyes adjusted. They were on the cliffs overlooking the city. The storm had begun to die down and flakes of the mineral fell quietly down from the sky. There was no more lightning. Boreas with his right arm pushed himself up.

He looked toward Aethor, who had transformed out of his disguise into Death. He stood above both Boreas and Lily, in his hulking shape and armor. His skin which had been tarnished and blackened by performing The End was now healed over. His inhuman gray eyes with their deep blue pupils flicked between the two of them. "I think that will be the last time I use my disguise," Death smiled. He held out the blade and the stone. It glowed purple and a haze appeared in front of him.

Immediately after she had recovered from the nausea, Lily conjured a dsc, and it flew toward Death. It hit the haze and a shower of sparks fell to the floor. Death cocked his head. "Come now, we don't have to fight," he said, "We have more important things to discuss."

Lily conjured another disc. She held it in front of her. She didn't trust her father. As Boreas shouldn't have. "We had a deal," Boreas hissed.

Death looked toward him. "We did," he said before shaking his head. "And now, we don't."

"Why would you break it?" Lily asked. "You both wanted the same thing." She stood up from the ground. She had been knocked over by being teleported. Boreas was sure the same would have happened, had he been standing up.

"What Boreas and I desire most are the same thing," Death said, "But, as I would never obtain it through the Annihilation Wave, Boreas could only get it through that."

"Then why did you betray him?" Lily asked. "Why would you take the blade and the stone if not to use it to end humanity."

"Oh, but I did, daughter," Aethor answered, "What Boreas and I desire most is not the destruction of humanity. I think you already know what I desire the most is. Piece the rest of the puzzle together."

Lily looked toward the ground confused for a moment and then looked toward Boreas. Boreas knew she had figured it out. He had been haunted by the day in his nightmares. And, the rage and pain in his life had become all he had known, from the day the ferry was destroyed. "We never found her body," Boreas choked out. He could feel a tear coming down from his cheek. "I would have only needed the Crimson Blade if we had. The North Wind was founded upon a lie, a ruse. I hid my intentions behind a mask few saw, and less knew the face behind it. Everything I had done was done for her." He choked out the last set of words. "To bring my daughter back to life."

Lily looked down upon the ground. She looked to Death. "You have done so much and hurt so many people," she sighed, "At least, honor your deal to him and bring back his daughter. Give at least one person solace."

Death sighed. He breathed in and said, "I never had to keep our arrangement. I never had to, because she never died."

"She was an infant lost at sea!" Boreas shouted. "She couldn't speak or walk, let alone swim.

She burned in the wreck or fell to the bottom of the waves."

"Boreas," Death whispered, "There has been an orchestrator, who has made the three of us stand on this cliff right now. We each have been visited by dead people we once knew, because of the Crimson Blade. Lily, you saw The Assassin in the caves. Boreas, you saw your wife. While at Death's Landing, as you saw your wife, I also saw The Assassin. He told me something I did not believe. Lily, while he saw your three friends' fears, he also saw memories of their pasts.

"And, one confused him, given my current situation. He saw Boreas in the memory, which I thought to be impossible. None of them were Sorcerers. He saw the ferry in her memory and the explosion. Her memory, as an infant, spawned her greatest fear she had: drowning. Deep water. It had always been that, because somehow she had survived."

"No!" Lily shouted. "She couldn't be his daughter." Boreas studied her face. Somehow, he knew that she was lying to herself. Boreas looked at Death. He raised the blade which was now violet. It glowed brighter and a flash of blue light appeared, and disappeared in an instant.

A girl had fallen to the ground in the daze of being teleported. Boreas saw it now. Her mother's auburn hair, and she had her same green eyes as she stood up. Boreas tensed. He had seen her with Lily at Sunlight Grove, at their spire in the Capital, in Victory Peak, and in the woods and cliffs on Torfaa.

His daughter stood up in front of them.

Chapter Twenty Six:
The Orchestrator of Annihilation

"Sage, I am so sorry," Lily whispered. She looked at Sage, who had stood up from the ground. Like Lily, she had felt the same brief nausea, when she had been teleported by the Reality Stone.

"Lily, why am I here?" Sage asked. Her eyes went wide, when she saw Boreas, but she nearly jumped, when she saw Death behind her.

"I am so sorry," Lily whispered once more. She looked toward her father. "Let her go," she said. She conjured a disc in front of her. She looked toward her side and saw Boreas do the same as her.

Death turned his head. "What do you think I am going to do to her?" he asked. "I am surprised you'd think I'd kill her out of spite, or some other gain. No. I have what I want and it would be quite easy to stop you." He looked down toward Sage. "You can go to them."

Sage slowly walked toward Lily. She walked through the haze in front of Death. She checked back toward Death to see if he would do anything, but he didn't move. When Sage came toward her, Lily grabbed Sage's hand. Lily pulled Sage behind her. "Stay behind me," she whispered.

"You are going to destroy humanity," Boreas said, "Permanently."

"Don't be so dramatic," Death replied, "But, despite me not having to keep our deal, I believe I will only adjust one part of it."

"What was his end of the deal?" Lily asked Boreas.

Boreas sighed. "I'd give him Haranae," he mumbled after a brief silence. He looked at the mineral covered ground, ashamed of himself.

"You were willing to let him kill all those people, for whatever you wanted with the blade and the stone?" Sage asked behind her. "You should be ashamed of yourself."

Lily could tell Boreas was ashamed. And the worst part was, now, she would know why he did it. For her. Boreas looked toward Lily. "She won't believe me, if I say it," Boreas whispered. Lily knew it was true. She didn't even want to believe it herself, and, yet, she knew that Death's explanation made sense.

Lily turned to Sage. "What does he mean?" Sage asked. She went from anger toward Boreas, to confusion toward Lily. "Why did you say you were sorry, when I came here?"

Lily tried to put it delicately. "You and I both grew up together, as sisters," she began, "I had come from another world and kept it a secret except to our foster parents. I always knew my mother had died, but I never knew who my father was, at the time.

"You, however, knew neither of your parents. You had been found by the sea, and we always thought you had been abandoned, perhaps by a mother who couldn't care for you, or a father who never wanted you. But your parents did want you, however. They did love you. Your parents were taking you to a new life for them. But, the ferry you were on was destroyed and your mother was killed. But, your father survived the attack, as did you."

Sage began to realize what it meant. Lily had told her what she saw in Boreas's memory of the ferry weeks ago. Her reaction had been the same as Lily's two years ago, when she had found out her father had been Death. First, she was shocked, then disbelief.

"No," Sage whispered. She looked from Lily to Boreas. "No," she repeated. Lily took her hand and hugged her. "It's not true, it can't be true." Lily could hear her voice crack, and she felt a tear hit her shoulder.

"I am sorry," Lily whispered, "I truly am." It felt like minutes before Sage let go over her, but neither of their fathers intervened. Lily knew Death understood. He had a daughter, who had never wanted him, once she found out who he was. Boreas didn't intervene either. He was just as broken as Sage was.

"How do you know for sure?" Sage asked Death.

"Let me ask you a question, instead," Death responded, "Has there ever been a time when you were unable to explain how you stayed alive? Such as how you inexplicably survived a moment you shouldn't?

"When we were in the jungle, we were attacked by a beast," Sage answered slowly, "I thought it was a flare that set its fur on fire, but it may not have been."

Death smiled. "Magic can do strange and powerful things, some that can't be explained," he began, "It can grow, it can evolve, and sometimes it can be left untouched without its host knowing of it. It kept you alive twice in your life, perhaps more times that you don't remember.

"It also affects the perception of time. A tenet we must understand with time is that it cannot be changed. There are an infinite amount of outcomes to every action we take, and yet time is already set in a flow of a river. We can see into the future as two of you have, but that doesn't change what you see in your dreams. You can find out a prophecy in your childhood but that doesn't change what happens after you run away. Time is sadistic and ironic. And, there is someone who understood this, as well as I." Death smiled. "All of this has come to where we are now, because of him. The Orchestrator of Annihilation. Do any of you know who it is?"

Lily looked to Boreas. He was just as clueless as her. She wondered who that one person could be. It had to be someone who tied to Death's resurrection, whether indirectly or directly. Someone who had changed the intentions of Boreas into resurrecting Death. It could only be her, which didn't make sense.

Lily could tell that Death did understand their befuddlement. Death smiled and looked toward Boreas. "Did your wife tell you anything at Death's Landing, which you did not understand?"

Boreas winced, when Death asked him. Whatever she had said must have been painful for him to her. "It was her last words," Boreas answered, "But, they were directed to me instead of…" He broke off and looked toward Sage. "My daughter. It was as if she knew I would see her again."

Lily could tell Death was bringing his point to a conclusion, because he smiled again. "Exactly," He said, "But, the question we must ask now was how could she know this conclusion? It is because of this." He held up the Crimson Blade which glowed purple with the Reality Stone embedded into the hidden eye. "The blade and the stone are connected with each other, despite being apart in unmeasurable distances. Boreas, you saw her shade because of the blade, and, therefore, she could know what the universe foretold with the other half that controls time and reality."

The blade and the stone began to glow in Death's hand. A shade formed beside Death. Except the shade wasn't a shade. While it's body was translucent, when it came, it's outline began to become clearer, and, slowly, he was real. The Assassin stood in front of them.

Despite being in his trademark black mask, Lily could tell he was smiling. "My own flesh and blood," he said in his calm voice. He began flexing his gloved fingers. He looked up toward Lily. "Hello, Lily. It's been a long time since the cave, and, finally, here we are."

"You knew what you were doing," Lily gasped, "You knew by setting me free we would end up where we are now." The Assassin was the Orchestrator of Annihilation. Had he not helped her get out of the cave, she would have been left with Boreas. He would have never chosen to resurrect Death, and, thereby, they wouldn't be here.

"Yes," The Assassin said, "I did. When I told you about the river of time, I said I was throwing a boulder into it. And, I did. I set the flow to where we are now. It's funny. While being dead, I was more powerful than ever. My influence was infinite, despite my conscious being alive for only minutes."

"I should never have trusted you," Lily said, "I thought you had changed, but you hadn't."

The Assassin shook his head. "Perhaps, you were naive," he chuckled, "Do you think death changes you? If you do, then you think of most people wrong. If given the chance to come back from the void, most people wouldn't change what they believe. Martyrs would fight for their causes, once more. The opposite would be believed for people who fight against a cause, and they would reason that they are brought back to stop change. Being dead doesn't change you."

His last words brought silence to the group. "If he is the Orchestrator of Annihilation, then who is the one giving Lily and I these dreams?" Boreas broke in. Lily thought it over. Despite bringing us to the point where they are now, it was in no way possible for The Assassin to give them the glimpses of the future. It was someone else. Lily turned toward her father and The Assassin. They looked just as confused as everyone else was.

Death held the blade and the stone, and they began to glow. Lily watched as their eyes began to flicker around, as if they were reading. They were peering through time. When the glow finished, both of them were confused. Whatever they had seen confused them even further. Death exchanged glances to both of them. "How could you not know?" Death asked. "How couldn't you know who was behind it?"

"What are you talking about?" Boreas asked. "How should we know who it is?"

"They don't," The Assassin said, turning toward Death. "I don't know how, but, somehow, they don't know who did it."

"Who was it?" Lily asked.

"That is something I believe you shouldn't find out by my own words," Death whispered. He looked between Boreas and Lily. "Goodbye, daughter."

Lily had dreaded this moment the second she had seen him hold the blade and the stone. The blade began to glow purple, as he raised it once more. Lily knew what he was doing now. He was about to conjure the Annihilation Wave.

Lily conjured another disc in front of her and whispered, "Ignysfire." The disc erupted into flames. The fire blasted forward, across the area in front of her, and crashed into the haze. But the fire spread out over the haze. It didn't break through.

A strange sound went across the air. She had heard it in her dreams. And, it was the Annihilation Wave. The light from the blade and the stone began to grow. Lily concentrated everything she had into breaking that haze, but it didn't shatter or disappear. The sound stopped.

The light faltered, but then grew incredibly bright. Lily shielded her eyes. A massive shockwave came from through the haze. In the last moments before it hit, Lily tried to conjure some sort of barrier in front of her to stop it, but she still felt the wind get knocked out of her. It blew her and Sage back, and the two of them fell a dozen feet from where they had just stood. Somewhere to her right, Boreas fell and rolled on the ground. The cliff began to crack and groan. She saw cracks form as far as where she was from the cliff's edge.

As her vision began to falter, Lily looked at the haze one last time. She saw Death and The Assassin looking at them. The haze disappeared. They were gone as the edge of the cliff began to crumble away.

Chapter Twenty Seven:
Aftermath

The cliff began to recede further. The chunks of blood red mineral continued to fall until only no more five feet was left between them and the open. Had Lily not rotated her body, her feet would be right at the edge. She wondered how many people now lay silent from the collapsing rubble. She added their unknown names to the list that now included billions. If what she thought Death had done he actually did, when he conjured the Annihilation Wave, she knew Death had won.

As she tried to stand up, she felt pain go through her body. When Death had finally reached Earth two years earlier with the blood matter, Lily had passed out from the pain she had taken while trying to stop him. She refused to let that happen this time.

Lily stood up, ignoring the pain in her chest. She walked over to the edge of the cliff. The last of the North Wind was retreating. The Annihilation Wave spooked them to the point that they disengaged. It was only a portion of the group that was running away through the streets. She doubted everyone who wasn't with them had died. They probably had surrendered. Despite the numbers, many of them were untrained for combat. It was the same end as the fighting at the Last City.

She looked over to Boreas. He gritted his teeth, as he pushed himself up. He was different from how she had thought of him just a few months ago. The cloth around his shoulder was blackened and she knew he was badly hurt beneath it. His long white hair was a mess around his face. His eyes were full of distraught. She would have said he was imposing even a few hours ago. Now, the only word she could think of was wounded.

She fell into the same trap at the Last City. She thought Boreas was trying to accomplish something he wasn't, and that small difference led to her failure twice.

He was looking toward Sage. Her hair had fallen all around her head and she was unconscious, although beginning to awaken. She had taken the full hit of the shockwave, as Lily hadn't managed to conjure the full barrier between them and the shockwave. Lily was amazed how Boreas was even conscious, between taking the full blast of it and his injury.

"She has her same hair," Boreas whispered. He was right, from what Lily remembered from the memory. He looked toward Lily. "I should have asked for your help the moment I decided to try and find the blade and the stone."

"I probably wouldn't have believed you," Lily said, "Twice, I thought you were going to destroy humanity. I finally understand two glimpses I had of the future. In the first, we were both there. I saw Death walking out with a younger girl, who I was when I was younger. I represented Sage. In the other, I saw two people wearing masks. One wore a black mask and one wore a white mask. They represented their face's intentions. When they took off their masks, I didn't see their faces, but the masks of the opposite shade. You were now in a white mask and my father in a black. I believed you were going to do something bad, and you didn't, whereas, I didn't focus on Death's intentions when I should have."

"Anyone who strives to find the power of a god must be stopped at all costs," Boreas whispered, "It is difficult to believe any man or woman would try to do something inherently good, when trying to seek that type of power. It's impossible to find someone who would use that power for selfless reasons, because a selfless man would turn them down. What difference does it make, however, if I am the man who brought the destruction of everyone, where I am the responsible for it, even if I never desired it?"

"It could make all the difference in the future," Lily responded. Lily thought she saw a brief smile form on his lips, but they were gone as quickly as they had come.

"It might, but if I am willing to risk annihilation of everyone to uphold my morals, then what difference does it make?" Boreas asked. He stared at the ground. "Did you learn about the other option?"

Lily nodded. "And, you were a fool," she whispered. Boreas didn't even bother to refute.

She looked over to Sage, who was beginning to wake up. Lily walked over and crouched down beside her. Sage looked up at her. "What happened?" she asked.

Lily didn't even want to answer her question. "We lost," Lily whispered. "Can you stand?" Sage nodded, although Lily knew she was probably in worse pain than she felt. She helped support Sage, as she stood up.

A lone figure was running toward them. Lily was ready to fight him when she saw that it was Percival with his left cheek covered in blood.

"You were wrong about Boreas," Percival whispered, as he scanned the three of them. "Weren't you?"

"You knew all this time?" Lily asked.

"I began to doubt him, but never fully," Percival answered, "I thought it might be too… well, too well intentioned to be true. I knew that if he did succeed then it wouldn't make a difference to everyone else. Who created the Annihilation Wave?"

His last question rang in her head. What was left of humanity would finally learn what happened on the cliffs. Lily didn't have to answer it though. Boreas did. "Death won."

Percival looked out where the edge of the cliff was, and sighed. He didn't even talk about it. "How easily can you walk?" he asked Boreas.

The four of them walked to the back entrance of the fortress. Lily was helping Sage walk and Percival was helping Boreas. None of them spoke to each other. The dread that hung over them was too much.

They walked back through the tunnel until they came to the end of the hallway. As Lily opened the door, Lily found that most of the hangar was quiet. The battle had ended. She looked over the railing and saw the vault which had been torn to shreds by the Crimson Blade. Among the rubble from the vault, she saw bodies where her father had fought through the guards. If she had been just a minute sooner, she may have been able to stop them from getting to the stone.

The four of them began walking down the flights of stairs. It was eerie in the quiet. Just minutes ago, the fighting had been in full force. Lily looked around at the dead bodies, if any of them were those that she knew. Few bodies were on the ground. Maybe, some had already been taken away, but Lily doubted that.

Soon, they came to the base of the hangar. The doors of the hallway that led to the entrance room of the base were open. They heard shouting coming from the entrance room. The four of them moved as fast as they could for their current states.

A group of guards were trying to fight Ariadne. She was pinned to the wall and was bleeding from a cut along her thigh and her cheek, but was still fighting. Pane was shouting at her to stop fighting while Graves was leading the group that surrounded her, although he was limping severely.

"Ariadne!" Boreas shouted.

She turned towards the four of them, as they entered the room. She didn't lower her weapons, as she spoke to them. "Come on, Boreas, let's take these morons!" She shouted at him. "Percival, the three of us can fight them off. I know we can." The group was now split between who to attack.

"We could," Boreas whispered. He raised his hands into the air however. "But, we shouldn't. We lost."

"They haven't beat us, as long as the three of us are still here," Ariadne said. She raised a knife toward one of the guards, but it stopped short. Boreas had conjured a disc in front of the guard. She looked at him, shocked he had stopped her.

"We all lost," Boreas said, "Only Death won. He played us all and won the game." The effect on those who understood what had happened was near instantaneous. They looked at the four of them with shock, expecting one to say it was a trick, even though it wasn't. Ariadne looked to the floor and raised her hands into the air.

"Where is Corvus?" Boreas asked.

"Dragged away by some of your followers," Ariadne answered, "He took a hit to his leg and was dragged back by them. They probably took him back through the city to the world engine."

Boreas nodded. One of the guards moved forward and put her arms behind her back and led her away. The battle was now over.

Pane looked toward the guards who had surrounded Ariadne. Many were confused by what Boreas had said. Pane turned toward them. "Leave us," he commanded quietly. The remaining guards left the room, confused but silent. Pane rubbed his eyes before looking at Lily. "Is what he said true?" Lily gave a small nod. Pane rubbed his eyes again, and swore. "Is there any way we can stop him in time, before he does the Annihilation Wave?"

"It's done," Lily mumbled, "He already did it."

"We'll think of something, right?" Sage asked.

No one answered. They all had nothing to contribute. "Let's make sure you're not severely injured," was all that Pane said.

"I suppose, you'll take me to prison now if you aren't going to kill me," Boreas said. He looked toward Graves. Lily knew Graves had his own personal vendetta for wanting to kill Boreas.

"We won't kill you," Pane said before Graves could respond. He looked toward Graves and told him to take him away. Graves nodded, wordlessly, and took him by the shoulder.

"I hope you treat the people I brought here well," Boreas mumbled, "I lied to them about why I brought them here, and the next thing they don't need to hear is that they are spending the rest of their life as prisoners."

"We'll find a compromise," Pane responded, "Secure him and get someone to look at his wounds." Graves scowled at the generosity, but took him away. Lily watched as Boreas looked behind him. Lily looked toward Sage, beside her, as Sage knew Boreas was taking one last look at his daughter.

Pane looked to the three of them. "Tell me what happened, exactly," Pane said, "And, what did he mean by that he lied to his supporters?"

Lily looked toward Sage. Sage just stared outside, where Boreas was being led away. She turned to Lily, when she realized she was staring at her. Her gaze went from Pane, then back to Lily, and she gave a small nod.

"Sage is Boreas's daughter," Lily answered in a whisper, "As unlikely as it seemed. He tried to bring her back with the Annihilation Wave, after he thought she had died, even though she never had." She looked over to Sage, who was now staring back out the door where Boreas had left. "I think it's better if I tell you everything else later."

Pane took a few seconds before he responded with anything. "We should get you both to some doctors," Pane said.

Lily nodded. The four of them walked out of the entrance room. Lily wrapped her arm around Sage, as they walked. Sage placed her head on

Lily's shoulder. They began walking through streets that had barely been touched during the battle. The storm above them had finally disappeared. The last of the clouds were rolling away from the city, as the night was ending.

They were traveling to the far side of the city. She looked up and saw the bell tower which had signaled the Sorcerers to attack the North Wind. The bell was faded and rusted, but it still had done its job.

Pane led them into a tower. The room was much larger than it had appeared from the outside. While it had probably no more than a ten foot radius on the outside, the room was at least ten times larger on the inside. It must have been enlarged by an enchantment in preparation of the battle. Along the room were dozens of injured fighters from both sides. Many were conscious, either getting wounds bandaged or being probed for other injuries like broken ribs. Others were unconscious on their beds, as doctors moved around keeping them stable.

Lily didn't want to keep count of the passing faces that were injured. There were hundreds in the room, at least. She didn't even bother looking at whether they were in the midnight blue cloaks of the North Wind or in the black of the Black Striders or in the golden armor of guards from the Capital. They were all on the same side now, regardless of whether they knew it or not. The side of life.

Pane led them up to a pair of stairs. The four of them walked up the stairs into another room with the same situation. Hundreds more were being tended to just like below. Just like last time, many were passing faces. She recognized no one. She hoped it would be the same for any level above her. She would recognize no one stone cold on a bed.

They continued traveling up the stairs, until they came to the third level. This was separated by a door and the stairs. Pane opened the door. In it was a row of beds divided by curtains, until the row ended next to a large window, where a yellow sky began at the other side of the basin. Lily knew everyone in this room.

On the first bed to her right was Reeves, who was shirtless while a bandage was being pressed against the front of his shoulder. Blood was already slowly turning the bandage red, but he was still conscious, so it wasn't worse. To the next bed was Anita, who had the bandage on her stomach removed that had been placed earlier. Lily could see where the blast of energy had hit, but the doctors were already tending to it. To the other side was Fonsesca. She could immediately tell he had been in a crashed dragonfly. He had small cuts all along his face, probably from where small shards of glass hit his face. And, he was being checked for broken ribs. Peter and John were beside him talking with him.

The three of them looked up. They were from Earth. Lily knew Peter and John must have both had families there. And now, they were gone. And, she'd be the one to tell them that. She dreaded when that time came.

"I'll bring in some doctors, just to make sure you are alright," Pane said. Lily nodded, and he walked out of the room. She looked back toward

Fonsesca's bed, and saw John and Peter rising from their chairs. Percival walked over to them, and cut them off. They began to talk in small whispers.

Lily looked over at Sage, who had walked over to the large window and sat down on the ledge. Lily walked over beside Sage and sat down beside her. Their fingers touched, and Sage took her hand. Sage put her head on Lily's shoulder. She felt a tear fall onto her hand. Lily looked out across the basin. The world engine was now gone. It had disappeared from where it had remained motionless for the battle. The sun was slowly rising above the cliffs and mountains on the other side of the basin. They watched the dawn of a new universe.

Chapter Twenty Eight:
Crimson Snow

A storm was moving east towards them. Lightning cracked and the wind was already swaying the thin, pale, leafless trees of the Forest of the Ghosts. At Death's Landing, thousands of Storm Riders were encamped along the grounds inside the fortress, and the flat area outside. Their fires danced in the wind. The hundreds of lights were the only ones in the black, cloudy night.

There was a rock that jutted above the rest of the snow and reached over the bulk of the pale trees' height. Only the thin tops of the trees were above them. Two figures stood above the rock. The first was in black and blended into the night itself. The other stood at nearly twice the first's height. He took out a small glowing red object from a pocket in his armor. The Crimson Blade. It glowed and a long staff at least his height was in his hand. At the ends, two foot long blades appeared. Death looked out at the fortress.

Other shadows began to glide through the woods. They moved incredibly silent, along the snow. Their dark grey cloaks didn't move, despite the intense wind. Specters. They moved through the pale trees into the edge of the woods. They were spread out, and at least a few dozen of them along the tree line.

Horns began to blare along the encampment. The battle was going to start. Death looked toward The Assassin. "Bring the demons," he commanded.

The Assassin walked down the rock. He appeared at the edge of the tree line along with specters. Portals appeared along the tree line. Black warping shapes flew from them and fell onto the ground. The demons landed on four legs. They lacked any facial features, except a large mouth with jagged teeth. Saliva dripped from their mouths and many let out strange howls into the night. Thousands of them waited at the tree line.

The Assassin joined Death, once more on the rock. "They'll increase their chances the longer we wait," The Assassin grumbled.

Death looked toward him. "You shouldn't be complaining," Death said, "You enjoy fighting, and we both need to make it, at least, a little closer to even grounds. I have the blade and the stone, but the

worlds will not build themselves anew with just them. In an instant, I can change aspects of the universe, but that doesn't mean doing it is right, even if I make it so."

"You have been quite the philosopher," The Assassin mocked, as he rolled his eyes. He looked up into the sky. "I do hope you rebuild the worlds that you left. You kind of blew two right out of the sky. That leaves five now. I hope you don't blow up another one, if you get bored or if you slip on a patch of particularly icy snow."

"You are tenacious, and that was a necessary precaution," Death sneered, "And, you know it. I destroyed Haranae and Torfaa so that the blade and the stone couldn't be returned to them if they are taken."

"But, you could, so easily, look into the future and see if they are," The Assassin mocked, "So, hopefully, you didn't destroy them because of that fact or I expect neither of us would live long past that."

"You are a very unlikable man," Death muttered.

"I am merely celebrating the miracle known as life," The Assassin said. If he hadn't been wearing a mask, Death was sure he would have been smiling. "And, soon, I am going to bring the inevitable knock on the door of death. It appears you like me even more than before, because you've stopped talking to me telepathically."

Death looked towards Death's Landing. All the people outside had left the encampment and, now, they were all behind the walls. Even from afar, he could tell the dozens of archers along the walls. He knew that inside, there would be hundreds of combatants waiting.

"Go knock on their door," Death commanded. He didn't need to command it. The Assassin moved down from the rock and toward their army with much more enthusiasm.

The night became silent. The wind stopped briefly and the snow began to fall gently onto the forest. If it wasn't for the mass of black shapes below him, it would have been peaceful. Death raised the blade in his hand as the wind blasted the thin trees once more.

The demons began to cackle and howl, and the black mass charged forward. The horde began to charge through the snow, sending up a fine powder behind them. Behind them, the cloaked specters floated along behind, gliding soundlessly through the night. The Assassin was in a run with the line of specters.

From the walls, firelights began to fly through the sky, at least a hundred flew in a moment toward the horde. The arrows began to strike the front of the horde, and more arrows followed. While the strategy may have worked against the Black Striders, it had little impact on the horde of demons. With exception of a well placed arrow to the head, the demons could take nearly a half dozen arrows before slumping to the ground and disappearing in wisps of black matter.

Within a minute, the horde made contact with the encampment outside the walls. The demons began to tear apart the hide tents and trampled over the campfires, but little was found. Everyone had been moved into the fortress.

Death walked down the rock. He began to walk among the last of the trees. He crossed the tree line into the open. The wind kicked the fine powder that had come up from the demons' charge and now he was surrounded by the thin haze.

The gates had been broken through by the charge of the demons, but a group of Storm Riders riding great elk and wolves the size of horses were cutting through the horde. Their losses, however, were massive. Despite the riders cutting through the demons, there were mounds of bodies, where bloody masses of men and elk and wolves lay on the snow.

Two riders had broken through past the specters, who had been preoccupied, and now were charging toward Death. One was riding a pale wolf whose maw could crush Death's skull in a second, and the other was riding an elk whose antlers were as tall as Death's own height.

As they came within a hundred feet of him, two spears were thrown at Death. He moved aside from the first, as it thrust through the snow behind him, and the next would have landed in his chest if he had not struck it aside with his spear.

The elk rider came upon him first. The rider had a longsword in his hand and swung it at Death's head, as he charged by. He ducked under the blade and swung the two foot long blade at one of the ends of his spear towards the elk. It cut through, like a sword through the snow, and Death heard the elk whine and collapse behind him.

The other rider had nearly come to him. The wolf lunged at him. Death moved to the side and he raised the spear toward it, as it slid through the snow. It growled toward him, showing its teeth that were the size of knives. It began to lunge toward him a second time. This time, he thrusted the spear through the wolf's chest. The body continued forward, but fell to his side.

He pulled out his spear and stabbed the rider in the chest, as he tried to bring his sword at Death's head. He slumped forward and dropped the sword into the snow. Death pulled out the spear and the body fell from the wolf's back onto the snow.

The first rider was limping toward him, with his sword out. Death walked toward him. The rider swiped first, and Death blocked the strike with the blade of the spear, cutting through half of the blade. Death pulled the spear edge away from the sword and slashed the rider across the chest, before he could attack again. Death turned back toward the fortress, but stabbed the rider with the other end of the spear. He fell to the ground.

Death began to walk forward through the snow, once more. Groups of Storm Riders were cutting through the horde, but anyone who broke apart from their group was soon thrashed by a pouncing demon.

Death soon came upon the carnage. A few hundred feet from the wall, the majority of the demons and storm riders were fighting each other.

Some demons had managed to break through the outpouring storm riders, and were now ransacking the inner encampment from the gates. Others in the horde were beginning to climb the walls of the fortress, and would only fall back into the snow once its body was impaled by arrows.

He soon began cutting through the battle. He cut down half a dozen riders, littering the ground with dead bodies and staining the snow before an arrow struck him in the chest, but bounced off his armor. He conjured a disc and sent a beam of energy at the group of archers, where the arrow had come originated, and blasted the section of the wall. The archers flew over the wall from the blast.

Death was never struck after that. He continued weaving out of the way from pouncing wolves and charging elk, as the fighting continued. He ducked out of the way of longswords, swung at his head, and moved from the spears that tried to impale his armor and heart. He cut down at least another dozen riders before he came upon the gates. He began to walk through and moved out of the way, as a rider charged at him with a spear. He cut down the elk and its rider tumbled across the snow until she was met by a demon.

He walked through the gate. A Storm Rider, on foot, finished stabbing a demon and ran toward Death. Death moved out of the way and slashed him across the chest with one of the two foot long blades. He fell into the remains of a tent that was set on fire.

Death saw few Storm Riders left among the horde of demons. He did, however, see the final four fighters inside the gates nearby. They were not mounted, but were cutting down demons nearly as quickly as Death was them. He recognized one as the leader of the White Ravens.

The Raven's Eye finished cutting down a demon with a large, thick sword. Death stabbed his spear into the ground. A flash of red light cut through the air. The demons all stopped fighting around him and spread out, forming a line around the remaining four and Death. The area between Death and the four Storm Riders was now empty. The demons snarled at them, but remained at the sidelines.

Death picked up the blade and looked toward them. The Raven's Eye charged toward Death, followed by the other three survivors moments later. Death raised his spear and blocked the swing of the sword that came first at him from the Raven's Eye. He was surprised by the force that came with it, but, then again, The Raven's Eye had survived this long. Death threw off the sword from the shaft between the two blades causing him to fall back.

Death began to block two of the other of his attackers, both swinging longswords in a rhythmic dance of steel. The cuts could be heard all through the courtyard. They began to push Death back, until he cut one of them across the chest with the end of one of the two blades. He barely felt any resistance, when he cut through his body and already slashed the other across the neck before she could respond.

Both dropped dead on the snow. The third came at him with a limp, that came with a slashed leg, and swung a great axe at Death. Death caught the attack before the axe could cut through his chest. He pushed the attacker back and stabbed him with the edge of the spear. He dropped the axe and slowly fell to the floor. Three were dead.

The Raven's Eye had pushed himself off the ground. Strands of his long white hair had fallen across his face. He looked around the courtyard. Death knew that The Raven's Eye knew that he lost. He ran toward Death, once more and slashed at Death. Death moved to the side as it cut through snow. The blade already swung back at him. He caught it with the spear edge and threw it to his side.

Death danced once more. While two of the dead Storm Riders had been able to hold Death off for some time, the Raven's Eye did even better than the two of his now-dead comrades by himself.

It wasn't until after a half minute that one of Death's spear edges cut The Raven's Eye, and that was through the back of his calf. The two of them continued, one with a trail of blood as he limped, until Death caught The Raven's Eye's wrist with one of the spear edges. He dropped the sword and it fell into the snow beside him.

The Raven's Eye looked toward Death, just as he pushed one of the spear edges into the center of his chest. The Raven's Eye fell onto his knees giving hoarse breaths. "You fought well," Death said, although he wasn't sure that he understood him.

Death pulled out his spear and The Raven's Eye fell forward into the snow. The snow of Death's Landing was crimson. The spear disappeared in wisps of red matter, and Death pocketed the Crimson Blade.

Death looked toward The Assassin, as he walked through the demon line. Blood covered The Assassin's body, although Death knew it was not his.

"The battle is over, I take it?" Death asked.

"He was the last fighter," The Assassin answered, "Damn strong one, at that, I might add." He looked out at the wall. "Some of them must have escaped, however."

"We'll find them soon enough," Death said. "Who else was here?"

"They must have brought every one in their clan," The Assassin answered, "I don't think anyone expected more than a few dozen Black Striders. There were a few elderly and crippled, a dozen or two children, and a few others who couldn't fight. What do you want us to do with them?"

"Are any of them Sorcerers?" Death asked.

"No," The Assassin answered, "But, there are two dozen or so captive Black Striders. In chains but, otherwise, unharmed."

"Leave the captives be," Death said, "I have a job for them to do when the time comes."

"A job I can't do?" The Assassin asked.

"One you certainly can't do," Death answered. He looked toward the Raven's Eye behind him. "But, there is something you can do."

"Anything fun?" The Assassin asked.

"On relative terms for you, yes, considering your definition of fun is cruelly sadistic for everyone else," Death whispered. "But, kill our captives, everyone." He added coldly. "There's a lake a few miles east from here, it is probably frozen over, however. Drop their bodies there."

The Assassin nodded and walked back through the demon line, where captives were being held. Death looked back toward the fortress and walked away, leaving the crimson snow.

...

The storm had descended upon Death's Landing. Death looked upon it from the balcony of a tower. Despite the snow flying across his vision, he could still see as far as the fortress wall that surrounded the courtyard. Specters floated slowly around the walls, their grey, hooded figures watching the surrounding area of Death's Landing, although he doubted they could see far. Below, the bodies were gone and so were the demons, who had returned to the Spectral Boundary after the bodies were disposed of. The crimson had been covered by the white that came with the storm. While the night was ending, the storm had only just begun.

As he watched below, he saw The Assassin ride into Death's Landing on one of the elk that had managed to survive the encounter hours before. He was followed by half a dozen specters gliding through the air above the snow.

Death walked back inside the room. He closed the doors off the balcony, and he still heard the howl of wind behind him. He sat down at a lone table with two chairs. Soon, The Assassin came into the room with a small wooden box in his hand. He took off his mask and set it on the table. A scar cut across his face leaving only one eye, which was an inhuman orange.

"The bodies?" Death asked.

"Gone," The Assassin answered, "We found two riders as we went. One was wounded, so they must have needed to stop only about a mile out."

"And?" Death asked.

"They are dead," The Assassin answered without any show of remorse. He opened the box revealing a checkerboard. He put one side in front of Death and began putting circular pieces on every other square. He moved his first piece. "It is a shame we won't use their bodies for our attacks. I'd expect they would be very useful. And, we can't use hollows anymore either, now that The End will not come, once more. And, you won't bring your people back from the dead, either. Three armies you won't use."

Death moved his first piece. "I will not use an army of the undead to fight for us," he said, "Nor will I try to create The End. If you are willing to cast it, that is another story, if it were not pointless now."

"Are you trying to get rid of me that easily?" The Assassin asked moving another piece forward. "I am appalled by your lack of feelings for me." Death moved another forward.

"I am appalled for your disregard for life," Death said. He watched as The Assassin took one of his own pieces.

"And, anyway, we are using demons and specters," The Assassin said, "Those are very questionable, morally. I find those much more divisive than bringing your own people from the dead."

"I will not resurrect my own people from the dead, solely to see more of them die once more," Death explained while moving another piece, "They fought their battles against humanity, and they lost. If I resurrect them for the sole purpose of fighting, then why bring them back. It would not be right to bring them back, solely to add more blood to the canvas of history than what I would be doing, regardless. When the time is right, I will rebuild my people."

"And, you brought me back to do the exact thing that you wouldn't for them," The Assassin said.

"You are different," Death said, "You enjoy all of this." He took three of The Assassin's pieces.

"Damn, I think you are going to win," The Assassin muttered. He moved another piece forward and looked up from the game. "And, when is the time for bringing them back?"

It was a few more turns off the game before Death answered. "The deed is done," Death answered, "I have won. But, now is not the time to celebrate victory. Nor is it the time to look away. There is a darker deed that has yet to be done. The pieces will soon be moved and before long, that will become clear." He took away the last of The Assassin's pieces. "To clear the board."

Epilogue

It had been some time since the battle at the Titan-World. A few days, maybe a week. She did not know or she chose not to know. The length of time between when it had happened made no difference. It happened. She had seen it in her dreams, but it made no difference. The outcome was, nonetheless, the same despite her attempts to stop it.

After the days had finally ticked by, Lily was able to bring herself to the place. Annihilation was strange. What had she chosen to expect? What had her friends and sister, behind her, had chosen to expect? Had she expected to see rubble, destruction, and decay? Were there to be bodies with expressions of pain and shock strewn across the ground?

It was none of that. Yes, it was annihilation, but it also created something new. The expanse of plains spread out across the miles of land. The grass had taken place what was once there. The sky was blue and, despite that it was winter, not a single cloud was across the sky. The mountains around them were beautiful, with snow covering the upper halves of them. A forest of pine could be seen from the valley, lacking all that stood in front of it. It would've been beautiful, if it were not for what was once there.

Alone, the few of them that stood on the hillside with the lone tree knew what had been there. They did, but it didn't matter, and the Annihilation Wave changed that. And everything was gone.

Christian Crow

23064184R00168